DATE DUE

DEMCO 38-296

Uneasy Relations

John Haylock

Uneasy Relations

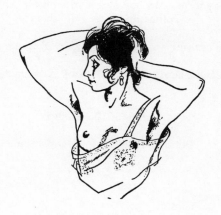

Peter Owen

London & Chester Springs

BLISHERS
lon SW5 0RE
uted in the USA by
Dufour Editions Inc. Chester Springs PA 19425–0449

First published in Great Britain 1993
© John Haylock 1993

The drawing on the title page is by Yuri Annenkov

A catalogue record for this book is available from
the British Library

ISBN 0–7206–0880–5

Printed and made in Great Britain

To
Donald Richie

Part One

· 1 ·

Sylvia Field took a taxi from her hotel near the moat of the Imperial Palace to her rendezvous with Professor Suzuki. The professor had offered to fetch her from the hotel, but she, not wishing to trouble him and wanting from the beginning of her sojourn in Tokyo to find her own way about the great city, had insisted on meeting him near the apartment which had been found for her by the university where she was to teach English literature. She had only arrived two days before and was still numbed by the flight from England in spite of a stopover in Bangkok.

'It is best if we meet by the Red Gate of Tokyo University, which is not your university, of course,' he had said over the phone, emitting a girlish laugh, high pitched. 'You say to the driver, "Take me to Akamon". Do not take a street car named Desire –'. A giggle. 'We do not have street cars anymore. I tell a lie. We have one.' More laughter. 'But no good for you. Let us say at ten-thirty. It not far.'

It was quite a chilly March morning, gusty, and the sky was grey. Sylvia put on a brown check tweed coat and skirt, and over the outfit a tweed coat. She wore a tweed hat too and brown brogues and looked more as if she were going to a point to point than to meet a future colleague at a Japanese university.

She was fifty, of medium height, blue-eyed, and thanks to regular treatment her hair was still blonde. She had a straight nose and a slightly prominent chin, underneath which its soft fellow

7

became visible when she lowered her head. After her divorce she had put on weight.

Her separation from her husband had been caused by his affair with his secretary in the publishing house of which he was a director. Sylvia, after twenty-five years of marriage, had felt so deeply hurt and humiliated by her husband's infidelity that she had insisted on a divorce. Mark, her only child, had tried to persuade her not to go to such lengths, telling her that the affair would pass. But her great friend and confidante, Betty Strutt, had advised her to take the irretrievable step and this she had done. Having become a divorcée she needed a job and it was Betty who had encouraged her to apply for a teaching post in Tokyo which had been advertised in the *Times Educational Supplement*.

'But I've never taught,' complained Sylvia.

'You have a good degree and you've published two volumes of poetry,' replied her friend. 'That ought to be enough for them.' And, surprisingly, it had been; Sylvia was accepted by the university. Betty had been right.

The excitement of preparing to go to Japan had acted as a balm to the wound inflicted by the ugly crisis she had experienced. Japan! Tokyo! They were so gloriously far away and, she hoped, they would be exhilarating and different.

Sylvia looked out of the taxi window. Yes, Tokyo was very different from London. Although the buildings seemed to be mostly concrete boxes, the ideograms that hung everywhere mitigated their ordinariness and imbued the city with an air of mystery. 'And that is what I want,' she told herself. 'Mystery. I want not to understand what is going on around me.' And yet when she saw a sign in Roman letters – Sony, Bar or Clinic – she felt comforted. She was impressed by the speed of the pedestrians, and distressed by the number of vehicles. Her taxi edged along, stopped and then spurted.

They entered a wide road, passed a bank, a busy crossing, shops and came to a halt opposite a vermilion gate with a heavy tiled roof, steeply sloping. A Japanese man in glasses and a grey raincoat hailed her; the traffic lights changed to a bluish-green and the man hastened over the road to the car, whose door had automatically opened. Sylvia fumbled for money, but before she had extracted one of the strange banknotes she had got from her bank in

London, the man said, 'No, don't get out. We go on some more.' Sylvia slid along the seat and was joined by Professor Suzuki, who produced his visiting card.

'Suzuki,' he said. 'I am pleased to meet you, Mrs Field.'

'How did you know it was me?'

'I have a nose for foreigners.' Suzuki let out the high giggle which Sylvia had heard on the phone and instructed the driver to continue down the avenue. 'This is Hongo Avenue,' he informed her. 'You will soon be well acquainted with this thoroughfare. On the right through those trees is Tokyo University; on the left is your *apāto*. Later, I show you.'

'Where are we going now?'

'We go to see Mrs Ota. She is the owner of your *apāto*. Her husband is very important businessman, company president, high up, at the top, you see.'

'Shouldn't I see the apartment first?' asked Sylvia. 'I might not like it.'

'It already taken for you,' replied the professor, firmly.

'I see.'

Obeying a brief word of command from the professor, the driver turned into a side street and stopped outside a pair of wooden gates. The professor paid.

Sylvia protested, 'I should pay for the taxi as all this is for me.'

'You are in Japan,' said Professor Suzuki. 'You are guest.'

Behind the gates was a short double drive up to a large house. There was a circular flower bed with a palm in the middle in front of the entrance which cars could drive round. Trees grew on either side. 'This is a Meiji period house,' explained the professor as he opened one of the gates. 'Very distinguished.'

Sylvia checked herself from remarking on the gloominess of the residence. She decided not to be critical. The professor went ahead up some steps to the front door; he took off his raincoat before ringing the bell. Presently the door was opened by a young man in a white jacket, a black bow-tie and white cotton gloves. The servant ushered them into the entrance, where Suzuki instructed Sylvia to take off her shoes and put on one of the pairs of slippers arrayed on the entrance step. 'Must I?'

'Yes, Mrs Field. It is our custom.'

Sylvia had to sit on the step in order to unlace her brogues; the professor was out of his shoes and into a pair of slippers in a flash. He stood on the entrance step while she dealt with her shoes and evinced impatience. Sylvia took off her overcoat and handed it to the servant, who seemed unready to receive it, but he did so hesitantly and then led the way down a dark passage, past a sitting-room full of armchairs and sofas with white covers to a small room furnished with a Persian carpet and imitation French chairs. In the bay window was a bureau, and on the walls were oil paintings of snowcapped mountains and lakes. The window looked on to a lawn on which was a gnarled and angular pine.

The professor and Sylvia sat facing each other in the narrow room. 'Mrs Ota will be here shortly,' Suzuki said.

'She likes to inspect her tenants before they move in, does she?'

'It is usual.'

There was a knock on the door and the servant returned with two handleless cups of green tea on lacquer saucers. He put them on an occasional table together with a plate of biscuits wrapped in plastic and bowed himself out of the room.

'Green tea,' explained Suzuki. 'Japanese tea.'

'I didn't know tea grew in Japan.' Sylvia put her fingers round her cup and withdrew them quickly. 'It's hot. There's no handle.'

'You take it like this.' The professor put his thumb on the rim of the cup and his forefinger on the base, raised the cup to his lips and sipped, slurping loudly. Sylvia flinched.

'I see,' she said, and copied her teacher, leaving out the slurp. She grimaced slightly as she put down her cup.

'You don't like it?'

'It's rather bitter.'

'Have a cookie.'

Sylvia took a biscuit, fiddled with the plastic wrapping, and failing to open it, she put it back on the plate.

'Mrs Field . . . 'Professor Suzuki began.

'She's arrived,' Matthew announced to his friend Jun as soon as the young man entered the sitting-room of the flat which they shared.

'Who?'

'Sylvia Field, the new English teacher in our department.'

'What's she like?' As was his custom when he returned in the early evening from the school where he taught, Jun went into the kitchen leaving the door open behind him.

Matthew raised his voice. 'Haven't seen her yet. Professor Suzuki is looking after her because he speaks English well, or has the reputation in the Faculty of being able to. Are you hungry?'

'Yes.' Jun came back into the room with a bowl of boiled rice which he had scooped out of the rice cooker.

'It's only six-thirty. Too early to eat.' Matthew was sitting in an armchair with the *TLS* on his lap.

'How old?' Jun sat on a stool by the television set.

'Fifty.'

'Younger than you.' Jun switched on the television.

'Twice your age, almost.'

'Married?' With his chopsticks Jun flicked some rice into his mouth.

'Divorced, I think. Her curriculum vitae mentioned a son, but not her husband. She was at Oxford. Has a degree in English literature. She's published two volumes of poetry. You'll spoil your dinner eating all that rice. Where have you been today?'

'School.'

'But school doesn't start until next week.'

'Meeting.'

'Oh, the Japanese and their meetings! Eternal meetings. Rarely a decision. I have to go to a meeting tomorrow to be introduced to her.'

Jun turned up the volume of the TV set and became absorbed in a bulletin of local news. Matthew began to read a review of a new biography of Proust. 'We're having chicken pilaff, so don't eat too much rice.'

'Huh!'

'It's your turn to cook dinner tommorow.'

'Huh!'

11

· 3 ·

'Mrs Field?'

'Yes, Professor Suzuki?'

'Your husband, where is he?'

'In London. But he is no longer my husband. We are divorced.'

'I see.' Suzuki skilfully opened the plastic wrapping round one of the biscuits and popped what looked like a wafery sweetmeat into his mouth.

'If my marriage hadn't broken up I would not have been able to come to Japan.'

The professor made no reply to this statement.

'I would have had to stay with him.'

'So his loss is our gain.' The professor laughed. Sylvia wasn't sure if he were laughing at his own cleverness in producing an apt English saying or out of nervousness.

'You do have divorce in Japan, don't you?'

'Yes, but it is not considered to be, to be . . . how shall I say? . . . to be a success.'

'I don't think it is considered to be a "success", as you put it, anywhere. But it is sometimes necessary.'

'In your case . . . '

Sylvia interrupted. 'Professor Suzuki, I don't think a discussion of my marital experience will serve any purpose.'

At that the professor closed his lips over his teeth and became solemn and silent.

After a minute or two, Sylvia asked sweetly, 'How long will Mrs Ota be, do you think?'

'I've no idea, Mrs Field. She is a busy lady.'

'Couldn't we go to the flat first and then come back here when she is free? It's near, isn't it?'

'She has the key.'

Another silence was broken by Suzuki, who inquired if Sylvia knew Matthew Bennet. 'He is in our department. He was at Cambridge University.'

12

'No, I don't know him. I was at Oxford.'

'You will meet him today.'

There was a light, diffident knock on the door and a diminutive, middle-aged Japanese woman with tidy jet-black hair entered; her face shone as if it had been polished. Professor Suzuki jumped to his feet and bowed deeply several times, his back seemingly on springs. Mrs Ota also bowed but less deferentially. Sylvia stood. After mutterings between the professor and Mrs Ota, Sylvia shook hands with her future landlady and the three sat down.

Mrs Ota was dressed in a simple black dress which, Sylvia noticed at once, was well cut; she also noticed that the Japanese woman wore no jewellery, not even a ring. She and Suzuki chatted together for a while and then the professor said, 'Mrs Ota is very sorry she can't speak English.'

Sylvia replied, 'Please tell her I am sorry I can't speak Japanese.' This was translated and Mrs Ota smiled at the English woman and then continued to talk with Professor Suzuki.

'Mrs Ota wants to know how many children you have.'

'Please tell her, and,' she added a little sarcastically, 'about my being divorced, if you like.'

There followed another conversation between the two Japanese which was brought to an end by further light knocks on the door and the entrance of the manservant with a tray bearing three cups of coffee and three slices of melon on plates with spoons. On seeing that her coffee spoon was on the left side of her cup, Sylvia automatically moved it to the right side. Mrs Ota frowned briefly and then indicated the sugar bowl and the milk jug. Sylvia helped herself to some milk but did not take any sugar.

The professor said, 'Mrs Ota ask you what you think of Japan.'

Sylvia laughed, 'Tell her that after two days, I haven't had time to think very much. I went for a walk yesterday along the moat of the Imperial Palace. A nice part of Tokyo. Quiet. Today I've been driven here from my hotel. The traffic seems as heavy as in London. There is one thing I have noticed: people seem to walk faster than they do in England. Everyone seems in a hurry. Am I right?'

· 4 ·

The Japanese side of the young bank clerk's visiting card read Yamada Toshihiko, his family name coming first; on the reverse side was Toshihiko Yamada, Foreign Department, Four Square Bank Inc., Hongo Branch, Tokyo, Japan. The bank's sign of four yellow squares was on the top left corner of the card, but its motto, 'We stand four square', was omitted. While Toshihiko's father and mother called him Toshi or Toshi-chan, his sister called him *onī-san* (elder brother); his close friends called him Yamada or sometimes Toshi, and his colleagues Yamada-san.

Toshi was twenty-six and had been in the bank since graduating from a Tokyo university four years ago. He had read economics and had got an A in English, although he could not speak the language very well. He found his colleagues congenial enough, but often he regretted his carefree university days and on occasions would recapture past joys by seeking out the company of a friend who worked in a certain club in Shinjuku, a quarter notorious for its eclectic night life.

· 5 ·

Jun left the apartment at 7 a.m. to go to his school, an hour and a half away by train and bus; Matthew, in bed, murmured as he was leaving, 'I have to go to a meeting too, but it's not until one o'clock. Should I have an early lunch here or a late one at the university, or should I indulge myself at the Cosmopolitan Hotel?'

'You must do what you think wise,' replied Jun, repeating the expression Matthew often used when asked advice.

'See you tonight!' cried Matthew when the front door slammed. He lay in bed for another half hour contemplating the day ahead. What would this new teacher, Sylvia Field, be like? A divorcée, presumably, with a grown-up son, fifty years old, which made her five years younger than he, quite striking according to the photograph she had sent along with her curriculum vitae when she had

14

applied for the post, blonde (dyed, no doubt) with good features, a firm chin. Matthew had recommended her. The other candidates, male and female Americans with degrees in linguistics, had been carefully considered, but Matthew had won the day. Or had it been the photograph that had done so? There were occasions when he wished he had not been successful in persuading his colleagues to appoint Sylvia. What with her credentials (she had published two books of poetry; he had published nothing except articles in minor Japanese magazines) and her looks he feared she might outshine him. He liked to think he was the department's favourite foreign professor.

Matthew rose from his bed, put on his dressing gown, went into the narrow kitchen and made coffee and toast. In his hurry Jun obviously had not breakfasted as no dirty cup and rice bowl cluttered the sink. He sat at the dining-table in the largish living room and perused the *Japan Times*, which Jun had thoughtfully put by his place, munched toast and marmalade and sipped the coffee. He liked to begin the day slowly. His classes never began before eleven. He decided that he would make some sandwiches and lunch in his room at the university, after the Faculty meeting.

At noon, Matthew, dressed in tweed sports coat and grey flannel trousers over which he wore a tweed greatcoat, set out for the university, three quarters of an hour away. He walked slowly; as he was stout, most of his movements were deliberate and contrasted markedly with the speed at which the Japanese did most things, except making decisions. Why run to catch a train when there was another in three minutes? What does it matter if one is a little late? He locked the door of his apartment, which was above his landlord's garage, descended the iron staircase and ambled down the slope towards the station.

· 6 ·

'Mrs Ota said you do not look like a teacher,' Professor Suzuki informed Sylvia. They were walking along Hongo Avenue towards the apartment that had been allotted to the new member of the Faculty of Literature, English Department.

'Am I to take that as a compliment?'

The professor gave a laugh in reply which made Sylvia wonder if he had understood the question. They crossed a main road and continued along the avenue on the left side of which were the massive evergreen trees of Tokyo University. Suzuki paused outside a large post office, a rectangular building of no architectural merit, and said, 'Post office. You can come here with your letters.'

'Convenient,' remarked Sylvia.

A bicycle whizzed between them. 'Heavens!' cried Sylvia. 'How dangerous! Why is he on the pavement?'

'Bicycles may only use the sidewalk.'

'Why?'

'There were so many accidents when they used the road.' The professor paused at the top of a street leading down from the avenue. 'Shopping street,' he said. 'Useful for you, maybe.'

Another bicycle flashed by. 'These bicycles will take some getting used to.'

They turned down a narrow road that ended after about sixty yards in an apartment block. 'Your mansion,' said the professor.

'Mansion?'

On the left of the apartments were a car park and a graveyard; on the right a modern Buddhist temple in concrete decorated with a sort of pebble dash. Above the entrance in Japanese and Roman writing was the name of the building: 'Sunflower Mansions'.

They entered a dark hall. On the left was an office in which an elderly man in a grey uniform was sitting and watching television. Suzuki had a word with the porter and led Sylvia towards the lift. 'Floor two,' he said, pressing a button. 'That is floor two for us, floor one for you.'

'Like in America,' said Sylvia. 'We hardly need the lift to go up one floor.'

'Lift for you, elevator for us,' remarked Suzuki with one of his laughs.

They arrived in a passage lit by fluorescent lighting with windows at either end, and when they reached Number 202, Suzuki produced a key. He put it in the heavy metal door and pulled it towards him.

This surprised Sylvia. 'Why doesn't it open inwards? In En-

16

gland . . . ' She stopped, reminding herself that she must not be the insular traveller and compare foreign arrangements unfavourably with those in her own country.

Suzuki went into the tiny hall, slid out of his shoes and mounted a high step at the top of which were two pairs of shabby, backless slippers. He put his feet into one of the pairs and said as Sylvia was about to place her shod right foot on the step, 'You must take off, I'm afraid.'

'Must I? In my own house?' Again Sylvia had to sit on the step to unlace her brogues. 'Must I wear these?' she asked, indicating the other pair of slippers.

'It is our custom.'

Sylvia stepped into the second pair of slippers, which looked very second-hand.

On the left was a six-tatami-mat room in which was a honeymoon size bed and a series of cupboards, a low table with a fluorescent office lamp on it, and a looking-glass on a low stand, designed for floor use. The windows which gave on to the passage were of frosted glass.

'Bedroom,' said Suzuki.

'I see.' Sylvia tried not to show her disappointment.

Opposite the bedroom on the other side of the hall was the bathroom, lavatory and an alcove containing a washing machine.

'Now, here is the living-dining-kitchen room, the LDK, as we call it.' He opened a door and they entered an L-shaped room. Against the back wall in a row were a refrigerator, a sink and gas cooker; above there were cupboards containing pans and crockery. A dining-table with four chairs stood two yards away from the 'kitchen', and down the long side of the L were bookshelves, empty except for a telephone on one of them. Round the corner was a space (the foot of the letter) in which were a Rexine settee, two imitation leather chairs with straps for arms, and a bureau. The space in the L was shut off by sliding paper and wood screens. Professor Suzuki slid back one of these to reveal a four-mat room containing no furniture. 'These doors are called *shōji*,' he said, and going to the window he added, 'and these are *shōji* too.' He slid open two of the screens which concealed sliding glass windows and a balcony, a vestigial construction, too narrow for use. 'I hope you are not afraid of ghosts.'

17

'Ghosts?'

'Well, we say that graveyards have ghosts.' He let out his high, girlish laugh.

Sylvia remained solemn. She was busy looking round the room, whose simplicity and dinginess rather appalled her. She joined her companion at the window. Below, a dumpy little woman in a cloth hat was sweeping the paths between the graves; beyond the cemetery were not unpleasant wooden houses with grey tiled roofs. It was quiet except for the faint rumble of traffic on Hongo Avenue. She turned from the window and saw the professor looking expectantly at her. 'There is a gas heater there,' he said. 'and an air cooler up here.' He indicated the appliances. 'I hope you are satisfied,' he went on, as if he had sensed her dismay. 'Accomodation is a great problem in Tokyo. This is very central.'

'What is the rent?'

'The university will pay the rent apart from a nominal sum, which will be taken off your salary, but you must pay the *kanrinin*.'

'The what?'

'The *kanrinin*, the, how shall I say? . . . the, er, the janitor, the maintenance man. You must pay him fifteen thousand yen a month for the services, taking in your mail, cleaning the passages, clearing away the garbage and so on.'

'Fifteen thousand? How much is that? One thousand yen is roughly four pounds, so that is sixty pounds. It seems a lot.'

'I am sorry.'

'No, I'm not complaining,' said Sylvia, hastily. 'When may I move in?'

'When you like.'

'I'll do so tomorrow. I brought some sheets and I saw there were blankets on the bed and a pillow. The hotel is so expensive. It is a waste to stay there longer than necessary.'

They left the flat. Suzuki handed Sylvia the key after he had locked the door. 'We will go to the university by subway.' he said, 'so you can learn the way.' He paused when they came to the Red Gate, their rendezvous earlier that morning, and pointing across the avenue at the vermilion, wooden, roofed structure, he said, 'That used to be the entrance to Lord Maeda's mansion, and is all that is left of it. His land was taken by the government for the building of Tokyo University, whose buildings you can see behind the gate. He was one of the richest feudal lords in Japan. He was known as "Million-rice-bags Maeda". He was given other land in another part of Tokyo, where he built another mansion. Now we have no lords. You have lords in England.'

'Yes we do, but they are not all that important.'

They passed a drinks shop, several small cafés and a number of bookshops. Sylvia stopped by each of the latter but expressed disappointment when she saw their windows displayed only Japanese books. There was one which had art books on show in several languages, and another with books on philosophy, mostly German. They came upon a Pachinko parlour outside which Sylvia stopped, amazed at the garishly lit place, the martial music that blared forth and the rows of pinball machines inside. 'Good heavens!' she exclaimed. 'The players look so absorbed.'

'They make money, sometimes,' said Suzuki, apologetically.

Next was a McDonald's hamburger joint. Its big yellow M framed in red stood out incongruously in the street of drab and assorted buildings. There was no harmony. Just past McDonald's Suzuki pointed out a little building on the corner of a busy crossroads. 'A police box,' he explained. Inside and almost filling it were two policemen in dark blue, wearing black leather Sam Brownes with revolvers attached to them. The couple waited for the traffic lights to turn green and then crossed the road with a posse of pedestrians, a mixed bag of walkers: young, old, middle aged. 'How they hurry!' Sylvia murmured to herself. On the corner across the street Suzuki indicated the Four Square Bank, where on the second floor Toshi was at his desk. 'I recommend that bank,' said the professor. 'You can open an account there so the university can pay your salary into it.'

The two continued along the busy street, sometimes one behind the other because of the hastening people. Sylvia was only able to glance at the shops they passed because Suzuki kept speeding ahead of her and she was afraid of losing sight of him. He turned down an alley of shops. Sylvia could not resist looking into the window of a shop selling coffee beans from all the coffee-producing countries in the world. 'You li' coffee?' asked Suzuki, who had retraced his steps.

'Yes, I do.'

'You want some coffee now?'

'No. I was just amazed at the wide choice.'

'In Tokyo you can buy everything. We take the subway here.' They entered a dingy ticket hall. Suzuki inserted coins into a machine and gave Sylvia a ticket.

'How much was it?' she asked.

'Nothing. I pay.'

'That's good of you. Thank you. But I want to know the cost of the ticket so I know how much to put into the machine when I take the train by myself.'

'One hundred and forty yen.'

While Sylvia calculated what the sum was in sterling, they descended a steep flight of concrete steps to a platform which was even murkier than the entrance. An amplified voice made an announcement. 'What's he saying?' asked Sylvia.

'He say a train is coming.'

'Isn't that what one would expect?'

'He also warn us about the danger and he tell us to stand behind the white line – that line there, you see?' Suzuki readied himself for the approaching train, which was red and looked as if it had been in service for many years. The professor waited for passengers to alight and then leapt into a carriage ahead of Sylvia and other travellers. This lack of gallantry irritated her until she saw its point, which was to secure her a seat. Dark eyes opposite and above her stared; they drank her in, and then having had a deep draught went on with reading or looking out of the window. The train had come out of the tunnel and was in the open. They passed a gigantic silver dome.

'What is that?' she asked.

'That is the Korakuen indoor stadium. They play baseball.'

'So huge!'

The train soon entered another tunnel and after two stops they arrived at Ikebukuro, their destination and a terminus. As the train was approaching the station a long announcement came through the loudspeakers.

'What is he saying?'

'He tell us of the other lines at this station and also he ask us not to forget anything, and he thank us for travelling by this line.'

'How sweet!'

Suzuki smiled weakly. He and Sylvia followed the crowd of passengers up a flight of steps to an underground concourse that was teeming with people hurrying in all directions.

'Lord, the crowds!'

'It is usual,' said the professor, who slipped his way through the throng like an eel. Sylvia followed, getting jostled.

'I don't think I'll ever get used to these crowds,' she said when she had caught Suzuki up. He was standing at the foot of a flight of concrete steps.

'God, more mountaineering! They look like a cliff face.'

Suzuki made no rejoinder.

· 7 ·

A few minutes before Sylvia and the professor ascended into the turbulent sea of humanity surging about the underground concourse at Ikebukuro Station, Matthew descended into the tumult from another line on a higher level. A plump old hand, he knew better than to climb the steps when advantage could be taken of the moving staircase that conveyed potential shoppers from the concourse up to the ground floor of the department store which dominated part of the west exit of the station. The escalator took him up to the women's shoe section. In spite of his having used this method of ascent to street level hundreds of times, nevertheless it was with a certain diffidence that he passed the rows of ladies' shoes and made his way past shelves of handbags manufactured by famous European houses to the door. In order to satisfy his conscience about not being a bona fide customer he reminded himself that he had often purchased things from the store. When he had told Jun how he felt about this way of leaving the station his friend had laughed. 'They don't mind,' Jun had said. 'But what if everyone did it?' 'Everyone they not do it,' had been Jun's reply. And yet Jun would not cross the road if the traffic lights were red and nothing was coming.

Matthew walked slowly to the university which was half a mile from the station. It was not yet term time, but quite a few students were wandering about in that aimless way that students the world over adopt on their campuses. Their gait was different from that of people who had entered their working lives. He arrived at a pair of iron gates, passed through and reached a building which was faced with red brick tiles, the Faculty of Literature. He nodded to the porter sitting in his office and went down a dark passage to his room. Before entering it, he looked at the door of the next room and saw that the name of the new arrival had already been put on it: Sylvia Field. 'They might have put Mrs or Ms,' he muttered to himself as he opened his own door. 'Some may not be sure of her sex. I wonder if we'll get on.' He sat at his desk which was at the head of a long table and took out of his brief case the ham, cheese and tomato sandwiches he had made that morning. He decided to consume them before the meeting.

· 8 ·

'What about a lunch?' Professor Suzuki asked Sylvia.

They were standing at the west entrance to Ikebukuro Station. Sylvia looked out at the square they were facing. It had two large ventilation ducts on one side and on the other a bronze trio of two women, scantily clothed, and a man, nude except for a slip, in the midst of treading a gentle measure.

'Oh, I like that!' declared Sylvia.' '"Homage to Terpsichore". Good.'

'What about a lunch?' repeated Suzuki, looking at his watch. We have about forty-five minutes. What kind would you like?'

'Kind?'

'Western style; Chinese – there is a noodle shop near, it serves good noodles; or,' he looked across the square where the yellow M framed in red shone out, 'what about McDonald's?'

'Why not something Japanese? I had some raw fish with rice at a Japanese restaurant in London and thought it delicious.' Suzuki looked uncertain, so Sylvia went on. 'After all, we're in Japan. Why not a Japanese meal?'

'Okay. You like *sushi*?'

'I'm not sure what that is. It sounds exciting. Well yes, please.'

Suzuki guided Sylvia across a road to a wide open space in front of a gigantic building with a huge glass portico.

'What on earth is that?' asked Sylvia.

'That's the new concert hall. In English it is called Metropolitan Art Space. It has three theatres as well as galleries for exhibitions. Inside a very big escalator like in your London subway.'

'Very impressive.' Sylvia looked at a big piece of abstract sculpture in front of the mammoth building, which was a mixture of styles: Pompidou Centre, concrete box and Doric columns. The sculpture was black and resembled a tuning fork with one of its prongs half broken. 'What's that supposed to represent?'

'I don't know.'

While waiting for the lights to change, Sylvia noticed on a nearby corner a department store with the sign 'OI OI' prominently displayed. 'Oi, oi!' laughed Sylvia. 'It sounds like a Cockney cry.'

'It mean *marui*, round. It's the name of the store.'

They crossed the road and entered an alley. An elderly woman on a bicycle whizzed by Sylvia, practically shaving her. 'Even the old do it,' said Sylvia. 'One needs eyes in the back of one's head here.' She laughed. She paused outside a new building that called itself Hotel City. 'A good hotel?' she asked. 'I might have stayed there instead of in that expensive place by the moat.'

'It's a "love hotel",' explained Suzuki.

'A "love hotel"? I see, a short-time place. How interesting!' She looked at a notice outside which had two prices on it: ¥4,500 and ¥6,500, and asked for an explanation.

Embarrassed, Suzuki said, 'One price for two hours, other price for one night.'

'How amusing!'

They turned into a short street and came upon a new-looking shop with model fish dishes in the window: rice balls wrapped in seaweed with a slither of raw fish on top, or a prawn, a piece of squid or a bit of octopus. 'Fascinating,' she said.

'This is where we eat.'

'Oh, good!'

As soon as they entered the restaurant, three men in white coats, aprons and hats cried out, '*Irasshaimase*!' and the professor

23

and his protégée sat on stools at the bar and faced a glass case full of fishy morsels. 'This is exciting!' exclaimed Sylvia. 'Now I feel I have arrived in Japan. You *are* kind!'

'What you like?' asked the professor. He seemed to have lost some of the buoyancy he had had earlier in the day. 'Can you eat raw fish?'

'Yes, of course I can. We have smoked salmon and Bismark herring in the West. They're practically raw; and as I told you I had some raw fish in London and adored it. What is that red stuff?' Sylvia pointed.

'*Maguro*. Tuna.'

'Let's have some of that. Please order a selection. And what about some sake?'

'You like sake, now?'

'Yes, why not?'

Sylvia carefully watched the man skilfully slice the lump of tuna with a large sharp knife and soon four slithers of *maguro* on top of wedges of rice appeared on the counter. Sylvia and the professor took one each in their fingers.

'Delicious!' exclaimed Sylvia. 'Absolute heaven! Food for the gods!'

Suzuki poured some sake into a tiny porcelain cup and handed it to Sylvia, who took it and waited for the professor to fill his own cup, but he just put a drop of the wine into it and placed the little porcelain decanter between them. '*Kampai*!' he said, holding up his cup. 'It mean the same as "your health".'

'*Kampai*,' echoed Sylvia, adding. 'This is fun.' She drained her cup and Suzuki refilled it at once. 'You're not having any?'

'I can't drink at midday.'

After biting in half her second piece of *maguro* and rice, Sylvia said, 'Do tell me something, Professor Suzuki, why did Mrs Ota knock on her own sitting-room door?' Sylvia put the other piece of *sushi* into her mouth and then tossed back her sake; again her cup was immediately refilled.

Suzuki seemed puzzled. Sylvia repeated. 'Why did Mrs Ota knock on the door when we were waiting for her in her own sitting-room?'

'Why she knock?'

'Yes, why she knock?'

'It is polite to knock. You do not knock?'

'Yes, we knock. We knock on bedroom doors, not on sitting-room doors. In a bedroom one might be in a state of undress or something, so we knock to warn the occupant, to ask permission to enter; but in a sitting-room one is supposed not to be in a state or a position that requires a warning. Her knocking suggested that you and I might have been up to something.'

'Up to something?'

'Doing something that we would not like anyone to see.'

'Sorry, I do not understand, Mrs Field. What kind of thing?'

'Well, kissing or something.' Sylvia hoped her laugh would alleviate the shocked look on Suzuki's face.

'Kissing? You think Mrs Ota think that you and I were kissing?'

Sylvia sighed. 'No, I do not think that Mrs Ota thought that you and I might be kissing, but knocking on her own sitting-room door suggests that she thought we might be doing something we needed warning to stop.'

'It is the Japanese custom to knock on door.'

'I see. Now, what is that the man has put on the counter?'

'Squid. We call it *ika*.'

Sylvia took one of the four wedges. 'Very good, but not as good as the tuna – what do you call tuna?'

'*Maguro*.'

'*Maguro*. I must try and remember it.'

Suzuki emptied the remains of the sake into Sylvia's cup.

· 9 ·

Matthew had finished his sandwiches. He had begun to read 'Isabella, or the Pot of Basil' in preparation for a tutorial with one of his M.A. students, a rather pretty girl. Why had she chosen Keats? Oh dear! They had read some of the odes last academic year and she had found 'Ode on a Grecian Urn' heavy going. He pulled his watch out of his trousers pocket: five to one. Time to go up to the meeting. He more and more frequently caught himself talking out loud when alone. Age. He rose, and picking up a notebook so as to be armed with something and to appear occupied, he left his room and took the lift up to the third floor. Would she be like her photograph? He went down the passage to the Conference Room. About half the Faculty was present. He sat in the vacant chair next to Professor Maeda, a kind man whom Matthew liked. He was the current chairman of the English section of the Faculty of Literature.

· 10 ·

Suzuki paid the bill while Sylvia was in the lavatory. She joined him at the door. 'Was it very expensive?' she asked.

'It doesn't matter.' He went ahead into the street.

'How much did it cost?'

'It doesn't matter,' he repeated.

'But I want to know for the future. I might want to go there by myself.'

'It cost about ten thousand yen.'

'Gosh! Did it really? That's about forty pounds. How frightful! And we didn't have all that much. I am sorry. I didn't mean to make you give me such an expensive meal.'

'Never mind.'

'Let me pay my share.'

'No, no. You are our guest.'

'It's very kind of you, but . . . '

They were walking on the narrow pavement towards the university. Again Sylvia was disconcerted by the bicycles which forced her to walk behind the professor. They entered the same building which Matthew had entered not long before. Suzuki spoke to the porter, who gave him a key with a wooden plaque attached to it marked No. 3 and they went down the passage. He paused outside Matthew's room and knocked on the door. 'You knock on office doors?' he asked.

'Yes, I think we do.'

'In case of kissing?' The professor smiled. This pleased Sylvia. It showed that he did have some sense of humour. She laughed.

'Not really.'

There was no answer since Matthew had gone upstairs a few minutes before. Professor Suzuki unlocked the door of the next room. 'This is your room.'

'How splendid! I have a room to myself?'

'Yes. This is your room. It is a very bad room. I am sorry.'

The room was murky. Its shelves were packed with Japanese theses loosely bound, and the windows were of frosted glass. Sylvia said unenthusiastically, 'It's fine. To have a room to myself is marvellous.'

'Now we go upstairs to meet the Faculty members.'

Sylvia took off her overcoat and hat. 'May I leave these here?'

'It is your room.'

She looked in the mirror, which was over a handbasin in a corner, and tidied her hair, licked her lips. 'Do I look all right?' she asked.

He seemed surprised by the question and made no reply to it. 'Let us go,' he said a little impatiently.

Suzuki knocked on a door on the third floor and without waiting for a reply led Sylvia into the conference room which was furnished with a long table around which were gathered the members of the Faculty, all men except for two women, one middle aged, the other elderly and grey. From the foot of the table with Sylvia beside him, Suzuki addressed the assembled professors in Japanese. His speech caused some laughter. Sylvia thought she detected the words *maguro* and sake and guessed that the professor had referred to their lunch. While he was speaking all eyes were on Sylvia: scrutinizing, they were like those on the train. Sylvia looked at her future colleagues in turn. She noticed a large, bald, benevolent-looking Westerner – Matthew smiled and nodded. When Suzuki had done, a middle-aged professor who was sitting at the head of the table uttered a few words which Suzuki translated. 'Professor Ishizuka, who is the Dean of the Faculty, welcomes you to our university. He hopes you will be happy among us. Please say some words.' Suzuki then abandoned Sylvia, leaving her alone at the foot of the long table, and took his place among his colleagues. She felt like a supplicant.

After an awkward silence, Sylvia said, 'First I would like to thank you all for appointing me. I can't tell you how much I have

27

been looking forward to coming to Japan, a country I have always longed to visit and one I never dreamed I would have the opportunity to live in. You have made my dream come true. Second, I must put on record my thanks to Professor Suzuki, who so very kindly looked after me this morning. He introduced me to some of the delights of the Japanese cuisine by feeding me on *sushi* and sake. I must say I liked them both enormously . . . ' (there were a few half-hearted laughs) 'and my liking them is a good omen, I think, for my visit to Japan and to this university . . . ' (more laughter). Sylvia smiled, 'And third, I would just like to add that I greatly look forward to beginning my job here, meeting the students and getting to know you all. Thank you.' There was a silence for some moments which was broken by applause led, Sylvia noticed, by the one foreigner present.

Matthew rose and joined Sylvia at the bottom of the table. He introduced himself and added, 'I've been delegated to show you round.' He bowed towards the Dean. Sylvia nodded and left the room with the Englishman.

· 11 ·

'Was I all right?' Sylvia asked Matthew as soon as they had left the conference room.

'You were fine.'

'Seriously?'

'Seriously.'

'I didn't know which note to strike.'

'You struck the right one. You made a good impression. I know that.'

'You are kind!'

'I mean it.'

'They don't seem to understand English very well, do they? I mean, Professor Suzuki couldn't grasp my remarks about Mrs Ota knocking on her own sitting-room door. I won't go into it now but we had a hilarious, to me anyway, conversation. Doesn't the Dean speak English?'

'Very little. He belongs to the French Department of the Faculty. He's an expert on Molière.'

'I wonder what *Le Misanthrope* is like in Japanese. I suppose it's been translated.'

'I expect so. I've no idea how it goes down in Japanese. Professor Maeda, who is the Chairman of the English Department, speaks English quite well.'

'There is a Dean and a Chairman?'

'The Dean is the head of the Faculty of Literature, which includes French, German, Japanese and Chinese as well as English. The Chairman is the head of the English Department.'

Matthew showed the newcomer round the campus, which with its purely functional buildings was not in any way outstanding. The place didn't have much atmosphere. He then took her to his room, where he made her a cup of instant coffee, apologizing for the fact that it was instant.

'How long have you been here?' Sylvia asked.

'Twenty years in Japan. Eight years at this university.'

'Quite a time. You like it, then?'

'Yes, on the whole, yes.' Matthew rubbed the side of his large nose with his left forefinger.

'I don't know if I'm going to like it. Professor Suzuki showed me my flat this morning. It's pretty awful. Very basic.'

'I know the place. I knew your predecessor, an American, who was there. It's not bad, and the university is paying the rent, which is more than they do for me, so . . . '

'So I should count myself lucky.'

Matthew smiled. 'That's right.'

'Do you live near the university?'

'About three quarters of an hour away. My journey includes a walk, two trains and another walk. Which is not bad for Tokyo. Professor Suzuki, for example, lives about two hours away from door to door, and so do many of the other professors.'

'I don't have to call you Professor Bennet, do I?' asked Sylvia, looking at Matthew, her blue eyes smiling.

'God no! I'm Matthew.'

'And please call me Sylvia.'

'You must come and have a meal some time.'

'Do you live alone?'

'No, I don't as a matter of fact.' Matthew did not reveal any more information about his private life, but he did blush.

Tactfully, Sylvia said, 'Now I must ask you some practical questions, if you don't mind. Professor suggested that I open an account at the Four Square Bank. Is that a good idea? I must say I love the name.'

'Its motto is "We Stand Four Square".'

'How lovely!'

They both laughed.

· 12 ·

Toshi was tired. He had had hardly any sleep and he kept nodding off at his desk in the foreign department of the Four Square Bank, Hongo Branch.

'Yamada-san!'

'Uh?'

A colleague informed him that there was a foreigner downstairs whom no one could understand. With some reluctance Toshi rose, put on the jacket of his dark-blue suit and descended into the main hall of the bank, where between the cash-dispensing machines and the rows of benches facing the counter stood Sylvia. She was trying to speak to an elderly bank usher in a grey suit with an armband. There was not a seat vacant. The benches were occupied, mostly by women who looked like housewives, busily flicking over the pages of magazines while awaiting their turn to be called to the counter by a clerk. Sylvia looked and felt lost and frustrated. The man could not or would not understand that she wanted to open an account. She showed him her book of traveller's cheques. He looked at them vaguely and said, 'Jus' a moment, please.' It was then that Toshi was called down from the foreign department.

'Can I help you?' he asked Sylvia.

'Oh, you speak English. Thank goodness! Yes, you can help me, or I hope you can. I want to cash these sterling traveller's cheques and open an account with the proceeds.'

'Proceeds?'

'The money I get from the cheques, the yen I get. I want to put it into an account at this bank.'

'Okay,' said Toshi. 'Please come upstair to my office.'

When the banking business had been completed and after a long wait during which Toshi went downstairs and up again several times, Sylvia was issued with a bank book and told that her cash card would be ready in a few days. The young man conducted Sylvia to the door and handed her his card. 'My name Toshihiko Yamada. You live Sunflower Mansions I see. May I come and see you, Mrs Field? I know Sunflower Mansions.'

Sylvia hesitated. She found this young bespectacled bank clerk charming, and he had been so helpful, taking such pains over her arrangements. She had had to think of a 'secret number' for her cash card. He had suggested the year of her birth, but sensing a ruse she had chosen that of her son Mark: 1969. This had surprised the clerk for a reason Sylvia had not been able to fathom. 'Yes, please come and see me. My apartment is 202 . . . oh, you know that from the address I've given you.'

'When?' he asked anxiously, his dark eyes earnestly looking into hers.

'What about the day after tomorrow, Saturday?'

'Okay. We finish work about one. Sometimes I must stay on. I come abou' five-thirty.' He stepped aside to allow a customer to leave.

'Make it half past six, can you? I'll give you supper.'

'Thank you very much, Mrs Field.'

She held out her hand which he took eagerly in his. His palm was soft and his fingers were limp. She attributed his weak handshake to the fact that he was probably more used to bowing than to shaking hands. She moved nearer the doors and the automatic glass panels opened. 'Goodbye, and thank you again,' she said, looking at him and then past him at the usher, who was quizzing them.

· 13 ·

When Toshi got upstairs he was greeted by a cry of 'Ahhh?', a teasing cry given on a rising note. One of his colleagues asked him what figures Sylvia had given as her secret number, and when Toshi told him, all the clerks laughed, and joked about women not wanting to reveal their age. The clerks decided that Sylvia was attractive and their teasing was spiked with envy. Toshi did not tell them about his Saturday engagement.

· 14 ·

On her way back to her flat, Sylvia wondered about Toshihiko Yamada as his card announced him. What did he want? Matthew had told her that there were some Japanese who sought out foreigners in order to try out the English they had spent years studying at school and the university. She guessed that he was about her son's age, twenty-three, perhaps a bit more; it was hard to tell, he looked youthful enough. Mark lived in Islington with Colin Sibley, a fairly successful actor who was twice his age and had recently formed his own company and taken on Mark as one of the members. Mark was stage-struck. Sylvia realized that the relationship was a homosexual one and she disliked that aspect of it. It made her feel that she had in a way failed as a mother. She had got as far as the Red Gate. She paused to examine the heavy, double-roofed construction; behind it, spoiling it and dwarfing it, rose the ugly, functional university blocks. She was amused by the notice which said, 'Don't make a bonfire' in Japanese and in English. As if anyone would burn their rubbish in the little garden by the gate! Or were pyromaniacs common in Japan? She waited for the traffic lights to turn green. Hongo Avenue was a busy artery. It was rarely free of traffic, it seemed. If only Mark would stop being the boy-friend of an older man! She crossed the road. She was getting used to being stared at. Being blonde, tall and plump, she felt she stood out among the Japanese like a cow among sheep. She would smile at a stare and thereby cause the eyes to look away; only occasionally would she get a return smile and then usually from women. She walked to her flat past the drinks shop, which no doubt would prove useful, wondering what she should provide for Mr Toshihiko Yamada of the Four Square Bank when he came to see her on Saturday.

· 15 ·

'What's she like?' asked Jun.

'She's not at all bad looking,' replied Matthew. 'I suppose she would be considered quite attractive. Not slim, but elegant. Out of the handkerchief drawer, as my mother would have said. A lady, if one dare use the expression today. Professor Suzuki was full of praise for her after the meeting. We must have her round.'

'You tell her abou' me?'

'No.'

'You ashame' of me?'

'No, darling, I'm not ashamed of you,' the teacher in him made him emphasize the ending of the word, and correcting his friend in a way counteracted Jun's criticism. 'But like you I don't want my inclinations known at my place of work.'

'But you invite her here?'

'Yes, one day. There's no hurry. I'll invite her when . . . '

'When I'm not here?'

'I didn't say that. I was going to say when I know her better.' In fact Matthew had thought of inviting Sylvia to lunch when Jun would be at school. 'We'll have her to dinner one evening. English women of her class don't care about one's tastes. They are amused by them, if anything.'

'Huh!' This was an expression of Jun's which indicated, as far as Matthew could fathom, a certain scepticism.

The following day Sylvia was almost an hour late for her appointment with Professor Suzuki in her room at the university. She got
lost at Ikebukuro Station going to the east exit instead of to the
west one. When she surfaced from the underground concourse,
she thought the square looked a bit different from the one she'd
been to the day before, but there were the bronze statues . . .
They were, though, not a man and two women in Terpsichorean
pose, but two gymnasts balancing on top of one another in an
improbable attitude, and the department store was different too.
She wandered about, crossed the square, set off down a wide
avenue, the pavement cluttered with shop wares and people. She
sensed she was wrong but went on hoping she wasn't. Soon she
had no doubt that she had missed the way and returned to the station
entrance. People were bustling everywhere. She approached a
middle-aged man, 'Excuse me, can you tell me where . . . ?' He
looked at her aghast and hurried away. Did she look a fright? She
walked along the outside of a store and came to what, thanks to
Suzuki's explanations the day before, she recognized as a police
box. Inside were three policemen in dark blue. Smiling, she asked
one of them for the university, and smiling back one of them in
halting English and with the aid of a map explained that she had
come out of the wrong exit. He guided her through a tunnel under
the railway lines – at its entrance was a plaque on which was
engraved 'We Road' in English – to the other side of the station
which was buried under the two immense department stores.
When they reached the other side, she saw the dancers, thanked
the policeman and found her way to the university.

Professor Suzuki did not show any annoyance at her lateness,
but she felt he was none too pleased with her. She met him in the
staff room on the third floor which Matthew had shown her. It was
a large room crammed with tables and a few armchairs; in one
corner sat a Japanese woman at a desk on which were a telephone
and a word processor; in another were cups and an electric kettle.
On the walls were posters and various notices, all in Japanese.
The professor first offered Sylvia some tea, which she declined, so
on his suggestion they descended in the lift to Sylvia's room. They
sat opposite each other and discussed Sylvia's timetable. She was

surprised that she only had to be at the university on two days a week.

'What am I going to do on the other days?' she asked.

'You can do *arbeito*, if you like.'

'*Arbeito*? What on earth is that?'

'Take a side job.'

'Oh, I see from the German, *arbeit*. I don't think I fancy doing that.'

'Most of us have side jobs.'

'I shall spend my spare time learning about Japan and exploring Tokyo.'

'We Japanese do not need to do that.'

'Quite.'

She and the professor went through her timetable and discussed books for her undergraduate classes and her seminar with graduate students. When they had finished, Suzuki took out of his fat briefcase a paperback edition of *Lady Windermere's Fan*. 'May I ask you some questions, Mrs Field?'

'Of course.'

He opened the book and turned over a few pages. 'Ah, I find! It is in Act One. Lord Windermere he is talking of Mrs Erlynne to Lady Windermere. I read: "Misfortunes one can endure – they come from outside, they are accidents. But to suffer for one's own faults – ah! – there is the sting of life." I'm not sure of the meaning exactly. What does it mean "misfortunes one can endure"? How can one endure misfortunes, if they are terrible?'

'May I see the text?' A little reluctantly, the professor handed her the book. The margin of every page was full of Japanese writing and many words were covered with transparent pink. Sylvia read Lord Windermere's lines. 'Wilde means,' she explained, 'that a misfortune, for example being in a train accident or having one's car stolen, one can endure because it is caused by someone else, an outside force, but when a disaster occurs due to something wrong one has done, it is then that one suffers.'

'I might suffer if I was in a train accident. I might break my arm.'

'Yes, you might suffer physically, but it would not be as hurtful as the mental suffering, the guilt feeling brought about by your own wilful wrong doing.'

'Please give an example.'

'Well, in Wilde's case, his "feasting with panthers".'

'His what?'

'His immoral acts. His liaisons with male prostitutes, for example. They brought him down in the end as no doubt you know. That he was tried and condemned was his own fault.'

'You think that Oscar Wilde was thinking of his, er . . . how shall I say? . . . his bad behaviour with boys when he wrote those lines?'

'Yes, possibly. But also what he says is true. When something goes wrong and no one is to blame but oneself, then it is more hurtful, more stinging, than if one can blame it on someone else or on an act of God. In this case, in the play, Lord Windermere is talking about Mrs Erlynne's running away with a lover. She suffered for it. It was her fault. It is the suffering from something that only oneself can be blamed for that stings.'

'I see.' But Sylvia felt that he hadn't understood. 'I see,' Suzuki repeated. 'That is very helpful. May I ask you some more questions?'

'Please.'

When the questions had been asked and, Sylvia hoped, satisfactorily answered, she said, 'Now I want to ask you some questions.'

'Please.' Suzuki seemed somewhat alarmed.

'Coming here, when I took the wrong way, I went under a tunnel called "We Road". What does it mean, "We Road"? Is it a mistake for "wee road", meaning tiny road?'

'It mean the road for everyone.'

'So it should be "Our Road"?'

'Maybe, it mean that.'

'And another question, what do Japanese people like to eat? I know they like raw fish, but what else do they like?'

'Sah!' Suzuki exclaimed. 'That is very difficult question.'

'What would you give a Japanese if he were coming to dinner?'

'I never do cooking. My wife she look after that.'

'Would he like steak, or would he prefer roast pork?'

'Yes,' replied Suzuki.

Sylvia gave up the idea of asking any further culinary questions. Instead she asked, 'Is Professor Bennet married?'

'No,' replied Suzuki.

'I thought he said he didn't live alone.'

'I've no idea.'

'It's of no importance. I just wondered. Maybe I misunderstood him. "Yes" can so often be confused with "No", don't you think?'

'No,' answered the professor, uncertainly. Then with an intake of breath, a profusion of thanks, and a bow he left her office.

Sylvia sat for a while under the fluorescent light in her room. She wondered how she could make her dungeon less dreary. Matthew, she had noticed, had improved his cell by sticking up posters advertising art exhibitions and reproductions of paintings by famous artists on his walls. She was amused but at the same time irritated by Suzuki's denseness about the lines in the Wilde play and his inability to answer her question about food. She wanted to know what to give Toshihiko Yamada when he came to supper on Saturday. Matthew had given her his telephone number. She picked up the phone on her desk and dialled the number, only half expecting him to be in as it was almost noon. He was in, however. When she announced her name, he sounded wary.

'I want your advice,' said Sylvia.

'Oh, yes?' He sounded even more wary.

'I've made a conquest,' she began and went on to tell him about Toshi. 'He's perfectly sweet,' she added in her slightly patronizing upper-class accent. 'But how should I entertain him? I invited him to supper. What should I give him?'

'Steak. They like steak,' advised Matthew.

'With vegetables?'

'Yes.'

'Rice?'

'Not necessary, though they adore the stuff, and feel they haven't eaten properly if they haven't had any.'

'I'd better serve rice then. And a green vegetable?'

'Salad. They like salad. Don't serve rice. You probably won't cook it in the way they like it. Give him fried potatoes and vegetables and then a salad.'

'Good. And wine?'

'Yes. They like wine nowadays.'

'What drink before the meal?'

'Whisky.'

'Scotch?'

'Oh, yes.'

'You wouldn't like to come and help out with him, would you?'

'Sorry. I'm never free on a Saturday.'

'I see. Another time then.'

'See you at the university next week.'

'Goodbye, Matthew. You solved my problem. Thank you so much.'

· 17 ·

'She's invited a bank clerk from the Four Square Bank to dinner tomorrow night,' Matthew informed his friend Jun, who was lying on the sofa with the remote control apparatus in his hand. He was about to settle down to an evening's television viewing.

'Why? She want to rend money?'

'Lend, Jun dear, and you mean borrow. No, I don't think so. She didn't say why she invited him. She rang me to ask what she should give him to eat.'

'Maybe she love him.' Jun changed the channel which was showing commercials.

'She's fifty.'

'Fifty isn't too ole for love, is it, Mattu-san?'

Matthew rose from his armchair. 'No, darling, it isn't. But in her case I doubt it. He must be young if he's a bank clerk. He wasn't the manager.'

'A *tsubame*, maybe.'

'I've only met her once. I don't know if she wants a gigolo. Anyway, I'm for bed.'

'I want to watch *Casablanca*.'

'That old thing?'

'I love it.'

'Ingrid Bergman and Humphrey Bogart?'

'Yes. Humphrey Bogart very handsome and sexy.'

'You think so?'

'Yes, and the story it suit us. We Japanese like that kind of story because it is the same as our life. Ingrid Bergman has choice between her lover and her husband, between her true feelings, love, and duty, between *ninjo* and *giri*. She choose *giri* and go off with her husband, and that is what a Japanese would do. He have to do.'

'What have you chosen, Jun?'

'Me?'

'Yes, you, Jun.'

'I have not chosen *giri*. You know that, Mattu-san. I have chosen *ninjo*, but sometime I am very worried I have not chosen *giri*. *Giri* is very important in Japan.'

'Please don't choose *giri*. You won't, will you?'

'Yes, I mean no. Not yet, anyway.'

'Good. I'm going to bed then.'

'Goodni', Mattu-san.'

'Don't be long, Jun. Switch off before Ingrid Bergman chooses *giri*.'

· 18 ·

On the Saturday morning Sylvia left her apartment with her handbag over one arm and a garish plastic duty-free bag she had got at Bangkok airport over the other. She made her way to Hongo Avenue, and after a few yards turned into the street of shops Suzuki had shown her. She came to a butcher's shop, which like most of the individual shops she had noticed so far, was open to the street. On one side a woman in a long white coat and a white hat was busily frying breaded pork cutlets; behind the counter were two men, also in white, one old, the other young – father and son, no doubt. Sylvia looked at the various cuts of meat in the glass case below the counter, and then, smiling, faced the two butchers. 'Steak, please,' she said, almost apologetically.

'*Sutēki*?' replied the younger butcher.

'Yes. *Hai*.' Sylvia had picked up the easy Japanese affirmative.

The young butcher smiled and brought out of a huge refrigerator a hunk of beef. Sylvia held up two fingers and then with her forefinger and her thumb indicated the thickness she required.

The steaks when cut looked enormous and their price was high. Sylvia nodded and the meat was wrapped in stiff grease-proof paper, put into a plastic bag and then into brown paper, and secured with an elastic band. The tidy parcel almost looked ready for posting. Sylvia paid, both butchers bowed, crying out their thanks. If all shopping was like this, she would enjoy it.

She passed on down to a large greengrocer's shop that faced up the street, which ended in a T-junction at this point. The name of the shop, which she couldn't read, was flanked by Coca-Cola signs. A business-like cry from the male and female staff welcomed her. She regarded the neat piles of fruit and vegetables and waited by a mound of potatoes until a girl had finished serving a housewife and approached her. 'Potatoes, one kilo,' she said, holding up a finger. The assistant weighed the potatoes and then put them into a brown paper bag, and after that Sylvia pointed to French beans, onions, tomatoes, lettuce and strawberries (she hoped Mr Yamada would like strawberries, for her always a treat), and the girl deftly weighed each item, filled more paper bags and jotted down the prices on a piece of grey cardboard. While the assistant was making rapid calculations on a pocket calculator, Sylvia noticed a young man standing near her with a box of aubergines in his arms. He wore a peaked cap with a number on it and a blue apron. Placing his box of the shining black vegetables on the floor, he smiled, showing a set of steel teeth. Sylvia paid the girl, who put Sylvia's purchases into her duty-free bag. Steel tooth noticed the bag and made a remark to the girl, who laughed.

Sylvia returned by the lane parallel to Hongo Avenue, buying a loaf and some ice cream from a jolly girl at a bread shop, and butter from a tiny, solemn woman in a little stall of a shop under the eaves of her apartment block. She and her equally tiny husband looked as if life were a struggle for them. But they had no rice. Well, Matthew had said that fried potatoes would do, so she'd give him 'French fries' as perhaps he would call them if he were English or American.

At six the bell sounded its two tones, which were like the first two notes of a chiming clock. Sylvia, wearing a plain sky-blue dress with long sleeves, shuffled to the door in one of the pairs of the backless slippers left behind by the previous tenant. She disliked this Japanese custom of taking one's shoes off inside the house for she felt undressed and unsmart in sloppy slippers, and the wrong height too. She went into the little hall, turned on the striplight, whose stark glare she hated, stepped into the well where shoes were discarded and pushed open the heavy, metal door. There stood Toshihiko Yamada bearing a parcel. He was not wearing his glasses.

'For you,' he said, handing Sylvia the parcel.

'Oh, how kind! But you shouldn't bring a present.'

'Japanese custom,' he replied, thereby rather deflating her enthusiasm. He stepped out of his black shoes without untying the laces and into the slippers Sylvia had placed on the step in the hall. He was wearing his bank outfit: a dark-blue suit, a white shirt and a maroon tie.

'Thank you very much for your kind invitation,' he said solemnly with a jerk of a bow.

'Not at all.' She smiled wondering if he would keep up this formal manner throughout the evening.

'Come in and sit down,' Sylvia said warmly. 'It is good to see you. I'm afraid my room is rather bare, but I hope to improve it.'

Toshi sat on the edge of one of the leather chairs in the foot of the L. He was blushing and his lips trembled when he said again, 'Thank you very much for your kind invitation.'

'Is it too warm in here?' Sylvia asked. The gas fire sat on the floor between the sitting part and the dining part of the room, not by a chimney, for there was no fireplace. This had worried her. It seemed dangerous and unsanitary. She was afraid of tripping on the rubber pipe that led to a gas point in the floor across the room.

'No, it fine,' said Toshi.

'It's rather chilly in the evening, isn't it?' remarked Sylvia. 'Is the weather cold for this time of the year?'

'Pardon?'

Sylvia was getting used to speaking slowly and articulating carefully. 'The weather,' she said, 'is it usual for the beginning of April?'

'It usual.'

'When shall I be able to put this ugly gas fire away?'

'Gas fire?'

'That.' She waved a hand at the fire.

'The heater.'

'Yes. When shall I be able to do without it? Next month?'

'Yes. Maybe.'

Sylvia wondered how long she could keep up this stilted conversation without laughing; perhaps he'd loosen up after a drink.
'What would you like to drink?'

'Juice. You have juice?'

'Juice? Oh, don't have a soft drink. Won't you have gin or
whisky?'

'You have?'

'Yes, I have. What about a whisky and water?'

'I like.'

'Good.' Sylvia rose and went to the kitchen area and poured out
a stiff whisky for Toshi and a gin and tonic for herself. She had
bought the spirits at the duty-free shop at Bangkok airport.

'Thank you,' he said when she gave him his drink; he rose a
little from his chair to receive it.

'Here's luck!' she raised her glass. He did the same, drank and
looked down.

Silence.

They sipped their drinks. Smiled at each other. Sipped again.
Sylvia couldn't think of anything to say. Toshi's face had become
red. Was he blushing? Or was it the alcohol? Her eyes wandered
over to the dining-table, on which she had put his present. 'Oh, I
haven't opened your parcel.' She got up and brought it to her
chair and sat down again and with a feigned excitement like that
she had assumed at Christmas over her son's gift to her, she said,
'What is it? How sweet of you to bring me something. I love
presents.' She slipped off the nylon ribbon round the box, undid
the paper wrapping and brought out of the box a tiny teapot and
two handleless cups in white porcelain, sparsely but artistically
patterned with blue and red flowers. 'How sweet!' She held up the
little pot. 'For a doll's – ' She checked herself in time she hoped.
Quickly, she added, 'For tea? Tea for one? It will do for my
morning cup.'

'It is for Japanese tea,' Toshi explained.

Sylvia examined the cups. 'Why is one cup bigger than the other?'

'Big one for man, small for woman.' Toshi blushed again, or
was it the whisky?

'I see,' said Sylvia, laughing, 'you only allow your women small cups, do you? In England that wouldn't go down very well. Women's Lib would be up in arms. Do you have Women's Lib in Japan?'

Toshi said, 'Sorry?'

'Never mind.' Sylvia looked into the box again. 'There's something more.' She brought out a round, dark-red tin with gold ideograms on it.

'Japanese tea,' he told her.

'Is it different?' She opened the tin. 'Why, it looks like – ' she was about to say 'dried grass' but she stopped herself in time. 'It looks different from Indian or China tea.'

'Yes,' he said. 'This green tea; that black tea.'

'I see. Thank you very much for your lovely present.'

'No,' he replied. 'Please.'

A silence set in again. Whisky was sipped again. An idea suddenly came to Sylvia. She got up. 'I wonder if you'd mind helping me with my bed.'

'Sorry?'

'I want you to help me move my bed. It's in the back room and I want to move it into this room.' She pulled open the *shōji* of the little alcove room. 'I've measured and it will fit. So please, will you come?' After a moment or two of hesitation he rose, put on his glasses and followed her into the back tatami room, in which she had spent two sleepless nights due to the fluorescent lighting in the corridor. Together they lifted the bed, but it would not go through the door.

'Jus' a moment, please.' Toshi thought for a moment and then said, 'I know.' He proceeded to take the bed to pieces, using his shoe as a hammer, and it was not long before the bed was re-erected in the inner room off the main one. After remaking the bed, Sylvia lay on it.' There, that's much better. I think I'll be able to see the trees in the graveyard when it's light. I like to look at trees when in bed.' Toshi watched her, amused. She got off the bed. 'Thank you very much, Mr Yamada. I am grateful. I don't think I could have borne another night in that horrid little room. And it smells too. Bad smell.' She held her nose. 'In that room bad smell.'

'Old tatami,' said Toshi.

'Is that what it is?' Sylvia closed the *shōji* round her new bedroom. 'Now let's have another drink.' When she had poured out another drink for Toshi and for herself, she sat on the Rexine sofa, and switching on what her husband had called her 'party smile', she said, 'Now, tell me something about yourself, Mr Yamada. Where do you live?'

'In Nerima.'

'Is that far from here?'

'Abou' forty-five minute.'

'Not too bad. Do you live with your parents?'

'No. They in Hamamatsu.'

'I'm very ignorant of the geography of Japan, I'm afraid. Where is that?'

'On the Tōkaidō line between Tokyo and Kyoto.'

'Have you any brothers and sisters?' She felt as if she were interviewing him for some job.

'I have one sister. She younger than me. She twenty-three.'

'The same age as my son.'

'You have son?' The young man seemed surprised, or was he pretending to be so?

'Yes. I am not a girl.'

'You look young. Your husband, where?'

'He is in London. We are divorced, separated.' She put her hands together and then pulled them apart quickly. 'It's over.' She shrugged and then rose. 'Now I must see about our meal. You like steak?'

'Yes, but I cannot stay.'

'But I asked you to supper. You must stay and eat your steak.'

'I mus' see my correagues.'

'See them when you've had dinner.' She looked at him, suspiciously. 'You haven't eaten, have you?'

'No.'

'Then sit there while I get things ready.' She went over to the kitchen area wondering why he had asked to visit if after under an hour he wanted to leave. Was it Japanese politeness? Was he disappointed in her? Had it been a mistake to ask him to help her move the bed? Surely not. He had carried out the task willingly and with an admirable practicality. When the meal was ready she called him to the table. They sat opposite each other in the middle

44

of the small, oblong dining-table. She had brought from England some white table-cloths and some crested silver (from her family) and old-fashioned knives with bone handles made in Sheffield. She loved this old silver and cutlery and was proud of it. Her husband had tried to filch it when they had parted. 'But it's mine!' she had protested and won. Toshi handled his heavy knife and fork awkwardly and he put butter on his bread with the butter knife. She poured some red Japanese wine she had bought from the local drinks shop into the tumbler by his side (there were no wineglasses in the apartment) and then half filled her tumbler. 'Here's luck,' she said, lifting her glass.

'Here's luck,' he repeated and looked into her eyes briefly and then sipped his wine.

'I know nothing about the wine here. I just chose a bottle. This tastes a bit sharp. What is the best Japanese wine?'

'I don't know.'

'Do you like wine?'

'Yes, I like.'

'I hate a meal without wine,' said Sylvia. 'Even when I'm alone I like to have a glass with my food.'

He ate his steak and vegetables quickly as if he were hungry or in a hurry. He did not offer any table talk. When he had finished he said, 'Very delicious.'

'The meat is nice and lean.'

'Lean?'

'Not fat.'

'I like fat,' declared Toshi solemnly.

Sylvia laughed. 'You mean, you like beef fat or fat bodies?'

'I like fat body. Japanese girl they too skinny.'

Sylvia didn't know whether Toshi was making a sly suggestion or simply stating his preference. For the first time since the young man had arrived her poise was put off balance; this remark suggested that he was perhaps less innocent than he seemed, that he could be in control of the situation if he wanted to be. The practical way he had used his shoe to hammer the bed apart was an indication of this.

'Very delicious,' he said again at the end of the meal when the strawberries and ice cream had been consumed. They returned to the armchairs on the other side of the room.

45

'Tea?' she asked. 'What about some of your tea?'

'I must be running along.'

Sylvia smiled at his use of an expression gleaned in all probability from a phrase book. 'I will not allow you to go until we have had some of your tea. I'll put on the kettle; presumably it needs hot water.'

'Hot water, yes.'

When the kettle had boiled, she brought it over and Toshi measured out some tea, using the lid of the tin to do so, and put it into the little pot into which Sylvia poured the hot water. He filled the big cup first and then the small one, which he gave to her.

'No, I want the big cup,' she said, playfully.

He handed her the big cup, but she said, 'No, I must have the small one, mustn't I? I was only joking.'

Like Suzuki he slurped his tea. Should she tell him it wasn't done to slurp? She decided not to. He was drinking tea in what was no doubt the Japanese way and they were in Japan.

'What do you usually do on Saturday nights?' she asked.

'I and my friends we go to a bar sometimes in Shinjuku, a karaoke bar and we sing.'

'Oh, do you sing? I should like to hear you sing.'

'Sometimes we play mah-jong.'

'Where are your friends tonight?'

'They go to a karaoke bar.' He looked at his watch. 'I said I meet them at nine o'clock. I mus' soon go.'

'Oh, don't go. I am enjoying your company.' She was. She found Toshi charming; his presence pleased her in spite of the banal conversation. Was this because she was lonely?

Half an hour creaked by with the talk becoming more and more desultory, and then Toshi rose. 'I have to go now,' he said. Sylvia rose too. 'Well, do come again, er, what should I call you? Mr Yamada sounds too formal.'

'Call me Toshi. My name Toshihiko but Toshi is better.'

She led him into the little hall, where he slipped into his shoes and took up his briefcase, which he had left on the step. She held out a hand. He took it, grasping it firmly, and then with rather a severe expression on his face, he stepped up into the hall again, suddenly put his arms round her and kissed her on the cheek. 'I love you, Mrs Field,' he said.

She laughed nervously. 'Don't be silly.' She was going to add the cliché, 'I'm old enough to be your mother,' but she didn't. He was the same height as she, unlike her ex-husband, who had towered over her, and Sylvia found the equality pleasing. Their faces were on the same level. His dark eyes burnt into hers, pleadingly. She laughed again and said, 'You're very sweet, Toshi,' and put a hand on his cheek.

'Excuse me,' he said and turned, pushed open the heavy door. 'May I visit you again, Mrs Field?' he asked on the threshold.

'Please do. Telephone.'

'Goodbye, Mrs Field. Thank you very much for the dinner.'

Sylvia locked the door and went back to the sitting-room, sat on the settee and laughed. He had been so funny and so sweet. Had she made a conquest? No man in his twenties had behaved to her as Toshi had, not since her Oxford days and her meeting with her ex-husband. What had Toshi meant by his hug, kiss and declaration of love? Was he sincere, did he hope for an easy lay, or was it merely filial? She rose and poured some wine into her glass on the dining-table. She felt rather excited.

· 19 ·

Toshi rang Sylvia the next morning, Sunday. 'Thank you very much, Mrs Field, for the nice dinner last night.'

'Not at all. It was a pleasure.'

'It was very good of you to go to all that trouble.'

'No trouble at all.'

'I very much enjoyed your kind hospitality.' Was he reciting or perhaps reading sentences from a phrase book? He might have been a teacher explaining to students how to thank for a formal entertainment.

'It was a pleasure to see you.' She felt that she too was beginning to sound like a phrase book.

'The food was very delicious.'

'It's kind of you to say so.'

'I apologize for my very bad behaviour.'

47

Did this mean the kiss? 'But you behaved perfectly.'

'I was very impolite.'

'I didn't think so.'

'What are you doing today?'

'I'm going to stay in and write letters.'

'May I come and see you?'

She paused. She didn't want to see him again so soon, and yet in some ways she did. But no; seeing him meant making an effort. She said, 'Sorry. I have so many letters to write and there are lectures to prepare . . .'

'I see. What about next Saturday?'

'All right. Come at seven, seven o'clock. Not before, please.' She didn't want him as early as six.

· 20 ·

It was Wednesday, the first day of the academic year, which, confusingly, began in April. The campus was alive with youth who, apart from their oriental faces and their uniformly black hair, looked in their jeans and sweaters, their long skirts, their short skirts, like students on most campuses in the world.

Sylvia had just had her first class, composition, and about one hundred and fifty students, a quarter of them men, had attended. There hadn't been seats for them all, so many had stood at the back of the class-room. Sylvia hadn't known what to do. She had expected twenty at the most and had planned to chat vaguely about writing. Flummoxed at the sight of so many flat faces which bore expressions of curiosity rather than eagerness, Sylvia had told them that being able to write a language was as important as being able to speak it. She wasn't certain herself if this was true, but this was a writing class and she felt she must emphasize the usefulness of being able to write in a foreign language. She went on to say that she wanted them to write a composition about a place they liked by the following Wednesday.

'It can be any place you like, a town, a village, a mountain, a room. You must describe it exactly and then give your reasons for liking it.' She wrote a plan for such an essay on the blackboard; this was copied diligently by some of the students into their exercise books, but not by all. 'Do you think you can write such a composition?' she asked one of the female students, a girl with a moon face and hair that fell to her waist. The girl her head down and did not answer. Sylvia then asked one of the males, a stalwart young man in a golfing jacket. 'Yes, I think so, Mrs Field,' he answered to her surprise. 'I don't see any difficulty in such an assignment.' After asking a few more students who either seemed too embarrassed to say anything or just muttered, 'Very difficult', Sylvia dismissed the class and went back to the Faculty building. She knocked on Matthew's door.

The Englishman stood up when she opened the door in response to his, '*Dōzo.*'

'May I come in?'

'Please, Sylvia. Do sit down.'

Sylvia took a chair near his desk at the end of the room by the window, which like hers was of frosted glass. 'How can I teach composition to a hundred and fifty?' she asked, indignantly.

'You won't have to.'

'But there was that number in the classroom just now.'

'They just came to see what you were like. Next week you'll have fifty, and that number will soon dwindle to twenty-five.'

'I set them a composition.'

'Then you may get none next week.'

'Really?'

'No, I'm exaggerating. You'll get some. Those who think that learning to write English may help them in the future. To change the subject, how did you get on with your bank clerk?'

Sylvia bridled a bit and then laughed. 'You're curious, are you?'

'I just wondered.'

'He was sweet. He helped me move my bed from that horrid little back room to the alcove that is screened from the main part of the room by those sliding doors.'

'*Shōji.*'

'Yes, *shōji.* I remember the name now. Suzuki told me. Anyway, it's much better and if I leave the *shōji* open I can see some trees in the graveyard from my bed. By the way, is there a swimming pool near here?'

'Yes. You swim, do you?' said Matthew a little enviously.

'Please tell me where it is some time.'

'Certainly. I'll draw you a map. You're free on Friday, aren't you? So am I. Would you like to come to lunch on that day?'

'Love to.'

'I'll tell you how to get to my station. Now, if you . . .'

· 21 ·

Sylvia was still uncertain about findings her way to the university and while on the Wednesday she had surfaced from the confusing concourse correctly and found the bronze dancers, on the Thursday, when she had to meet her graduate students, she had on ascending to ground level come face to face with the gymnasts. She remembered the 'We Road', found it and got to the side of the perpetual dancers. Thank heavens for them!

Returning home was easier. She descended the steep steps, went straight ahead towards a news-stand behind which was her subway line. There were only three stops before hers so she didn't mind standing. When she did get a seat, no one would sit next her. She felt a pariah and wondered if to the Japanese she smelt. She enjoyed the walk to her apartment from the station at Hongo in spite of the many pedestrians and the threat of the bicycles. She always looked across the street at the Four Square Bank and thought of Toshi.

On her way home she would buy some supplies. The woman in the drinks shop with the tired eyes said to her on her second visit, 'Your husband, where?' Sylvia had not known what to say. The question was so direct. She had smiled, shaken her head and said, 'No.' The woman's English was very rudimentary and anyway why should Sylvia satisfy her curiosity?

'You alone?' the woman had persisted, and Sylvia, cross, had answered rather loudly, 'Yes, I alone.' The man in the shop, round-faced, young, fat, and becapped, with an inane grin had readily offered to deliver her order to the flat. And when he had arrived and dumped the crate of various bottles on her inner step, she sensed he wanted to look into her apartment. To see what? Her husband? Her lover? She offered him a coin, which he refused. No tipping in Japan, that was something. Plenty of nosiness, however.

· 22 ·

Matthew was waiting at the ticket barrier when Sylvia arrived about half an hour late for the luncheon appointment. 'So sorry. That station at Shinjuku is such a maze.'

'The whole of Tokyo is a maze, my dear. One has to learn various *points de repère*, like a sign in English, or a greengrocer's shop.'

They began to ascend a gentle slope with shops on either side of the narrow street. They passed a bar called 'Dorian' and a convenience store called 'Lawson', then crossed a main road and turned into a lane with apartment houses and private dwellings with small gardens well fenced in.

'It's pleasant here,' remarked Sylvia. 'Less towny than my district.'

'Yoyogi Uehara is very upmarket,' joked Matthew. He led her into a short cul-de-sac. On the left above a private garage was an apartment reached by an iron staircase.

'Here we are.' Matthew guided her up and into his flat. Sylvia went straight to the window of the large sitting-room and looked out.

'How good to have a view of a garden! Better than a cemetery, much.'

'Now I must put a soufflé into the oven and then we'll have a drink. What will you have?'

'Gin and tonic, please.' Sylvia took off the coat of her two-piece outfit and sat on the capacious sofa opposite the television set. She looked around. There were two telephones on the desk that divided the room into sitting and eating areas, and a typewriter that had a sheet of paper in it, with a pile of books and a dictionary by its side. On the walls above overloaded bookshelves hung copies of Beardsley prints, some of which would have been called *risqué* by Sylvia's mother.

One of the telephones rang. Matthew hastened into the room, saw it was the instrument on the right side of the desk, disregarded it and returned to the kitchen. The phone was still making its presence known when he reappeared with a gin and tonic in each hand. Sylvia looked questioningly at the phone.

Matthew said, handing her a drink, 'I don't answer that one.' The ringing ceased. 'I can never understand why people who know one lives in a small place let the telephone ring and ring as if one had to go down a long passage and up several flights of stairs to reach it. Cheers!' He raised his glass.

Sylvia was puzzled, but she made no further comment about the two telephones.

'Are you going to like it here, d'you think?' Matthew asked, taking a swig at his gin and tonic. He sat in one of the armchairs.

'I don't know. I find it all very fascinating. How about you? I suppose the fascination has worn off. But you're still happy here?'

'Oh yes,' Matthew answered. 'Definitely yes. When the fascination has worn off, one becomes accustomed to the oddities. They no longer seem odd.' He gave a weak smile.' One accepts, one realizes that Japan is not at all a bad place to live in. It's expensive, very, but one is well paid. I save, even. And above all Tokyo is safe. You can wander about drunk at night with impunity, which you can't do in most big cities these days.'

'It doesn't seem a very relaxing place.'

'It isn't. It's a restless place. The Japanese are restless. They wriggle about all the time, even in – ' he was about to say 'even in bed' but stopped himself in time. 'I, being congenitally lethargic, find it stimulating.'

'The first thing I noticed was that everyone seemed to be in a tearing hurry. Much more so than in London.'

Matthew leapt out of his chair. 'The soufflé!' he cried as he sped into the kitchen. He reappeared and called her to the dining-table at the head of which he stood bearing a soufflé dish on a tray. 'Please sit here, Sylvia.' He indicated the place on his right, and after putting the soufflé on the table, he returned to the kitchen and came back with a bottle. 'Wine?'

'Please. Muscadet, I see, and Sur Lie.'

It pleased him that she knew the meaning of the French nomenclature. 'There's a good wine shop one stop from Ikebukuro. Worth knowing about. Now, do help yourself.'

After Sylvia had made conventional noises of praise for the cheese soufflé, she said, 'Professor Suzuki's a funny little chap, isn't he?'

'He's one of the best, actually.'

'He's a bit dense. It took me about half an hour to explain some simple lines in *Lady Windermere's Fan*.'

'I can tell you what the lines were: "Misfortunes one can endure . . ."'

'Yes,' Sylvia interrupted, 'that's right.' She laughed.

'He asked me about that epigram the other day.'

'He was sort of comparing our versions, was he?'

'Not quite trusting mine.' Matthew laughed and so did she. He liked her for laughing. So few people laughed today. 'How amusing! I was also amused to hear from his speech at the meeting that he gave you *sushi* for lunch. You know it's very expensive.'

'How was I to know? I asked to have a Japanese meal and he suggested noodles or *sushi*. Naturally I chose *sushi*.'

'And you had sake too, apparently.'

'Yes, but he only took one sip and left the rest for me. Was that because of the expense?'

'No. It was because he was going to a Faculty meeting and he didn't want to have a drink flush. He has a reputation of being quite a toper.'

'Toshi, that's the name of my bank clerk, got quite red in the face after one glass of whisky. It made him look self-conscious.'

'It's called *akai kao* in Japanese. Red face. It's due to a deficiency in the pigment of their skin. The Chinese have it too.'

'Poor things. It's a give-away then. What do the Japanese usually have for lunch?'

'*O-bentō.*'

'What's that?'

'Cold boiled rice, seaweed, pickles and a few oddments; often leftovers like a piece of fried chicken, a slice of ham. Their wives put the ingredients in a lacquer box – *bentō* – and arrange them prettily. My fr – '

'Yes?'

'I was going to say. . . . No, never mind. Have some more wine.' He refilled Sylvia's glass.

'What were you going to say, Matthew?'

'I forget now.' He scratched the top of his bald head, and then took a sip from his wineglass. 'How's your bank clerk?'

'I'm seeing him tomorrow. I think he's in love with me.' She gave a shy laugh.

'That may well be.'

'He's very young. He seems about the same age as my son, Mark. He may be a bit older.'

'They like the not-so-young sometimes.'

'Do they now? Anyway, at my age it's fun, it's pleasing to be admired. By the way, there's something I want to ask you about. I've noticed that if I get a seat on the train and there's a vacant place next to me, no one will take it. Why? Is it xenophobia? Or do they think I might pong?'

'A bit of both, probably. I've asked about this habit. Jun, er, a friend of mine says that they don't sit next to one as they are afraid one might ask them a difficult question, one they cannot answer, and not being able to answer it would embarrass them.'

'How absurd!' Sylvia laughed. 'Why on earth should they imagine we would ask them a difficult question? Do they think one would suddenly ask them what they thought about hieroglyphics or the quantum theory?' She laughed again.

'They are genuinely shy of foreigners. Perhaps that's the real reason.'

'Shyness is a frightful handicap. Shy people often miss out in life.'

'The Japanese certainly haven't done that.'

'You're right there, Matthew. Oh yes, there's another thing I want to ask you. You said you'd tell me the way to the swimming pool.'

'I'll draw you a map. Have some salad first.'

They ended lunch with cheese, and after coffee, which they had in what Matthew called 'another part of the forest' (by which he meant the part where the armchairs and sofa were), Sylvia asked if she could go to the loo. Matthew directed her to the bedroom, off which was the bathroom, and while she was in the lavatory he quickly hid the two pairs of men's pyjamas, one on each of the twin beds. He hoped she hadn't noticed as, he told himself, 'one never knows with women'.

· 23 ·

Sylvia was disconcerted when Toshi arrived at six on the Saturday evening. She was in the midst of preparing the meal and still in her peignoir and hadn't even done her hair.

'I did say seven,' she said sharply.

'This for you.' Toshi took a little parcel out of his briefcase and handed it to her.

Sylvia melted. 'Not another present! You mustn't bring a present each time you come.'

'You say you like presents.'

Sylvia laughed. She was quite disarmed. 'I do. But you gave me that pretty teapot last week. Look, Toshi, I've several things to do, would you mind sitting over there and reading the newspaper or something.'

Toshi took himself off to the corner. He was not wearing his spectacles. Sylvia turned on the standard lamp near his chair and gave him that day's copy of the *Japan Times*. 'Now you sit there,' she commanded. Her age and his declaration of love the previous week put her in a superior position.

'You not going to open your present?' he asked winsomely.

'Later.' She dropped the parcel on the dining-table on her way out of the room. Should she be flattered by his early arrival or had he just come along from the bank when his work was done? She wished he had not caught her in *déshabille* with her hair all over the place.

'Can I help you, Mrs Field?'

'No, thank you. I'm going to dress now.' She left the main room, banging the door behind her, and went into the dingy matted cell that she used as a dressing-room; its one advantage was a capacious cupboard which ran the length of the wall that divided it from the living-room. She sat on a leather stool at the two-foot high dressing-table designed for floor-level living and leant forward to attend to her face. Toshi's premature arrival had put her out. On purpose she took time over her toilette. She did not wish him to take her for granted, to use her as a convenience.

'Mrs Field!' Toshi's cry was one of anxiety.

'Yes?' she answered, irritably.

'You okay?'

'Yes.' Although she was now ready, she purposely stayed on in the stuffy cell, putting her clothes away. She wasn't usually tidy; it was only Toshi's impatience that made her so that evening.

'Mrs Field!' The voice was nearer.

'Yes, I'm coming.' Sylvia left the little room and opened the door of the main room on to Toshi, who must have been standing by the door. 'What is it?' she asked.

'I'm hungry,' he said in such a pathetic, boyish manner that Sylvia laughed. She noticed that he had had his hair cut, which made him look even younger.

'It's not yet seven.'

'Every day I eat at six or six-thirty.'

'How awful! I hate an early dinner; it makes the evening so long.'

'I like.'

'Now you go and sit down again and I'll make you a sandwich and give you a drink.'

Toshi obeyed. On her way to the kitchen area, she picked up his present from the dining-table and as she opened it, he watched her. It was a box of coffee crystals.

'How lovely!' she exclaimed, not really thinking so. Granulated sugar was more suitable for her functional room, which did not call for such refinements as coffee crystals.

'Do you like it?' he asked as if the gift were something special.

'Yes, very much.' She was beginning to realize that she would have to tread carefully over the closely laid land-mines of the young man's feelings.

The whisky and the ham sandwich seemed to help Toshi to unwind. He smiled and said 'Very delicious' when she took his empty plate away from the occasional table by his side. She went back to the kitchen, checked the beef stew she had prepared that morning, poured herself a gin and tonic and joined him.

56

'Do you like my pictures?' she inquired for want of something to say. She threw a hand towards the three horses galloping through space, the trio of girls in pointed helmets playing exotic instruments, and the royal barge, rowed by similarly helmeted oarsmen, churning through the water making fish jump, with Wat Arun, the Temple of Dawn, in the background. She had that morning received back from a nearby frame shop the rubbings she had bought at Wat Po in Bangkok on her way to Japan. She had guessed that the walls of her apartment would be bare, and she loathed a room with no pictures. She had bought the rubbings on sale in a courtyard of the building that housed the famous statue of the Sleeping Buddha.

Toshi screwed up his eyes. 'Pardon?'

'The pictures on the wall there by the desk.' She pointed and then it occurred to her that Toshi could not see them properly without the glasses which he had taken off for reasons of vanity.

'I bought them in Bangkok,' Sylvia went on, 'where I spent a few days on my way here, staying with friends. They were very cheap. I've just had them framed at that shop opposite the Red Gate. The frames cost exactly fifty times more than the rubbings. I worked it out. Indicative of our age, don't you think?'

Toshi said nothing. Sylvia realized that he had only half understood what she had said. The young man's face had taken on that drink flush she and Matthew had talked about – or was he blushing? He had finished his whisky.

'Let's have another drink.'

After Sylvia's second gin and Toshi's third whisky and water, Sylvia suggested that they ate.

They sat opposite each other as they had done on the previous Saturday. As soon as she had served him with a helping of stew and had pushed the dish of mashed potatoes towards him, he helped himself and then began to eat greedily. Sylvia poured some wine into both glasses and then raised hers. 'Here's to you, Toshi.'

'Thank you, Mrs Field,' he replied, mouth full.

'I hope you like this, Toshi.'

'It's very good, Mrs Field.'

'You don't mind my calling you Toshi, do you? You did suggest I should, last time.'

'Yes, please.'

'Do you mind my calling you Toshi without the *san* attached?'
'Yes, I don't mind.'
'And please call me Sylvia.'
'All right, Mrs Field.'
'Go on, say it.'
'Say *it*?'
Sylvia laughed. Toshi looked puzzled. 'Say Sylvia,' she coaxed.
'Siruvia,' he said shyly.
She raised her glass again. 'To you, Toshi.'
'*Kampai*, Mrs Field, Siruvia.'
They clinked glasses.

· 24 ·

At the same moment that Sylvia and Toshi were toasting each
other across the dining-table in Hongo, Matthew Bennet was
walking up the slope to his flat in Yoyogi Uehara. He needed to
round a slight bend before he could see if Jun had returned home;
if he had, the lights in the bedroom and the bathroom and those
that lit the iron staircase up to the front door would be burning.
He walked on the right side of the road so that he could see at the
earliest moment if the lights were on. They were. Matthew didn't
mind the waste of electricity because lights meant presence. He
quickened his pace, ran up the iron steps, burst into the flat and
into the chubby arms of his lover. Jun was short, stocky; his coarse
black hair covered his ears and the back of his shirt collar. He was
cheery. Matthew called him a sanguine, pyknic type tempered by
Japanese melancholy and introspection. He had explained this at
length to the young man, who had listened attentively and then
said, 'I am just a Japanese man, well, sort of man,' and his jolly
chuckle had rung out.

The meal was over, the bottle of wine empty. Sylvia and Toshi were sitting side by side on the settee facing the white *shōji*, which he had carefully slid to.

Sylvia broke almost ten minutes of silence by saying, 'I find these white paper shutters, whatever you call them, depressing. I would prefer curtains. I wonder if I could have curtains in front of them, or would that be a transgression? There's something warm and friendly about curtains. These *shōji* are so cold, so austere, so clinical, don't you think?' He was asleep. She looked at his long face. The flush had subsided and his complexion had returned to its normal off-white colour, a Spanish pallor one might call it, not unhealthy. She admired his long dark eyelashes, tidy, well-spaced eyebrows, firm lips and slightly prominent chin. Two strands of his straight hair had tumbled over his forehead and now that he had had a haircut she could see his ears, which were well shaped and close to his head. He slept sitting up as if in a train, chin on chest, hands on knees. Should she wake him? It was ten-thirty. No. Let him sleep.

She rose and went to the sink and did the washing-up as quickly as she could; she hated leaving it until the next morning. When the dishes were done she went back to the settee and stood over the sleeping Toshi. Should she wake him? No. She gently lifted his legs and swung them on to the settee, then she loosened his collar, put one of her pillows under his head and covered him with a blanket. Apart from a grunt or two, he slept soundly throughout these ministrations. She wondered why he was so tired. It was only just after eleven. The drink, perhaps. He was unused to it, probably.

Sylvia didn't feel sleepy so she picked up the Japanese novel she was reading, *Singular Rebellion*, by Saiichi Maruya, which had recently been translated and won high praise by some British critics. It was about a businessman, a widower, who married a fashion model much younger than himself.

While Matthew and Jun were eating the hard-boiled eggs sliced in half and topped with salmon's roe that Jun had prepared (it was his turn to cook the dinner), Matthew said, 'Sylvia is entertaining her bank clerk tonight.'

'You told me.'

'I wonder if he'll succeed in bedding her.'

'You met her. I didn't. What do you think, Mattu-san?'

'She seemed to have an amused attitude towards him, as if it were all a joke. Do you think a young bank clerk would want to have sex with a fifty-year-old English woman?'

'It depend what he like. Maybe. Some Japanese young man they like ole lady, and they like foreign lady to try.'

'Just as some Japanese men – *men*, Jun – we have plurals in English – like old foreign men.'

Without making a rejoinder, Jun rose from the table and took the empty plates into the kitchen.

'What's next, Jun?'

'Chicken piraffu.'

'Good.'

27

Sylvia would have read on if she hadn't felt sleepy. She found the novel entertaining and also instructive about the Japanese way of living: how, for example, to the Japanese, the floor seems as comfortable as a chair. She shut the book and regarded the sleeping Toshi. Should she wake him and send him home? She liked his sleeping there. He looked so calm and his presence comforting. . . . Although she hated Graham, her husband, for his infidelity, she often thought of him and missed him, missed his companionship, missed not having a man to look after, to think about, to sleep beside her. She looked at Toshi and wondered what he thought of her, and then went into the back room and prepared herself for bed. She gave the sleeping man another look when she returned to the sitting-room clothed in her night-dress and dressing-gown. Her hand hovered over his face, but she stopped herself from stroking his hair and his cheek.

She switched off the gas fire and the lights, went into the alcove and got into bed. She could hear Toshi's gentle breathing on the other side of the sliding paper screens. To sleep so soundly in a strange flat must mean that he felt at ease, and his being there did not give her any qualms at all.

• 28 •

Neither Matthew nor Jun had done the washing-up as both of them preferred to do it in the morning. 'Washing-up during or directly after dinner is antisocial,' Matthew would say. 'It spoils the evening. To do it in front of guests as some people do makes them feel they should go.' Instead, Jun took up his habitual post-prandial pose, supine on the sofa, eyes on the television screen, the remote control instrument within his reach. Matthew sat in an armchair with his feet on a stool. He was in view of the screen but on his lap he had a paperback edition of *Pride and Prejudice*. This year he was reading Jane Austen with his seminar class.

At the moment Jun and Matthew were captivated by the week's 'real-life drama'. It concerned a young man who, enamoured of a girl, managed to get a copy made of her door key and, when she was asleep, stole into her room, undressed, slipped into her bed and began to make love to her. She awoke and screamed. 'Silly bitch,' murmured Matthew.

'She not like you,' said Jun.

• 29 •

Sylvia awoke and started. She could see in the faint dawn light glowing through the *shōji* that Toshi was standing over her. He was wearing only his undervest. She was unable to discern the look in his eyes but she could sense a passionate desire. He stretched out a hand. She took it in hers and he guided it on to his erect prick. 'You like?' he asked.

'D'you want to get in?'

'Get in?'

'Into bed.' She threw back the bed clothes. 'Come on, then.' He slipped in beside her and gave her a boyish kiss.

'It safe?' he asked.

'Safe? Do you mean will the porter look in or your bank manager or someone? Why should they?'

'No,' replied Toshi, timidly. 'I mean this.'

'This?'

'To, to make a love with you.' He put his forehead just above her breast; like a child, he was.

Sylvia bridled. 'Do you mean have I got a disease?'

'No, but if I . . . will you . . .?'

Sylvia chuckled. She didn't mind his youthful fears. 'Become pregnant? No, of course not.'

'I love you, Mrs Field.' He pulled up her nightgown.

'You're very sweet, Toshi, but for God's sake call me Sylvia.'

'Siruvia.'

'That's not quite right, but it's better. Just a minute.' She pulled her nightgown over her head and threw it on the floor.

He kissed her on the mouth. 'First time,' he said, but the kiss was sensual and experienced. His prick pressing against her abdomen was like a little iron rod. He withdrew his lips from hers and nibbled her nipples. She groaned in ecstasy. Toshi pushed back the bedclothes, knelt between Sylvia's legs and entered her. He made love vigorously.

'Not so fast,' pleaded Sylvia, but soon came the cry *'Iku, iku'* and the rise and fall of Toshi's neat, firm buttocks ceased. He remained on top of her while his prick shrank. 'Good,' said Sylvia. 'Not the first time, I think.' Toshi rolled off Sylvia's body and was soon asleep.

They slept, woke, made love again, slept again. When it was nearly noon, Sylvia stirred and crept carefully over the young man's naked, dormant body. It was Sunday, nevertheless she had a conscience about staying in bed so late; she felt more guilty about rising late than she did about sleeping with Toshi. If he had been English then she probably would have had misgivings; he could not be much older than her son. His being Japanese and therefore different made the sin seem venial. His young, smooth, virile body was so exciting. She had not experienced anything like it. Her husband's in comparison had been so coarse and hirsute.

Because of her strict C. of E. upbringing, Sylvia even after being married to an atheist still felt a bit conscience-stricken if she didn't go to church. Mark had none of his mother's respect for Sunday and after leaving school never went to church except to attend a wedding or a funeral. While Mark and his father were having a Sunday lie-in, Sylvia would slip round the corner to the Sung Eucharist. But in Japan it was different. Sunday wasn't Sunday and going to bed with a young man half her age didn't somehow seem to count as a sin. The day seemed like a secular holiday, a bank holiday. She looked at her banker lying in her bed and smiled to herself.

She had a shower and dressed, taking trouble with her make-up and her hair. She put on an apple-green dress and a string of pearls and without realizing it she looked ready for church. When she returned to the main room, a cry, a pathetic cry, came from the bed, now screened off by the *shōji*. 'What time?'

'It's almost one o'clock. Get up, Toshi.' She slid open a paper door and entered the bedroom chamber. Toshi was lying on his back, eyes open. She sat on the bed and placed a hand on his head. 'Get up, Toshi. I want to go out.'

'Go out?' He looked at her with alarm, noticing her dress.

'It's a lovely day. I want to go for a walk.'

'Work? You have work?'

'No, a walk.' She wiggled two fingers.

'Ah, a work.'

'A walk, yes.'

'I am hungry.'

'Would you like ham and eggs, coffee and toast?'

'I like.'

'Run along, then, and have a shower while I get it ready.'

'Run? I must run?'

'Go quickly.'

Toshi picked up his undervest from the floor and covering his genitals with it went into the bathroom; a few moments later he returned with a towel round his slim waist, one which would not go round Sylvia's. 'Have you feather?'

'Feather?'

'I want shave my face.' Toshi felt his chin.

'You mean a razor.' Sylvia examined Toshi's face. 'You don't need a shave, but if you want to have one, I have a sort of razor.' She went into the bathroom followed by the young man and produced her underarm razor, a little pink, plastic implement with a curved blade. 'Will this do?'

Toshi examined it suspiciously. 'I try,' he replied, taking the little razor. 'What it for?'

'For under the arms.'

'Oh.' He smelt the blade and felt his chin. 'Okay, I try.'

At breakfast Toshi sucked his fried egg off his fork as if it were an oyster and he put marmalade on his ham. Sylvia did not reprove him; she was amused like one of the fond mothers she had seen outside the flats watching over her toddler's little antics. After the meal when Toshi said, 'Okay, thank you very much, I go back my home now,' Sylvia felt a pang of loneliness, and countered this declaration with, 'Aren't you coming for a walk with me?'

'Yes, I come. But soon I must go my *apāto*.'

Toshi willingly took the polythene bag of rubbish which Sylvia was holding and they left the flat. He deposited the bag in one of the bins at the end of the passage and preceded Sylvia down the two flights of steep, concrete stairs. When he was about to pass the office in the hall, he accelerated and shot through the swing doors into the driveway that led up to Hongo Avenue. Sylvia, following, noticed the doorman registering Toshi as he hastened by. Did it matter? Was the porter also a spy? Would he report her to the university? She caught up with her new friend.

'Where shall we go?'

'I show you.'

Toshi led the way across the avenue, obediently waiting by the drinks shop for the traffic lights to change. The drinks shop woman saw Sylvia; their eyes met. Sylvia smiled weakly, the other only looked, a cigarette in her mouth. Was she hostile? Toshi and Sylvia went through the Red Gate on to the campus of Tokyo University. 'Is it allowed?' she asked.

64

'Of course.'

They passed several large, grim buildings of no architectural merit; there were trees on either side of the road that led to another block with untidy flower beds in front of it.

'Were you a student here?'

'No,' replied Toshi emphatically. 'I was at a private university.'

'In Tokyo?'

'Yes. My university not bad, but not good like this one.'

They descended a path that took them to a muddy pond on which some ducks were swimming; in the middle of a narrow bridge a boy lay on his stomach, dangling a line into the water. Here and there were students in casual clothes strolling and chatting; a group sitting at the far end of the pond were talking loudly and now and then emitting guffaws. Without being asked, as if dutifully carrying out an appointed task, Toshi told Sylvia in his hesitant English the legend of the pond.

'We have a writer,' he said. 'His name Natsume Sōseki. His picture on the thousand yen bank note. You see?'

'Yes, I have noticed a middle-aged man in a high, stiff Edwardian collar and a black tie with a heavy moustache and a wistful look, but I didn't know he was a writer. I took him for the founder of the bank. Does he like being on a bank note?'

'He dead. Japan's number one story writer. He study in Rondon and he write a book about a student his name Sanshiro. He country boy, like me, and love very beautiful woman, but she not love him enough and she go to marriage with another man who is rich and important, so he walk round the pond thinking about his love problem. So the pond is called Sanshiro Pond. His name Sanshiro, you see.'

Sylvia looked at Toshi. His eyes were moist. Was this visit to the pond made for a reason? Was he seeing himself in the part of Sanshiro? 'Did the boy throw himself into the pond and drown?'

'No, but his life very sad.'

They walked round one side of the pond and then ascended a path that took them up to ground level where they continued their tour of the campus. 'Why must the buildings be so ugly?' complained Sylvia.

Toshi did not reply and they went on past the huge university hospital and then out of the grounds to a busy commercial street

65

of even uglier buildings. A network of wires roofed the thoroughfare. A big poster of an epicene young man with a made-up face
advertising a shampoo commanded a curve in the road. 'Who's
that?' asked Sylvia, pointing at the poster.

'Kenji Kaneko. Famous pop star. You like?'

'Like? He looks pretty androgynous to me.'

'He what?'

'Looks like a homosexual, gay.'

'He gay, maybe,' said Toshi, quite naturally.

They passed a mammoth apartment block, a gigantic cliff of a
place, and then turning, came to a park. While waiting at the
traffic lights before crossing into the park, Toshi said, 'This Shinobazu Pond.'

'Another pond? Is there another story?'

'Yes, Mori Ōgai write about this pond in his story called "The
Wild – ", the name of a big white bird. I do not know.'

'Swan?'

'No.'

'Goose?'

'Yes, I think, yes. "The Wild Geese".'

'And is it a love story?'

'Yes. A medical student he love a woman and she love him, but
she not tell him she love him and he go to Germany to study, like
Mori Ōgai.'

'Is that all?'

'Yes.'

They crossed into the park and joined the Sunday crowd:
couples, a few arm in arm, small family bands, proud fathers throwing balls to tiny sons, fussy mothers doing up unwanted overcoats,
old men strolling, young ones in track suits jogging, kids on bicycles
watched by anxious parents. Here and there, lolling on benches,
sitting in groups were big men with beards and shabby clothes.
'They don't look Japanese,' remarked Sylvia to Toshi.

'They from Iran.'

'Iran?'

'They come here for work, but do not find sometimes.'

'Rich countries inevitably attract those from poor ones, I suppose,' she said. How they contrasted with the indigenous inhabi-
tants, who were well dressed and who looked well fed!

When people flicked their eyes at her, Sylvia wondered whether her being foreign made them do so or the fact that she was in the company of a young Japanese. 'Do people look because . . .' she allowed the unfinished question to die on her lips.

'Sorry?'

'Nothing.' Sylvia thought it was wiser not to ask the question. She did not wish to make Toshi feel self-conscious because he was in her company. How did he feel? He must notice the stares. Was he braving them since he liked her? They half-circled the pond, full of lotus plants which were no more than sticks in this season, and then they left the park by a narrow lane that led past a cinema outside which was a poster of a nude Western couple in the throes of a lustful embrace. 'You have movies like that in Rondon?' Toshi asked.

'Yes, we do. They revolt me.'

They passed another cinema, an underground one with stairs leading down to it; at the top was a similarly lubricious poster. 'What sort of district is this?' asked Sylvia.

'There is a famous park over there. Ueno Park. You see the trees?'

'Another park? Is it connected with another story of unrequited love?'

'I don't know. Its cherry blossoms very famous, now finish. Museum here and Bunka Kaikan, concert hall.'

They crossed the road by the cinema and went into the park, where there were more Sunday promenaders, players of catch and hide-and-seek, and Iranians than in the other one.

'Zoo here. You want see?'

'No, thanks. Don't like zoos. Animal prisons, I call them.'

· 30 ·

While Sylvia and Toshi strolled through Ueno Park, Matthew and Jun began their habitual Sunday constitutional to Shimokitazawa, where Jun caught a train to Shibuya, one of Tokyo's railway and shopping centres. It was Jun's custom to visit his parents in Yoko-

67

hama on Sunday afternoon and spend the night in their house. Monday for him was a free day. Although this walk meant that Jun was going away from him, Matthew enjoyed it. He wondered if he had caught the Japanese penchant for the sweet sorrow of parting. Jun was only going away for one night but it was a parting nevertheless. Matthew would try to delay the separation by sitting on a bench in a small public garden round which they usually walked. Now, about the garden where Jun and Matthew sat, children romped, squealed and blubbed, fathers smiled admiringly at their toddling sons while worried mothers watched, schoolboys hurled baseballs into the gloved hands of their mates.

Jun said, 'What about Mrs Field?'

'What about her?' replied Matthew, lazily. He had shut his eyes and was enjoying the warmth of the April sun on his eyelids.

'Do you think the bank clerk stayed the night?'

'No, I'm sure not. Sylvia wouldn't be attracted by someone so young.'

· 31 ·

Sylvia and Toshi were sitting opposite each other in a basement café near Ueno Station. There were little lamps with pink shades on each of the tables which were covered with pink cloths. The lighting was dim; the crepuscular atmosphere of the place was intended, it seemed, for discreet assignations. They had finished their coffee and cream cakes. Toshi was smoking. No word had passed between them for some minutes. Toshi seemed to have retreated into a private Japanese world. Was he embarrassed to be with a middle-aged foreigner? The other tables were occupied by whispering couples, most of them in their twenties. Sylvia felt compelled to break the silence.

'Do you come here often?'

'First time.'

'So this is your second "first time" today.'

'Uh?' Toshi looked puzzled. Had he forgotten the words he had uttered just before they had made love that morning?

'Your second "first time",' Sylvia repeated, smiling.

'So,' Toshi said.

Was he cross at being reminded, or did he simply not realize what was being referred to?

'You've had your hair cut since I saw you last.'

'Yes,' he said, putting a hand to his head.

'I don't think it's an improvement. I liked your hair long.'

'I like too. My boss he tell me to cut my hair. He say not good to have long hair in my job.'

'But it wasn't all that long. How absurd! Why shouldn't you wear your hair as you like?'

'In Japan, we Japanese must to obey the boss.'

· 32 ·

Matthew knew that he and Jun looked odd when walking together and he wondered if their relationship was obvious. Not only was he much older than Jun, but he was a foreigner too, and therefore could not possibly be taken for the young man's father, elder brother or uncle. Jun had never walked ahead as some young Japanese did when in public with their foreign lovers; even after six years, though, Matthew was still not certain about the impression he and Jun made on the passer-by; prying eyes often darted at him, then at Jun, and then back to him.

The two made their way through the narrow residential lanes, which were almost void of traffic, to Shimokitazawa, a suburban shopping centre where, as had become their custom, they parted at the station.

'Goodbye, my dear,' Matthew said to Jun at the bottom of the station steps.

'Bye,' returned Jun cheerfully. 'See you tomorrow night,' and up the steps he ran, but always he turned twice or three times to wave. He waved three times that afternoon. A good sign, thought Matthew as he slowly weaved his way past the housewives in the crowded shopping alley. 'He's a dear boy,' he muttered to himself.

Toshi looked at his watch. 'I must go my room,' he said. He and Sylvia were standing outside Ueno Station. It was six o'clock; dusk was gathering; lights were lit. 'You want catch taxi?'

'No. I'll walk back.'

'I come with you. I take the train from your station.'

'No, you take the train from here. You've wasted enough time with me.' Sylvia wanted him to go; she was beginning to find Toshi's youth, his naïvety, his broken English a strain.

'You sure you find the way?'

'Yes, easily.'

They shook hands formally, Toshi bowing slightly as they did so. 'Thank you very much, Siruvia-san. I have very nice time.'

'So did I. Thank you.' Sylvia smiled into the young man's dark, soulful eyes, and when at last Toshi released her hand, which he seemed reluctant to do, he turned and walked swiftly into the station hall; just before he was swallowed up by the crowds, he looked back and waggled the palm of his hand a few times. Sylvia waved back. A similar feeling to the one she used to have when seeing Mark off to school at Waterloo Station came over her. She wondered now, as she had wondered about her son, if Toshi would be able to cope with life's problems. He was childish except when in bed. Sylvia told herself as she retraced her steps past the sex-film theatres and into the path round the pond, that she did not want to play a sort of mother figure. She climbed the hill past the big apartment block wondering if she wanted a boy lover. She wished she had a confidant.

As Matthew meandered down the little lanes that took him home from Shimokitazawa, he wondered, as all lovers wonder, if Jun were faithful. Even after six and a half years, he wasn't absolutely certain. But yes, he was sure really, for hadn't Jun blurted out that morning, 'I love you', when Matthew had been trying to talk about the week's arrangements and had muddled the Japanese words for Tuesday and Friday; sometimes Matthew would speak to Jun in Japanese. Such impulsive exclamations were reassuring and because of the difference in their ages, their cultures, Matthew needed reassurance, now and then. He prayed that his affair with Jun, the longest he had ever had with anyone, would last.

Part Two

· 1 ·

Sylvia had settled into her new life in Tokyo fairly well. Her week had become a pleasant routine and so had her weekend assignations with Toshi. In spite of his constant telephone calls she kept him firmly to Saturday nights only, and had refused his request to let him visit her on Wednesday nights too. Her excuse was that she had a heavy day's teaching on Thursday and liked to have an early night on Wednesday. Toshi had accepted this but not without turning on childish sulks. She suspected that his mother had spoilt him.

She liked her students (at least most of them), especially the graduates and felt that she was slowly developing a good rapport with them. Professor Suzuki was a frequent visitor to her room in the university. He usually called when she was about to have her lunch. She copied Matthew and made herself some sandwiches which she ate in her room. She approved of his rule to spend the lunch hour alone, away from students and professors with questions. 'I lock my door,' he told her. 'Pretend I'm not in. I disregard knocks.' He did not tell her that the main reason for confining himself was to have forty winks. Sylvia wasn't as strong-minded as Matthew, and in any case she was not so well entrenched. He had tenure, while she was on a two-year contract, which had to be reviewed after one year. Feeling a bit on sufferance and that she had to prove she was worth her high salary, she responded to all requests for help. One of these was to answer

75

Professor Suzuki's lunch-break questions, or interruptions, as she called them. He would tap on her door, poke his head into the room and say, 'I hope I not disturb you, Mrs Field,' though he could see that she was in the middle of consuming her sandwiches.

'Not at all, Professor Suzuki,' Sylvia would lie and put her sandwiches away.

'May I impose on you for a little while?' he would ask, entering the room, shutting the door and placing his briefcase on the table. He would then pull out the paperback edition of *Lady Windermere's Fan*. Today Sylvia was asked to explain the patronizing attitude of the Duchess of Berwick with regard to Mr Hopper. Suzuki seemed to be fascinated by Sylvia's imitation of the Australian accent and the fact that the Duchess would regard Mr Hopper as inferior. She also brought in the deprecatory reference to Australia in *The Importance of Being Earnest* and Algernon's outburst: 'Australia! I'd sooner die.' Suzuki seemed genuinely interested in Sylvia's exegesis and he always thanked her profusely.

On the spur of the moment one Wednesday lunch-time, Sylvia invited Suzuki to dinner in her apartment. 'And please bring your wife. I would so much like to meet her.' Suzuki seemed delighted and it was agreed that he and Mrs Suzuki would dine with her on the following Saturday. After the professor had put his textbook into his bulging briefcase and left, Sylvia realized that she would have to put off Toshi. She would ask him to come on the Friday. He sometimes had Saturday off; in any case if he were on duty next Saturday her flat was nearer the bank than his. She asked Matthew if he would like to come to dinner with the Suzukis. He declined. 'Saturdays are sacrosanct,' he said. 'I never go out over the weekend.'

When Toshi telephoned Sylvia and she suggested he come on Friday instead of Saturday, he told her he was not free. 'Going out with your friends, are you?' she asked.

'On Friday I have *arbeito*,' he answered.

'I see,' she said, although she didn't. Suzuki had used this word to denote extra work, a side job. But what *arbeito* could a bank clerk have? Or was *arbeito* a euphemism?

'Sunday okay?' asked Toshi.

Since he had rebuffed her suggestion for Friday, she replied, partly out of pride, partly out of pique, 'Sorry, on Sunday I'm busy,' and put the phone down.

Sylvia had learnt how to shop in the basement of the department store which had a wide selection of comestibles, both Japanese and Western. The counters, though, were so abundant, the aisles so narrow, and the shoppers, mostly determined housewives in a hurry, so numerous that as well being bumped and pushed she frequently lost her bearings. She had several landmarks in the confusing sea of people and displays of food: these were the cheese counter, the pizza stand and the breadshop. If she found one of these she could orientate herself and proceed to the next section or the escalator. But often she couldn't find them and she struggled up and down the aisles where peculiar Japanese ingredients like pickles, seaweed and beanpaste cakes were on sale, until at last she came upon one of her landmarks. It seemed to her that the Japanese liked confusion and an illogical arrangement of the wares on sale. She never bought vegetables in the store because they were more expensive and less fresh than those at the local greengrocer's.

On the Saturday morning Sylvia set out from Sunflower Mansions with her duty-free bag, now rather tired and crinkled, to buy locally the rest of the items she required for the dinner party in honour of the Suzukis. The azalea and the daphne shrubs were in bloom on the campus of Tokyo University on this fine May morning. She was becoming inured to the bicycles that skimmed by her on the pavements of Hongo Avenue, but she was still disconcerted by them and the everlasting stream of hurrying people.

She turned into the little shopping street, passing the butcher's as she had bought chicken breasts at the store. At the greengrocer's she was served by the man with the steel teeth. She noticed that the plaque on his blue peaked baseball cap had the number 0–546 on it. He served her willingly and courteously, smiling when she pointed at the potatoes, saying *poteto*, and *ingen mame* when she indicated the French beans, *retasu* in reply to her handing him a lettuce she chose, and *ichigo* when she picked up a punnet of strawberries. The vegetables were weighed and put into bags which in turn were popped into her bag. He added up the prices on a pocket calculator, showed her the total and she paid.

'*Arigatō gozaimashita*!' he cried and the cry was echoed by the other shop assistants. She knew it meant 'thank you', but she didn't know what the correct reply was so she smiled and received from Mr Five-Four-Six a warm silvery grin. His dark eyes dipped into hers for a moment.

· 2 ·

It was Matthew's turn to cook dinner. To please Jun he had made onion soup, and to please himself he was going to grill some lamb chops. Jun didn't much care for lamb. He said it smelt. Nevertheless, when softened up by his favourite soup, he would eat the chops.

After one spoonful of the soup, Jun muttered '*oishī*!'. Matthew did not feel complimented for he knew well that pronouncing a dish to be delicious was no more than a formality. In reply, he said, 'Sylvia is giving dinner to Suzuki and his wife tonight.'

'At her *apāto*?'

'Yes. She's giving them a chicken casserole followed by strawberries.'

'What are we having?'

'Lamb chops.'

'Huh!'

'One of the two telephones on Matthew's desk rang.

'Which one is it?' asked Matthew. 'Yours or mine?'

'Mine.' Jun hurried across the room to the telephone on the left of the desk, which was for his incoming calls and which only he answered. This arrangement had been made so that if a colleague rang he would not learn that Jun was living with a foreigner. It was a necessary precaution against gossip. The Japanese did not have the habit of calling upon one another without warning, and so there was not much danger of anyone who would not be sympathetic towards Jun's life style turning up.

Matthew went into the kitchen to deal with the chops.

· 3 ·

The two-tone bell sounded exactly at seven, the hour Sylvia had invited the Suzukis. When she opened the door she was surprised to find a smiling Suzuki, not with his wife on his arm but instead a pot containing an azalea shrub; his inevitable briefcase dangled from the other arm. He handed Sylvia the azalea.

'How lovely! How kind! But where is your wife?'

'She is very sorry. She has a runny nose and cannot come.' He stepped out of his shoes and into a pair of slippers.

'I am most disappointed,' said Sylvia. 'I was looking forward to meeting her.' Sylvia led the professor into the sitting part of the room. He sat in one of the leather armchairs and put his briefcase on the floor.

Still holding the azalea, Sylvia said, 'Thank you very much. I love azaleas.'

'You said you liked them.'

'And you remembered. I am touched. But you shouldn't have brought me a present.'

'We Japanese love to give presents.'

'That shows a generous nature. What may I get you to drink?'

'I do not wish to trouble you. Have you whisky?'

'Yes.' Sylvia went to the kitchen area to pour out a whisky for the professor and a gin and tonic for herself. When she returned, she found Suzuki with his glasses on his forehead peering at the rubbings she had bought in Bangkok.

'I like these. Where are they from, Cambodia?'

'Thailand. That's Wat Arun, the Temple of Dawn.'

'Oh yes, of course! How stupid am I! Yukio Mishima called the third volume of his tetralogy *The Temple of Dawn*. Have you read any of Mishima's works?'

'I read *The Temple of the Golden Pavilion*.'

'His best, undoubtedly his best. It was based on a true incident, you know.'

'I did know that.'

'The boy who set the temple on fire is now out of prison.'

'I hope prison cured his pyromania.'

79

Suzuki did not respond to this remark, so Sylvia asked, 'Is Mishima highly regarded today?'

'As a writer, yes; as a man, I think we Japanese are rather ashamed of him. The less said about his miserable end and his ridiculous Shield Society, his army of students, the better.'

'You mean his *harakiri*?'

'Yes.'

'Quite horrible.'

'The newspapers used to call his *Tatenokai*, his band of followers, toy soldiers. He paid for their uniforms.' Suzuki put down his glass on the table by his side and brought out a packet of cigarettes. 'Do you mind?' he asked, holding up a cigarette.

'No, please smoke.'

'Would you like one?'

'No, thanks. I gave up some years ago.'

'So you did smoke?'

'Almost everyone has smoked at one time in their lives. Now it's rather out of fashion. At parties in London you see very few smokers. Excuse me, I must look at the food.'

· 4 ·

Jun was still on the phone when Matthew returned from the kitchen with the chops.

'Can't you tell him you're in the middle of dinner?'

Jun continued to talk and now and then to hoot with laughter. Patiently, Matthew waited until Jun had finished his telephone conversation before beginning his chops.

'Who was it?'

'Masa.'

'What did he want?'

'He want me to meet him in Shinjuku.'

'Tonight?'

'Yes.'

'Where?'

'At "Mr Lady".'

'That awful drag place?'

'Yes.'

'You going?'

'Yes, for a little.'

'That means for most of the night.'

'Mattu-san, I must see my friends sometime.'

'I agree, but why do you have to meet them in such a frightful place?'

'I like "Mr Lady". The master is my friend. Masa he go there, and Shinichi. There I feel freedom.'

· 5 ·

'Very delicious,' said Suzuki after his first mouthful of the chicken casserole.

'It's the first time I've used the oven,' said Sylvia, who was sitting opposite him, her back to the bookshelves.

'We do not have o-ven in Japanese house. Not many that is.'

'I must have an oven. There are so many dishes that need one. Have some more wine!' Sylvia refilled Suzuki's wineglass (she had recently bought six wineglasses from a shop near the station) with the red Bordeaux she had got from the local drinks shop.

'*Kampai*!', she said raising her glass.

'*Kampai*!' repeated the professor. 'So you remember the word?' He seemed pleased. 'You will soon speak Japanese like a, er . . . how shall I say . . . like a . . . er, like a Japanese.'

'I doubt that. I'm too old to learn such a difficult language.'

Sylvia looked at him while he ate his helping. She thought that if he didn't wear those heavily framed spectacles that screened half his face, and his hair speckled with grey wasn't so frizzy, his eyes were a little larger and didn't become slits when he smiled, and his teeth smaller and not quite so protruding – then he would be good looking. A pity, she thought. It would be easier to have an affair with him than with Toshi. Suzuki was much more articulate in English than the bank clerk. But Toshi had sex appeal, while for her the professor had none. Toshi was young and lusty; Suzuki was middle aged and though probably capable of being lecherous, not in the least attractive to her. Besides, he was married. These thoughts were interrupted by the telephone, which was on one of the empty bookshelves just behind Sylvia's chair. She rose, turning her back to the table.

'Hello? Oh, hello, Toshi. How are you? She began to blush.

'I come see you now, Siruvia-san?' Toshi sounded as if he had been drinking.

'No, not now. I am entertaining Professor Suzuki.' She spoke softly into the mouthpiece, though she knew that Suzuki, being so near, could hear what she was saying and possibly what Toshi was saying too, since he, probably telephoning from one of those phones in a shop open to the street, almost shouted.

'I come at twelve o'clock?'

'Not tonight.' She was not going to let him have his way.

'I come at one o'clock?' This proposition was followed by raucous laughter.

'No, Toshi.' Drink seemed to have caused him to lose both his diffidence and his politeness.

'I come tomorrow.'

'No, please telephone on Monday.'

'Okay,' Toshi said, crossly, and rang off.

Sylvia put down the receiver and still blushing, took her place opposite her guest. 'My banker,' she explained. 'It seems that he works late even on Saturday nights.'

'*Ah sō*,' said Suzuki, doubtfully.

'I am having a certain amount of difficulty over some banking arrangements I have been trying to make.'

'You should ask me to help you, Mrs Field. It is not right that the banker should disturb you so late at night.'

'He's very diligent, anxious to help. Do have some more wine, Professor Suzuki.'

'Thank you.'

'More chicken?'

'No, thank you. I have had quite e-nough.'

Sylvia Rose. 'I have strawberries next. I've done them with sugar and brandy. I forgot to get any cream. I don't like cream much anyway.'

'It sounds very interesting. It is very bad that the bank should telephone you so late. I shall call the manager on Monday morning and complain. Is it the Four Square Bank near Hongo Station?'

'Yes,' answered Sylvia from the kitchen area. 'I mean, no. It's a foreign bank that is dealing with some, er, some foreign business, a remittance I asked for.'

'I see.'

The telephone rang.

'Oh, damn,' exclaimed Sylvia.

'Your bank again,' suggested the professor.

Sylvia went to the bookshelf and picked up the receiver. She wished she had a portable instrument so she could wander off to the other side of the room with it, out of earshot.

'Hello?'

'Oh, hello, Sylvia. I just rang to see how you were,' said Matthew.

'Professor Suzuki is here. We're having dinner.'

'Oh, I'm so sorry. I forgot you were giving him dinner tonight. My engagement fell through.'

'Come to lunch tomorrow.'

'Sorry, I can't. Sunday is always difficult. Well, I mustn't keep you. See you at the university. Give my regards to Professor Suzuki and his wife, please.'

'That was Professor Bennet,' explained Sylvia, taking her place again at the table. 'He rang, to see how I was. He's been very kind. I hope you like these strawberries.'

'They are excellent. Professor Bennet is a kind man. We like him very much. He is not married. It is said that he doesn't like women. Did you know?'

'I guessed he was gay. There are two telephones in his flat. One for him, and one for . . .'

'His friend. He's a teacher.'

'Did you know?'

'We all know. We do not say we know. It does not matter. He does not pray with the students.'

'Pray? He's not in the least religious.'

'Pray around.'

'Oh, I see, play.'

'Yes, pray.'

'That is good.'

'It is not good to be gay,' said Suzuki, pompously. 'We do not mind, but we think it is not good.'

'Shall we sit a little more comfortably in the other part of the room? Would you like some coffee?'

Suzuki was on his feet. 'No, thank you, Mrs Field.'

'A brandy?'

'No, thank you.'

'I have some Japanese tea. Would you like some of that?'

'You have Japanese tea? Green tea?'

'I was brought some.'

'I see. No, thank you.'

'Are you sure you wouldn't like some brandy?'

'Well, perhaps.'

Suzuki sat on the settee and Sylvia, when she had given him a wineglass half full of brandy, on one of the leather armchairs.

'*Gochisosama deshita*,' said Suzuki, giving a little jerk of a bow. 'It mean something like "thank you for the feast".'

'The feast?' Sylvia laughed. 'It was hardly a feast.'

'We Japanese always say that even after just an ice cream.'

'How sweet!'

'Mrs Field, may I ask you some questions?'

'Yes, please,' answered Sylvia, a little apprehensively.

Suzuki took a copy of *The Importance of Being Earnest* out of his briefcase. 'Now what does Rady Blacknell mean exactly when she says: "What between the duties expected of one during one's lifetime and the duties exacted from one after one's death, land . . . gives one position and prevents one from keeping it up." Now the second "duties" I understand, it mean tax. But what "duties" would be expected of the landowner during his lifetime?'

Sylvia explained and then Suzuki after making notes in his textbook continued to ply her with questions. After Sylvia had attempted to explain the aphorism 'All women become like their mothers. That is their tragedy. No man does. That's his.' Suzuki suddenly took off his glasses, leant forward on the settee, and putting a hand on Sylvia's knee, which was peeping out of her skirt, said, 'You are very kind, Mrs Field; also, you are very beautiful. I er, I er, how shall I say . . .'

'I've no idea.' Sylvia moved her knee, too rapidly she felt when she considered her reaction afterwards.

Suzuki put away his book and rose. 'Well,' he said, adjusting his glasses, 'I must be running along.' He was as good as his word. Stepping into his shoes, snatching his raincoat off the hook in the entrance hall and repeating the phrase, '*Gochisosama deshita*', without looking at Sylvia, he made a hasty exit.

<h1 style="text-align:center">· 6 ·</h1>

The 'Mr Lady' bar didn't encourage foreign custom. This was not because the Master-san and his clients were particularly xenophobic, but because it was a place where the Japanese customers, all of whom were men (or, as Jun would say, 'sort of men'), and some of whom were distinguished, could feel at ease. Many Japanese, due to their insularity, are incapable of being themselves and behaving naturally in the presence of *gaijin* or foreigners. There are exceptions, of course, and Jun was one of them, but even he enjoyed a Japanese-only night now and then.

'Mr Lady' was no bigger than a large sitting-room. It was on the fifth floor of a tall, thin erection in the *ni-chōme* district of Shinjuku, a quarter notorious for its night life, multifarious and tolerant, catering for all tastes. The building, called 'Queen of Heart', was entirely devoted to bars, there being two on each of its eight floors. Opposite 'Mr Lady' on the other side of the landing was 'Club New Love', a host bar which provided young partners for lonely middle-aged women, mostly neglected wives of rich and busy husbands.

While the customers of 'Mr Lady' never patronized 'Club New Love', the hosts of the latter bar would occasionally look in at the former to have a change of scene. They did not ask for the treatment if they were going back on duty.

The treatment was not compulsory; however, to join properly the ambience of the bar it was necessary to have it. It consisted of going into a dressing-room at the back of the bar, sitting in a chair at a table whose mirror was fringed with lights and having one's face made up by one of the bar boys who usually wore drag.

Some customers came to 'Mr Lady', had their faces made up, or made them up themselves, sat at the bar, ordered a drink, admired themselves in the looking-glass for half an hour, went back into the make-up room, removed their slap and then, correct businessmen again, picked up their briefcases and set off to the station to catch a train home to their families. For a short while they had escaped from their existence of conformity and convention into a land of fantasy. There were some customers who kept a suitcase in the bar containing an outfit of drag, and as well as farding their faces they would don stockings, a wig and a dress. There was very little sexual play in the bar; only sometimes when the Master-san was a bit high would he turn down the lights and then skirts might go up and pants come down. As a rule at 'Mr Lady' the behaviour, if not the conversation, was decorous. The bar provided an outlet for escapists and narcissists. Without realizing it, the Master-san showed there was truth in the Wilde dictum: 'Give a man a mask and he'll be himself.'

Just before Matthew telephoned Sylvia and while she and Professor Suzuki were eating their strawberries, Jun was ascending in the lift to 'Mr Lady', together with a handsome young man he had not seen before. On the landing they paused, looked at one another and then Jun turned to go into 'Mr Lady'; the young man went towards the door of 'Club New Love'.

Screams of 'Junko!' greeted Jun and he in turn welcomed Shuko (Shinichi) and Masako (Masa). Some of the older customers, their faces painted, joined in the general campery, which was high-pitched and shrill; other senior members remained inside their temporary shells of femininity and gazed at their reflections in the mirror behind the bar.

On Saturdays there was a cabaret, and tonight Michiko (Michio) was going to do his striptease act. Michio worked in the Ministry of Trade and Industry and he confessed to owning more than thirty dresses. It was amazing that at the age of thirty-seven he had managed to remain at the Ministry without conforming with the rules of society and getting married. His brilliance as a statistician, and an understanding department chief who relied on him, were the reasons.

Pop music roared, drink flowed and the bar boys in miniskirts shrieked. Junko, Michiko and Shuko listened to the Master-san, who this evening wore a blouse and trousers and no wig. He recounted tales of scandal about customers, ex-customers, and one of the hosts from next door who had visited 'Mr Lady', made up his face, returned to 'Club New Love' and was immediately asked to leave. The patronesses did not want their hosts to be *maquillé*. The Master-san, an accomplished *raconteur*, made much more of the simple story of the host who became a hostess than truth demanded.

The familiar yet haunting notes of Ravel's 'Bolero' began and out of the dressing-room came Michio of the Ministry of Trade and Industry. He wore a purple dress which was slit up the sides as far as his thighs like a whore's *chongsam*; instead of a wig he had done his hair in the style of the twenties with a curl over each cheek; in his ears were large green plastic earrings; on his hands were long purple gloves.

He did a *pas seul* on the small stage where customers sometimes performed, and after throwing 'come hither' glances at the audience he slowly pulled off one glove, threw it across the room and then did the same with the other; he kicked off his shoes, and then with the lissomeness of a gymnast, he stood first on one leg and then on the other to peel off his stockings and toss them over the bar. Throughout he kept up coy looks, rolling his eyes and stroking his breasts and his thighs.

As Ravel's music quickened, he spun round and suddenly took off his dress to reveal a brassière and the briefest of slips, which bulged impressively, and above which peeped the beginnings of a dark forest. His body was firm and hairless, not in the least flabby. Off came his brassière and then with one large hand he eased off his slip keeping the other hand over his genitals. He turned sideways and removed his hand for a second, the lights dimmed, he stuck out his buttocks and disappeared into the back room.

The applause was polite; there were a few guffaws. The performance, like most amateur turns, was given more for the gratification of the performer than for that of the audience, many of whom had seen it or a similar version before. It was kind of the Master-san to let Michio do his thing. He knew well that giving his act meant a lot to Michio; it allowed him to escape for a while into a realm of fantasy, an escape which made his hours at his desk in the Ministry more bearable, because now and then he could break the tedium of calculation with thoughts of what he would wear on

87

Saturday night at 'Mr Lady'. The same was true of many of the customers who didn't go as far as Michio and were content with applying *maquillage* to their faces and wearing it for an hour or so. There was no viciousness in the atmosphere in the bar, no drugs, no great outrageousness. Once their make-up was removed, the customers became ordinary salary-men again.

· 7 ·

A contrite Toshi telephoned Sylvia on the Monday evening, and apologized for his uncouth conduct. Sylvia, of course, forgave him, and their Saturday meetings continued. He arrived about six – it was impossible to get him to come an hour later – and then they had drinks, supper, watched television. With his assistance one Sunday afternoon she had bought a TV and had embellished her flat with a proper sofa, two armchairs and some rugs. This was followed by a fairly early bedding down.

Sylvia felt fitter than she had for years. She was enjoying her teaching (especially the graduate classes), and the composition class, as Matthew had predicted, had shrunk to a manageable number. She was sure that her regular sessions with Toshi and her thrice weekly swims in the nearby pool were the reasons for her feeling in good shape.

The pool was twenty minutes' walk from the university, through the busy streets, along the railway lines protected by a high fence on which were hoardings advertising "love hotels" – 'Duet', 'Casablanca' and 'La La' –, over a bridge, down some steep steps, past a row of makeshift dwellings that seemed to double as factories producing shop signs and paper decorations, and then opposite a raised motorway, was the large building with a curved roof. Inside the entrance were a few computer-games machines, a small restaurant serving snacks (curry rice was a favourite dish), and the office, where Sylvia joined for a month. On the ground floor was a skating rink which changed into what was called a *mammothu poolu* in July. Up a steep flight of stairs were the dressing-rooms, and down another steep flight were the showers and the pool.

Sylvia usually went for a swim around 4 p.m. when the lunch-hour swimmers had gone and the evening ones had not yet arrived. There was often in progress a class of housewives practising synchronized swimming. With plastic clips on their noses, they submerged and then stuck their chubby legs out of the water. They were friendly to Sylvia. In the dressing-room they evinced a curiosity about her body, staring at her breasts and trying to peep at her genitals. Sylvia didn't mind this prying since it seemed perfectly guileless.

Sylvia was a good swimmer. She swam the crawl in one of the lanes reserved for those swimming lengths, often sharing it with a man who always did the backstroke and wore goggles and a black cap. She struck up an acquaintance with Mr Ogawa and while resting in one of the plastic chairs beside the pool would chat to him. He spoke English fairly well, better than most of her students. She was getting used to speaking slowly and restricting her vocabulary to simple words. Mr Ogawa seemed a lonely soul. He told her he was separated from his wife and ran a little business in the district which didn't do very well. He was about forty, she guessed, and well built with broad shoulders, a muscular chest and a flat stomach. His figure was more robust than Toshi's, and sometimes she wondered whether Mr Ogawa would make a more satisfactory lover than her present one; but in spite of his fine physique he lacked Toshi's sex appeal and charm, and all the time he was serious and worried about his situation. However, whenever she went swimming she looked forward to seeing Mr Ogawa, as she always called him, and missed him if he weren't there. She felt she had failed to break through his carapace of shyness and although they held their conversations when they were almost naked their relationship was very formal.

· 8 ·

Professor Suzuki hadn't visited Sylvia's room in the Faculty of Literature since he had dined with her. This worried her as he was an important member of the Faculty. She presumed he was annoyed with her over the rebuff she had given him, and embarrassed too.

Matthew had told Sylvia that he didn't mind her visiting his room during his sacred lunch hour and he told her he would open his door if she gave it three sharp knocks. This she did one lunch-time a few weeks after her repaired relationship with Toshi.

'Sorry to disturb you, Matthew.'

'That's all right, Sylvia. I said you could. Come in.' Matthew let Sylvia into his room and then shut the door and locked it. With a dramatic gesture he indicated that she should sit in the chair by his desk. 'This is where my graduate students sit,' he said. 'I call it the confessional seat, not that they have much to confess, except the non-completion of a task I've set them.' He smiled and sat at his desk, his back to the window of frosted glass.

'I have something to confess, as a matter of fact.'

'Oh?' Matthew leant forward as he did when students wished to confide in him. He was rather priest-like, thought Sylvia, when he put his elbows on the table and clasped his hands.

'I'm worried.' Sylvia shifted in her chair. 'Suzuki hasn't been near me to ask his usual silly questions about one of Wilde's plays since he dined at my flat.'

'Isn't that rather a relief? The less I'm pestered with questions, the happier I am.'

'Also he's been avoiding me. Just now in the staff room, he got up and left as soon as I entered. I think I know the reason.'

'Oh?'

'After dinner he made a mild pass which I rebuffed.'

'Oh dear!'

'What do you been by that, Matthew?' Sylvia asked sharply. 'Do you mean that I shouldn't have rebuffed him or that he shouldn't have made a pass?'

'By "oh dear", I meant what a pity it happened.'

'Indeed.' Sylvia paused. 'I suppose I'd better tell you everything that happened that evening.'

'Did something happen after the pass and the rebuff?'

'No, before.'

'Before?'

'Yes, Toshi, my bank clerk friend, rang in the middle of dinner. You know how near the telephone is to the dining-table? Well,

Toshi was a bit drunk and shouted down the phone. I'm sure Suzuki could hear him.'

'Did he say anything indiscreet?'

'Yes he did in a way. He went on asking if he could come and see me; first he suggested he came at once, and when I said no, he said, "I come at midnight", and after a further refusal, he said. "I come at one o'clock" and laughed lasciviously. I managed to get him to ring off. I told Suzuki it was a call from the bank and he said he'd ring the manager and complain on my behalf.' They both laughed. 'It isn't funny,' Sylvia insisted. 'I imagine that Suzuki guessed it wasn't a bank clerk at all, and he thought that this gave him licence to make a pounce.'

'I see,' said Matthew, serious again.

'What should I do?'

'Nothing,' advised Matthew. 'What can you do? Let it ride.' He said nothing for a while and then shot the question, 'Is he your lover?'

'You mean Toshi, the bank clerk?'

Matthew emitted an affirmative grunt.

'Yes, but it's not an affair. Quite frankly I enjoy going to bed with him and that's about it.' Her blue eyes were defiant.

'I see.' Matthew pursed his lips in a matronly manner. 'I wouldn't worry about Suzuki. You've got your contract, haven't you? You'll be all right for two years, provided you get through the first year without any trouble. The first year is probational, isn't it? It usually is.'

'Yes. They have a right to terminate my contract after the first year, if they find me unsuitable.'

'I'm sure they won't do that. They're lucky to have you. They don't mind about your private life, provided you don't parade it on the campus.'

'Am I likely to?' She was silent for a moment and then said, 'I hope you don't mind my asking, but what about your private life?'

Matthew unclasped his hands and began to rub his upper lip with his forefinger. 'I don't parade it on the campus,' he said.

'Could you come to lunch on Sunday?'

'Difficult.'

'You could bring your friend.'

Matthew blushed and shifted in his chair. 'You guessed?'

'When you didn't answer the telephone in your flat, I wondered. I knew you were gay, of course.'

'How?' Matthew looked concerned.

'Women sense these things. Anyway, Suzuki confirmed my suspicions.'

'Suzuki?' Matthew seemed alarmed. 'Oh, Lord!'

'He told me that everyone knew and that it didn't matter. You didn't play with the students, he said; actually he said "pray", which confused me at first. I was surprised to hear that you were religious or that you were some kind of missionary!' She laughed, but Matthew remained solemn. 'In any case, it doesn't seem to worry anyone. Now what about coming to lunch on Sunday, and bring your friend, if you like.'

'I'll suggest it to him, but I don't know if he'll want to come. Let's make it another Sunday, not next Sunday.'

When Sylvia had gone, Matthew felt depressed. His illusions had been crushed.

· 9 ·

The following Thursday evening Toshi rang to say he would not be able to see Sylvia on the Saturday as he had to go with a group of his colleagues to the bank's holiday hostel by the sea. For the second time Sylvia proposed that he came on the Friday evening instead and again he told her he couldn't. She wondered about this Friday engagement and assumed it must be some family obligation.

On the Saturday afternoon, a wet afternoon in the rainy month of June, Sylvia, on her way back from shopping, saw the greengrocer, who had not been in his shop, about to mount his motorcycle outside Sunflower Mansions. Once under the eaves of the building, she collapsed her umbrella and smiled at the young man, who, she supposed, had just delivered an order to one of the flats. He was wearing a capacious rubber raincoat.

'*Konnichi wa*,' he said, coming towards her, glinting his steel teeth. She knew this meant 'good afternoon' and she replied, '*Konnichi wa*', and returned his smile. Whereupon he took her not very full shopping bag from her, accompanied her up to the flat, and without any hesitation followed her inside, kicking off his shoes. There he was, still smiling, and still wearing his cap with the number on it (she had never seen his head uncovered) and his dripping, black rubber raincoat, which seemed heavy for the sultry day. Sylvia said, 'Thank you,' meaning to dismiss him, but he remained staring and smiling and came in past the *genkan* into the K part of the LDK. He put the shopping bag near the sink, turned and looked at Sylvia lustfully, almost leering. He approached her, unbuttoned her raincoat and pulled loose the knot of her head scarf.

'What do you want?' she asked nervously, having no doubts about his intention.

He helped her off with her raincoat and began to undo the front of her dress. 'No,' said Sylvia, but feebly, 'You'd better go. Go!' He took off his 0–546 cap and his raincoat, and flung them on to the floor, and then he did the same with his shirt, trousers, socks and underpants. He came towards her, and with a '*Gomen nasai*' (excuse me) gently led her into the bedroom alcove. Before going out she had closed the *shōji* so there was no danger of being seen from the graveyard. Without his cap (he had a full head of coarse, black hair, short like the pelt of a cat) and out of his greengrocer's clothes he was rather attractive – about thirty, Sylvia surmised – and his body was spotlessly clean. Perhaps she submitted because it was exciting to be so suddenly desired at three in the afternoon, and the pouring rain outside somehow induced desire.

In the midst of their violent act of lust, the telephone rang and she made a move to push him off her. '*Chotto dake*,' he said, holding her more firmly. The instrument rang and rang. 'I must answer it,' she muttered, turning her lips from his. 'No!' It was the only word he uttered in English throughout.

Then all at once, several times he almost shouted '*Eeku: okā-san, eeku, okā-san, eeku, eeku, eeku.*' The telephone stopped ringing. She realized that he had slaked his passion. He pulled himself off her, donned his pants, his shirt, his socks, his trousers with speed and hurried into the *genkan*, where he stepped into his shoes, put on his cap and raincoat. '*Dōmo arigatō*,' he said, making a little bow, and left. He hadn't been in the flat longer than seven minutes.

Sylvia's first reaction to his intimate though lightning visit was to laugh; he had been so funny in a way, so determined, so serious. Her second reaction was to feel ashamed. Would he tell everyone in the neighbourhood that she was an easy lay? Would her doorbell be rung constantly by libidinous louts? Oh God, she wished she hadn't given in to his blandishments, or rather obeyed his command. Would she dare go to the vegetable shop again? Not having anyone to tell was so depressing, but who in the world could she ever have told? There was no one.

She put on her dressing-gown and without remaking the bed or unpacking her purchases, which were still in the bag by the sink, where *he* (she didn't know his name) had put it, she sat in one of her new armchairs and cogitated upon the little lust scene she had just enacted with what her mother would have called 'a trades-man'. What was it that he had said? *Chotto dake*? She had heard *chotto* often, and she knew it meant 'a moment' and usually came together with '*chotto matte*' meaning 'wait a moment', but *dake*, was it *dake*? It could hardly be 'duckie', although 'Just a moment, duckie' would make sense. Giggling to herself, she rose and fetched from the bookshelf her Japanese-English dictionary and from out of her handbag her reading glasses, and then settling herself again into her chair she flicked over the flimsy pages. '*Dake*,' she read, 'only; alone; no more; merely'. So *chotto dake* meant 'only a moment'. Well, that made sense. But what was the other word he had pronounced with such feeling at the moment of climax when the telephone was ringing? It had sounded like *eeku*, but perhaps was spelt *iiku* in the unsatisfactory romanization of the ideograms. Under that word she found 'culture of will'. It could hardly have been that. Perhaps it was *iku*. She flipped over the pages until she came to the word and found three entries: 'Iku ~ *Yuku*; Iku: awe, reverential fear; to be struck with awe; Iku: some, how many (much)', and then came some examples with characters which she couldn't read. Perhaps it was the second *iku* and he meant he was awestruck. She felt flattered. Was it a Japanese custom to declare that one was filled with reveren-tial fear at such moments? How sweet that the greengrocer, Mr Five-Four-Six, should have been so moved! But what about the first one, the *iku* that seemed to be derived from *yuku*. She turned to 'Y' in her little dictionary. *Yuku* (1) meant 'go', 'betake

94

oneself to'; *Yuku* (2) meant 'go well' (smoothly, all right) – feasible? *Yuku* (3) meant 'running water' – a euphemism? And a fourth *yuku* not belonging to the group of three meant 'die, pass away, depart his life'. No, that could not possibly be the word. She decided that it was probably the awestruck *iku*, but she hoped to find out. Who could she ask? Matthew? But it might be a slang expression only used in such circumstances and inquiring about it might give away what she had been doing. After *iku* he had said '*okā-san*', which she knew meant 'mother'. This disturbed her as it made him seem kinky, or was he just turned on by an older woman? After all, Toshi seemed to be. His final words '*dōmo arigatō*' meant 'thank you'. She had learnt to say them herself.

The telephone rang.

'Hello?'

'I call but no answer.' Toshi sounded distraught.

'I was out shopping. Where are you? I thought you'd gone on a trip.'

'We are going soon.'

'Where are you?' Had he possibly seen her enter her building with the greengrocer?

'Near my bank.' He never rung her from his desk on which there was a telephone. 'Are you alone?'

'Yes, of course.' Had he sensed something? 'Why do you ask?'

'I wonder.'

'I am alone.'

'What will you do this weekend?'

'Just laze.'

'What is that?'

'Do nothing. Well, goodbye Toshi. Have a good time!'

'I no have good time without you.'

'Don't be silly. Ring me in the week, okay?'

'Okay.'

She rang off. Poor boy, he really was quite lovesick, unlike the greengrocer, who probably never suffered from that complaint and had possibly already forgotten about her. She opened the *shōji* and resettled herself in the armchair from which she could see the drenched trees in the cemetery and occasionally hear the loud, raucous voice of the funny, dumpy little woman who looked after the graves and even in the rain guided visitors to their ancestors' tombs and sold them greenery to put on them. Had she seen her and the greengrocer enter the apartments together? Would she bawl about her wantonness to all the graveyard visitors? 'See that flat up there? That's where a foreign whore lives.' Sylvia felt ashamed. She had behaved like a neglected housewife who has 'backdoor' sex with the milkman. She had never done such a thing before. But, however reprehensible, she had not, like the proverbial housewife, enticed him. She felt gratified in a way because for the first time for years she seemed to be wanted: by Toshi, definitely and sincerely; by Mr Five-Four-Six, perhaps only on impulse, but wanted nevertheless; by Professor Suzuki . . . but it was best to forget about him. And there was Mr Ogawa at the swimming pool.

During the last few years of her marriage she had felt the opposite – unwanted. She knew before the affair reached boiling point that Graham's secretary had become his mistress and she had suffered. How lonely she had been! Mark had gone to live with Colin and he provided no solace; all he had said was: 'Oh, I expect it'll blow over. Father's of the age when that sort of thing happens. He's having the male menopause.' 'And what am I supposed to do? Nothing?' 'Bide your time and he'll come back to you.' But he hadn't. He had asked for a divorce and Sylvia had agreed, finding it humiliating to try to hang on to him when he no longer needed her.

Now in Tokyo, even though Sylvia felt she had degraded herself, rather in the fashion of Belle de Jour in Luis Buñuel's film, she also felt less ignored than she had done in London, just before and after her divorce. She was a bit lonely, yes, and needed a friend, but Toshi seemed fond of her and that was a comfort. Sometimes she thought of Mr Ogawa at the swimming pool. Would Mr Five-Four-Six be a source of trouble? Seven minutes! He had been in the flat no more than seven minutes. Could such a brief act of intimacy, which was in retrospect more risible than anything, have any repercussions? After further meditation on the incident of that afternoon, she decided that although it was an experience she wouldn't regret (for in a way it had been thrilling), it was not one she would ever boast of.

One afternoon while swimming up and down the pool, Sylvia thought about Toshi, in spite of the fact that Mr Ogawa splashed past regularly. Several times she had offered to buy Toshi pyjamas as he would put on his underwear after making love to her. He had said that he didn't need any. When she had completed her stint of twenty lengths, five hundred metres, she sat by the pool in a plastic chair and was soon joined by Mr Ogawa. The life-guard, who sat on the seat at the top of a ladder, blew his whistle, as he or one of his colleagues did every hour on the hour. He began his routine announcement, which never varied and which lasted nearly as long as the five-minute interval.

'What does he say?' Sylvia asked, not for the first time as the amplified voice rang round the pool, fluent, expressionless, and meaningless since it was made so often.

'He say it is rest time,' replied Ogawa, also not for the first time.

'He must say more than that.'

'He thanks us for coming. He tell us swimming is good exercise but it tiring and we must have rest time.'

'Don't you think it's rather silly?'

'Yes, it silly. But we Japanese like instruction.'

'Do you like to be told what to do all the time?'

'Me?'

'Yes, you, Mr Ogawa.'

'I no like. But many they like.' Ogawa smiled.

Sylvia thought that he would be attractive if he didn't have such large teeth. How often dental arrangements spoilt a Japanese face! Toshi had regular teeth but they were more grey than white. The greengrocer's teeth of steel were awful but . . . the less she thought of him the better, she told herself.

'Mr Ogawa, do you wear pyjamas?'

The Japanese looked surprised. 'Sorry?'

'At night, when you go to bed, do you put on pyjamas?'

'Yes, I put.' He looked very puzzled. 'I like pyjama more than *yukata*. You know *yukata*?'

'No.'

'It is cotton like kimono style. I do not like in bed, it come up, so I put on pyjama.'

'I see. They sell pyjamas here then?'

'In departo store they sell. You wan' I help you buy?'

'No, thanks. I can manage. I want to send some pyjamas to my son in England.'

'I see.'

But Sylvia wondered if he thought there was any ulterior motive in her question about pyjamas. As usual he waited until she was dressed and they left the building together bidding each other goodbye at the bottom of the steps and going their different ways. She liked him. He was much easier than Professor Suzuki, who would have given his high-pitched giggle if she had asked him if he wore pyjamas in bed, and would have answered in a way which would not have told her whether he wore them or not, and then he would have gossiped about her inquiry in the way he had announced at the Faculty meeting what she had had for lunch on her first day at the university.

On her way home Sylvia went to the department store on the west side of Ikebukuro Station. In the men's section she asked a young salesman in a blue suit for pyjamas. The young man, who seemed to be not much more than a schoolboy, smiled bashfully, dropped his head, muttered 'Jus' a mo-ment, prease' and went off. He returned with another young man, older and taller, about Toshi's age, who also wore a blue suit, rather shiny, and had a neat head of hair, wide-set eyes but discoloured teeth crammed into a small mouth.

'Can I help you?' asked the new young man.

'Yes, please. I want two pairs of summer pyjamas,' said Sylvia slowly and clearly and stressing the season.

But the salesman didn't understand for he replied, 'Summer?'

'Yes, summer pyjamas. Thin ones, cotton ones.'

He understood cotton. 'Ah so, cotton,' he said, and then added, 'This man section.' The 'schoolboy' was beside the older man watching and trying to keep a straight face.

'Yes, I know. I want man's pyjamas, man's pyjamas for the summer, cotton; size medium.'

'For your husband?'

'No.'

'Your husband want L size,' said the man looking at Sylvia knowingly and nodding.

'I want M size. Please show me some.'

'For your son?'

'Never mind who they are for,' replied Sylvia, angrily.

The two assistants went off to fetch the pyjamas. Sylvia sighed and thought how much easier her life would be if she knew Japanese. This assumption of knowing what one wants better than one knows oneself was annoying. She had met it before. The young men returned with a pile of pyjamas in plastic wraps and she began to go through them. 'But these are all L,' she complained.

'I think you want L.'

'No. I don't want L. I want M size.'

'Your husband, he Japanese?' asked the young assistant.

'No, he is not,' she answered firmly.

'Then you want L.'

'No, I want M. Have you got M?'

'Yes, we have.'

'Then bring M, please.' The exasperation in her tone was understood and the 'schoolboy' was packed off to fetch medium-size pyjamas.

'Your husband not big-size man?' asked the older assistant.

'The pyjamas are *not* for my husband,' declared Sylvia, astonishing herself by the emphasis she put on the negative. Did she do this because the very idea of buying a present for the now hated Graham appalled her, or did she subconsciously wish to tell people about Toshi? The boy returned with a pile of medium-size pyjamas in plastic envelopes. Sylvia took some time to choose. To see what the colours would look like on a Japanese, she asked the assistant to hold several jackets up against his chest. She chose a dark-red pair and hesitated over a yellow pair striped with dark green. 'What do you think?' she asked.

'He is Japanese?'

'Yes.'

The young man smiled as if he had guessed her secret. 'I think blue better,' he said and selected a dark-blue pair and held it up against him. He was right, the blue pair and the dark-red pair looked better than the yellow pair. Dark shades suited the Japanese colouring better than light ones, she decided. The assistant's attitude changed. He became friendly, not impudent, but warm and willing to allow her to change her mind. Sylvia felt that her taking his advice and buying the dark-blue pair pleased him, for he had succeeded in asserting his will. The two pairs of pyjamas were skilfully wrapped by the junior assistant in the green and white paper of the store, while the senior one went off to cash Sylvia's banknote. She took her change from the plastic saucer proffered by the senior assistant and the carrier bag containing her parcel from the junior one and returned their bows with a smile and a little wave. She left the shop, content with her purchases and with the service of the shop assistants. She was convinced that they had tried to do their best and succeeded, and that the preliminary misunderstanding was simply due to the Japanese habit of anticipating one's needs. She left the shop pleased with Japan.

That evening when Toshi rang from a street telephone near the bank, she told him about the pyjamas and suggested he come round to try them on. 'So I can change them if they don't fit,' she said. 'Come along now, have a meal and then go home, if you must.'

'Sorry I cannot.'

'What are you going to do?'

'I meet my university friend.'

'I see. What will you do?'

'We just meet and talk.'

Sylvia had to accept this, but she did wonder what he did in the evenings. Then she thought of Mr Five-Four-Six and chided herself.

· 11 ·

Sylvia had managed to persuade Matthew to bring Jun to lunch. It was nearly noon on a Sunday morning, and Toshi was still in bed. A certain amount of cajoling had been necessary to get Toshi to agree to her inviting the two guests, not for any other reason, as far as Sylvia could gather, than it would mean his having to rise, shave and dress by one o'clock instead of lounging around in pyjamas (the shop assistant had been right, the dark-blue pair suited him) until well into the afternoon. Sylvia wondered if his fatigue was due to a riotous night on Friday; he had never explained his Friday engagement.

'Oh Toshi!' she cried from the kitchen. 'Do get up. They'll be here in three quarters of an hour.'

No answer.

· 12 ·

'Oh Jun, do get up,' cried Matthew from his desk in the sitting-room. He had already woken his friend three times and received grunts in reply; he knew he would get up eventually and spend an inordinate time in the bathroom washing his hair and shaving under the deluge of hot water in the shower. Matthew had advanced the bedroom clock by fifteen minutes. The clock was an adapted dinner plate with a blue and white Delft design (made in Japan, a gift from Jun), but this was not a new ruse and Jun knew the clock was fast. Matthew disliked the timepiece and would have thrown it away if Jun hadn't given it to him; Jun was rather proud of his gift and would sometimes admire it in the way that the young admire their own presents. 'Isn't it a nice clock,' Jun would say, 'and you like ceramic.'

'I like it because you gave it to me,' Matthew would say, truthfully.

It was nearly noon and Matthew was stuck over his article on a comparison between Jane Austen's and Anthony Trollope's use of dialogue, a subject he had been asked to write about for a Tokyo literary magazine and one he needed to publish to maintain his academic reputation at the university. No one would read it probably, but to get it printed was the thing and to present a copy to the Faculty.

'Oh do get up, Jun. It's not polite to be late. It'll take us three quarters of an hour to get there.'

'Toshi, please.' Sylvia was sitting on the bed, a hand stroking his dark hair that just showed above the sheet. 'It's twelve-thirty and they'll be here in half an hour.'

'Uh?'

'It's time to get up, darling.' She pulled back the sheet a little and saw half his face: one fine, thick eyebrow, one closed eye guarded by long lashes, and half his nose. The eye opened, saw her, then shut. 'You are awake.'

'I sleep.' A smile made the visible corner of his mouth curl upwards. Sylvia put her lips to his forehead and gently kissed it. 'Get up,' she whispered.

Suddenly he turned on to his back, threw down the bedclothes and revealed his stiff cock. He pulled her on to the bed. 'Oh Toshi,' she said, half-laughing, and between kisses, 'Don't . . . my dress . . . there isn't time.' He then moved aside, undid his pyjama jacket, kicked off his trousers and with a determined hand pushed her head down to his groin. 'No, Toshi, they'll be here at any moment!' 'Not take long.' He was right; he didn't. The bell sounded its two notes three times. 'God, they're here!' exclaimed Sylvia. 'Run to the bathroom quick. I've put your clothes in the back room.' He jumped out of the bed and dashed out of the room, pyjama jacket flying, and into the bathroom.

The bell sounded again. She closed the sliding doors that screened the bedroom from the living-room, tossed her hair into shape, and smoothing down her dress went to the door. There stood Mr Five-Four-Six, silver teeth glinting. The geyser roared, the shower pelted and Toshi started to sing a Japanese song. The greengrocer smiled. He was wearing a blue suit without a tie, his white shirt buttoned at the collar, and no numbered cap. Sylvia shook her head and an open hand at him. 'Okay,' he said, and throwing her a silver flash went off down the passage. Sylvia shut the door.

'They come? shouted Toshi from the bathroom.

'Not yet.'

'Who?' Toshi demanded, gruffly, as if he were the master of the house.

'No one.' Sylvia opened the bathroom door and regarded the soap-sudded body.

'Who?' He squinted through the hat of white froth on his head.

'Just the man from the drink shop.' It was the first time she had told him a direct lie to his face.

'What he want?'

'Empty bottles.'

'Shut the door. It cold.'

· 14 ·

'Jun, are you washing your hair?' asked Matthew through the bathroom door.

'Yes.'

'Well, hurry up. It's nearly one.' It was in fact twelve-twenty.

Matthew went on with his task of making the twin beds. He and Jun preferred singles to one double because Jun was a restless sleeper and kicked out in the night. Matthew picked up a ball of tissues from the floor, went into the kitchen and with a frown dropped them into the rubbish bin. He returned to the bedroom and shouted into the steamy bathroom, 'Are you going to wear your contact lenses?'

'Yes.'

'That'll add ten minutes to your being ready.'

'No, it won't.'

He plugged in the hair dryer and put it on the dressing-table. 'I've put the hair dryer out.'

'Thanks.'

'Do hurry.'

'All right.'

'What shall I take Sylvia as a present?'

'Take that bottle of Mateus Rosé Bill-san gave you.' Bill was an American friend.

'Good idea.'

At a quarter to one Matthew with a plastic bag containing the bottle of wine and Jun were walking down the road towards the station. Jun was in jeans and a white T-shirt. Matthew was wearing a light-blue open-necked shirt and blue summer trousers. It was a warm July morning. Jun stopped at a cigarette machine into which he inserted two coins. 'I don't want to go. I don't want to meet the lover boy.'

'Don't say that now. You could easily have refused.'

'I go to please you, because of you. I think you want to see what he is like.'

'In a way, yes.'

Jun picked the packet of cigarettes out of the machine and they continued their walk to the station.

· 15 ·

'Thank God, they're late,' said Sylvia. 'It's twenty past one.'

Toshi was sitting in the tatami room on the low stool in front of the dressing-table and Sylvia was kneeling by his side drying his hair with the dryer.

'I wish they not come.'

'Oh Toshi, you said you wanted to see them.'

'I see them because of you. I don't wan' meet gay people. I not gay.'

'You don't act or look in the least gay, Toshi. You did say you didn't mind meeting gay people.'

'I say I don't mind because of you. I like to be alone with you on Sunday afternoon, our Sunday afternoon special time.'

Sylvia was touched. 'They won't stay forever. We can continue our Sunday afternoon as soon as they've gone.'

'Thank you. You very kind.' He rose from the stool and Sylvia got up from her knees, not in one lithe movement like a Japanese, but in two clumsy stages as she held on to the dressing-table for support.

'That man who he?'

'I told you.' She went into the main room and opened the oven door to look at the roasting joint of pork.

Why was he so persistent? Did he suspect? He couldn't possibly know. While prodding the meat with a fork, she repeated her lie. 'The man from the drink shop. He had just delivered an order farther up the passage, I think. He wanted to know if I had any empty bottles. He's very obliging and helpful. I much prefer him to the woman in the shop.'

'Maybe he like you.'

There was no time to find out what exactly Toshi meant to insinuate by those words as the two notes of the bell rang out again. How nastily insistent the sound was! She gave a start. Her lie made her do so. Could it be Mr Five-Four-Six, who had mistaken her gesticulations for an invitation to return later?

'I go to the door,' said Toshi.

'No, I'll go. Better.' Sylvia carefully shut the living-room door when she had passed into the little hall and opened the front door with relief to find Matthew and Jun waiting below the outside step; they knew the door would open in their direction.

'Sorry we're late,' said Matthew.

'No matter. No matter at all.'

'This is Jun Sakamoto. Jun, Sylvia Field.'

'How do you do?' She shook Jun's hand. He gave a slight bow.

'This is for you.' Matthew handed her the plastic bag.

'A bottle. How sweet! You shouldn't bring a present. The meal won't merit one.'

'It's nothing much,' said Matthew.

'How I hate the two-tone bell,' said Sylvia. 'There's something horribly genteel about it, don't you think?' She opened the door into the living-room. 'As if an ordinary bell were vulgar and this sickening ding-dong mitigated the urgency of the summons.'

'Most bells in mansions are the same,' said Matthew, entering the room.

'Now, Matthew, this is Toshi Yamada. Toshi, Matthew Bennet and Jun, Jun, er . . .'

'Sakamoto,' Jun provided his name for her.

'Jun Sakamoto.'

Toshi, now dressed in his tidy banker's blue with a white shirt and a blue and red tie, shook hands with Matthew and jerked a bow at Jun, grunting. 'Come into the body of the church,' said Sylvia, nervously, in the hostess's voice she had put on so often in the past for duty parties she and Graham had given. She directed

105

her guests towards the sofa and the chairs. Matthew looked out of the window. 'I used to come here sometimes when your predecessor lived here. Do the tombs bother you? He hated them and would keep the *shōji* closed. He was a bit neurotic.'

'They don't bother me at all,' answered Sylvia. 'I no longer notice them. I look at the trees and those not unpleasant houses beyond, and rejoice in the fact that I don't look on to someone else's laundry or bathroom, to use the American euphemism. What'll you drink, Matthew – gin? Jun, gin? "Jun-gin" sounds rather lovely.' She laughed. She seemed unnaturally elated, in forced high spirits. Matthew wondered if the affair had sailed into rough waters – Sunday morning could be difficult, he knew well.

'Gin and tonic would be fine,' said Matthew.

'And you, Jun? You don't mind if I call you Jun, do you?'

'No, please. The same, gin and tonic.'

'Toshi?'

'Gin and tonic.'

While Sylvia was preparing the drinks, Matthew sat heavily on the sofa – he was no lightweight. 'Jun,' he called, 'why don't you sit here?' He patted the place by his side, but Jun was absorbed in conversation with Toshi by the window, not quite in the sitting-room area. Sylvia arrived on the scene with a tray of gin and tonics. She gave one to Jun. 'A gin for Jun,' she said. 'Toshi, you take this one. And Matthew, here's yours.' Matthew slightly raised his bottom when taking his drink. Sylvia picked up her own gin and tonic, which she had poured out for herself before Toshi had awakened, from the low table by the sofa. 'Cheers!' she said to Matthew. She raised her glass in the direction of the two young Japanese men standing by the window, but they were too busy talking and laughing to take any notice.

'It's not too cold in here, is it, Matthew? I could turn the cooler off.'

'It's fine.'

'I've got the boringest of lunches for you.'

'I'm sure you haven't,' Matthew replied, rather formally.

Sylvia turned to the Japanese. 'Toshi, why don't you take off your jacket?' she said in a motherly way. Her lover replied by giving her a frown and turning his attention back to Jun. 'Hey, you two, why don't you come over here?' she cried, and reluc-

106

tantly they broke off their conversation and joined the foreigners. Again Sylvia suggested that Toshi remove his jacket; again he frowned.

Jun obeyed Sylvia's signal to sit on the side of the sofa near her, and Toshi sat near Matthew, who said, 'I believe you work in a bank.'

'So.' He brought out a visiting card and gave it to Matthew.

Sylvia said to Jun, 'In two weeks' time holidays begin. What will you do?'

'I go to England.'

'Oh? How nice! Will it be your first visit?'

'My third visit. Will you go to England?'

'No. I've only just arrived. I don't know what I shall do.'

While Sylvia was acting the polite hostess to Jun, Matthew asked Toshi if his bank kept him busy.

'Yes, I busy.'

After a pause, Matthew said, 'Does your bank have background music?'

'Yes, not upstair in foreign department. I work in foreign department.'

'Don't the clerks get tired of it?'

'They don't hear it.'

'You mean they are so used to it that to them it is just a noise.'

'It is for the customer.'

'It would drive me crazy.'

Sylvia got up. 'Let's have lunch.' She led her guests across the room to the dining-table, now screened from the kitchen equipment by a curtain she had bought at the same department store where she had got Toshi's pyjamas. Matthew admired the curtain.

'It does improve the room. I hated seeing the sink and the stove all the time.' Sylvia placed Matthew at one end of the table and the two Japanese opposite each other in the middle, and went behind the curtain to fetch the first course, but when she reappeared with four plates of eggs mayonnaise with anchovies, she found that Matthew had changed places with Toshi and was on her left. 'Why change the *placement*?' she asked as she handed round the plates. 'Better for conversation,' said Matthew, and looking at his eggs he remarked, 'I'm glad you don't serve soup for luncheon as so many do these days. Japanese restaurants especially, with their table d'hôte menus.'

'Nor do I hunt south of the Thames,' Sylvia replied, laughing. 'I've often thought,' she went on, 'that one could add to the list those who dislike salad. "Let us"! I've learnt to say "let-us" for lettuce.' Mr Five-Four-Six came into her mind and she blushed.

'It isn't "let-us", exactly,' said Matthew. 'It's *retasu*.' He noticed her blush and wondered why a reference to salad brought it on.

Neither Toshi nor Jun knew what their foreign friends were talking about, but this didn't matter as they were talking to each other in Japanese, and two conversations went on throughout the meal in the two languages. Now and then Sylvia, like a mother to whispering children, tried to interpolate with 'What are you two talking about?', but she got no response. When the *fraises Escoffier* had been consumed, Matthew exclaimed, 'Marvellous. Jun, we must do this.' 'Aren't the strawberries heavenly here!' said Sylvia. '*Oishī*!' said Jun. '*Oishī*!' echoed Toshi. Sylvia said, 'Now let's go to the other part of the room,' and they settled down again on the sofa and in the armchairs. But this time Jun sat at one end of the sofa with Toshi next to him in an armchair, while Matthew sat at the other end by the other armchair where Sylvia sat after she had served the coffee. Again two separate conversations struck up. During an English silence, Matthew, who understood Japanese fairly well, said to Jun, 'Are you telling Toshi about *ni-chome*?'

'What is *ni-chome*?' asked Sylvia, eagerly.

Jun, without answering, continued his conversation with Toshi.

Sylvia distinctly heard Toshi say 'Crub New Love' in the middle of a Japanese sentence. 'Toshi, what are you talking about?'

Toshi gave Sylvia a fierce glare and continued with what he was saying to Jun.

'Do they always divide up like this, Matthew?'

'Yes, if they get on, and these two seem to.'

'Why can't we all talk together?'

'If we did we'd have the same stilted conversation we had before lunch. While I talk happily with Jun when there's no one else around, and you presumably to Toshi when you're alone with him, at a time like this when there is a mixed party, the Japanese always like to talk to one another, and the foreigners do likewise.'

'But that's frightful – unnatural,' protested Sylvia.

'It may be frightful but it's not unnatural. The age difference has quite a lot to do with it, the generation gap.'

'I don't believe in the generation gap. I don't feel old.'

'If they were our age, then things might be different, but I doubt it. You have things to say to Toshi, private things, and so do I to Jun, but what do you have to say to Jun, or I to Toshi? Nothing of any consequence. We can exchange banalities, that's all.'

'But there're a lot of things I'd like to say to Jun.'

'Just conventional questions, probably. The Japanese are practical. To them conversation among themselves is far more profitable than conversation in a foreign language, which inevitably must be limited because they don't really know it, will never know it properly. I mean Jun, who teaches English, would not have understood your reference to hunting south of the Thames, if he had heard it.'

'But he would have done, if it had been explained.'

'Explaining jokes is awful.'

'But Matthew,' insisted Sylvia,' we have to explain. That's what we're here for.'

'But not on a social occasion. No, let them chatter in their way, let us chatter in ours, in our own languages.'

'So that never the twain may meet?'

'Not on a conversational level, if the talk is to flow, and table talk should flow, but on other levels the twain meet all right, don't they?' Matthew sniggered, but Sylvia was serious: she seemed to be pondering the problem. Matthew looked at Jun, caught his eye and he nodded, and after a few moments simultaneously they rose, and then came the usual thanks and goodbyes.

'Did you like Jun?' Sylvia asked when the couple had gone.

'Yes. He good man.'

'What did you talk to him about?'

'Nothing.'

'Just platitudes, empty talk? But you seemed to have a lot to say. I heard you mention some club.'

'Yes. We talk about a crub.'

'What club?'

'Just a crub.' He turned on the television set and began to watch women playing volley-ball.

It suddenly occurred to Sylvia that possibly the club was where he went on Friday nights. 'What is this club, Toshi?'

'It is crub.' He kept his eyes on the screen.

Exasperated, Sylvia crossed to the television set and turned it off. She stood over her lover. 'Now tell me, Toshi, what is this club? You go there on Friday nights, don't you?'

'How you know?'

'I guessed. What is this club?'

'It is host crub. It call "Crub New Love".'

'Why do you go there?'

'I host.'

'Host? What on earth do you mean?'

'When I a student, I was host as *arbeito*. My university friend he is Master host. Now I work in bank, he ask me to be host on Friday when I am free. So I go. I good host. The customer they like me.'

'What do you do as a host?'

'I talk to the customers. I dance with them. I pour their drink.'

'Who are the customers?'

'Ole women, some married, some not.'

'Do you sleep with them?'

'Sorry?'

'Do you go to bed with them?'

'No, I never.'

'Toshi, I don't believe you.' Sylvia, who had begun to seethe with jealous rage, hesitated, then she said in a voice tight with emotion, 'Toshi, please go.'

'You wan' me to go?'

'Yes.'

'Okay.' He rose, collected his briefcase from the back room and left without giving her as much as a glance.

· 16 ·

Matthew and Jun were walking towards Hongō-san-chōme station. 'You know,' Jun said, '"Mr Lady" bar is opposite "Club New Love"?'

'You told me.'

'One night I went up in the elevator with Toshi. I didn't know

who he was then. He went into "Club New Love".'
'And you into "Mr Lady".'
'Right.'
'When was this?'
'Few weeks ago.'
'So it was after Sylvia met him.'
'I don't know.'
'It must have been, if it was only a few weeks ago. So Toshi is a host, then. How interesting! How unusual for a bank clerk! But I thought that most hosts were gay.'
'Not all.'
'I see. I wonder if Sylvia will find out.'

· 17 ·

When Toshi had gone Sylvia washed the dishes angrily and noisily, and then, in spite of the humid heat and the wine she had had at lunch, she took herself out for a walk through the grounds of Tokyo University and down to Shinobazu Pond. She liked the walk, the one which Toshi had introduced her to after he had become her lover for the first time, and she often went on it. By the time she had reached the pond and begun to cross the causeway that divided the lake into two parts, one for boating, the other for lotuses, her anger had abated. Why shouldn't Toshi have his own private life? She had submitted to the greengrocer's peremptory advances. But she had not searched him out, while Toshi had had his Friday night fling with 'ole women' (how old? older than she?) for some time. It was possessive of her to want him for herself only. But wasn't that love: to want to possess. Was she in love with Toshi? She passed a bench on which a red-faced man was lying full length in ragged trousers and a torn shirt. An empty bottle of cheap whisky was on the ground by his right arm which dangled down. One of the few who had opted out, she supposed. A young couple rose from a bench just as she was passing it. She turned back and sat down. It was absurd for her to think that she, at fifty, could hold a young man only half way through his twenties. She gazed at the electric boats and the rowing boats on the lake; in nearly all of them were young couples. Toshi should have a girl friend who was about twenty, not a woman twenty-five years older than he. Yet he must have a penchant for older women if he enjoyed the company of the patronesses of the host club. Or did he do it for the money? Presumably a young bank clerk wasn't all that well off and Tokyo was so expensive.

She got up and walked towards the temple on an island joined by causeways. It was dedicated to Benten, the only female goddess of luck. She passed the eaves of the octagonal building, whose roof resembled a fancy-dress Chinese hat, and she went round to the front, where there was an open space and steps into the main hall, to which the quaint octagonal building was attached. There was an urn filled with sand in the middle of the space into which joss sticks had been stuck. A few people clapped their hands and muttered a prayer at the bottom of the steps after throwing coins into a receptacle at the top. Sylvia went up the steps, bought a joss stick, lit it at a burning candle, descended to the urn and stuck the smouldering stick into the sand. An old woman in kimono stood over the urn and with a hand wafted some of the smoke arising from the burning joss sticks on to her shoulders. Sylvia, without knowing the reason for the old woman's action, copied her. Should she wish? If so, what for? She wished she could be rid of her thoughts about Toshi. She walked away from Bentendo, past the little stalls selling food and purses and stuffed birds and plastic masks of pandas, babies, spacemen and cats that lined the main entrance to the temple, and when she came to the end of the causeway, she turned right and joined the pedestrians on the path along the lotus side of the pond. She felt uncomfortably hot. She was wearing a sleeveless cotton dress, but there was a damp patch of sweat on her chest and she was sure there was one on her back. She hailed a taxi as soon as she got outside the park. On the way up the hill, an idea came to her. Had it been sent by Benten, the goddess of luck?

· 18 ·

'There's a rumour going round about you,' Matthew told Sylvia. He had called on her at her room in the university.

'And what is this rumour?'

'That you're having an affair with one of your students.'

'I can guess who is responsible for that.'

'Professor Suzuki.'

'Right. Who told you about this rumour?'

'Professor Maeda, you know, the Chairman of the English Department. I'm sure he only told me so I could warn you.'

Indignant, Sylvia said, 'What am I supposed to do? You know it isn't true. Should I go to Suzuki and have it out with him?'

'No, I don't think you should.' Matthew, not a decisive, domineering person, was inept at giving advice and hated doing so.

'Suzuki is obviously out for my blood because I rebuffed him. I think I'll go to the Dean and tell him the truth, about Suzuki, and about Toshi. What gossips they are!'

'Gossip is not uncommon at a university. The trouble is that some of the students have been talking about it, apparently.'

'What should I do, Matthew? You've been here long enough to give me some guidance.'

'I should do nothing. Term ends this week. It'll blow over by the time classes start again.'

'You think I should ride the storm then?'

'It's not a storm, not even one in a teacup. It's just a rumour that is best ignored.'

· 19 ·

Sylvia suggested to the students of her seminar class that they come to an end-of-term party in her flat. There were five girls and two men in the class, so to balance the sexes she invited three of her male students, who were writing their M.A. theses and whom she saw separately. She liked these three men. One was writing about George Eliot, another about D.H. Lawrence, and the third about William Faulkner.

With the seminar class she was reading Forster's *Where Angels Fear to Tread*. She was never sure whether they appreciated the story or found it boring. They were cleverly evasive when a definite answer was required, and would seem bewildered when asked to say what they thought about a character, or a situation. 'But what do you *think*?' Sylvia would insist, and their non-committal answers suggested that they didn't think very much.

The men who attended her tutorials singly had at first been diffident and tense, but gradually they had become self-confident and now they behaved naturally. The most mature of these was Mr Matsuda (Sylvia always addressed her students as Mr or Miss). He was over thirty, quite tall, married and had a part-time teaching job in a school. His pale, pasty complexion was enlivened by a humorous twinkle in his dark eyes, and the corners of his well-shaped mouth would flick upwards when he smiled. He had a deep voice which made him sound more serious than his occasional smile suggested. His thesis was to be on *Middlemarch*. He would ask Sylvia pertinent questions, questions that were the product of careful thought. Sylvia enjoyed her fortnightly hour answering Mr Matsuda's considered questions about the behaviour of the characters. During the last session before the vacation, they discussed Dr Casaubon and his marriage to Dorothea.

'Are there people like Dr Casaubon in Japan?' Sylvia asked, thinking of Suzuki.

Mr Matsuda thought for a moment and then said, 'Yes, I suppose so.'

'Are there any professors like Dr Casaubon?'

'You mean at this university?'

'Yes.'

'I've no idea.'

'What about Professor Suzuki?' asked Sylvia recklessly, and then wished she hadn't.

'I've no idea.'

'Or Mr Bennet?'

'Mr Bennet? You mean Mr Bennet in *Pride and Prejudice?*'

Sylvia laughed. 'No, the Mr Bennet here.'

'Professor Bennet, you mean. He is English. You must know better than me, Mrs Field.' Matsuda was obviously embarrassed, but Sylvia persisted. 'What do the students think of Professor Bennet?'

'They think he is a very kind man.'

'And what do they think about me?'

'Who?'

'The students and the professors.'

'They think you are a very kind lady.'

'Kind? Is that all? What do they think about my ability?'

'I've no idea.'

Sylvia was about to ask Matsuda what he thought about her, when he firmly changed the subject back to *Middlemarch*. 'Do you think that Dorothea is really intelligent?'

Sylvia nearly said, 'I've no idea', but she took the hint and the tutorial returned to its proper course. Matsuda was a diligent student anxious to get the most out of the lesson. He did not like time to be wasted on gossip.

The students' party passed off fairly well; fairly, because Sylvia wasn't sure if they enjoyed it. Matsuda did not attend although he had said he would, and this worried Sylvia, who feared that her indiscreet questions had disconcerted him. She told herself she should have known better than to expect him to be disloyal about the university professors or about Matthew, who had been his tutor last year and had read Jane Austen with him.

At the party the students did not become very relaxed. They behaved much as they did at the seminar, the girls fidgeting with their long tresses – a silly fashion, Sylvia thought, and unsuitable for travel in crowded trains and for the summer heat. They told her that they washed their heads everyday and did not believe her when she said that too much shampooing might be beneficial for the cosmetic company but was not good for the hair. They often thought they knew best like the salesman in the department store where she had bought Toshi's pyjamas, which now lay washed and ironed but unworn in her cupboard. The girls, she had learnt, all wore contact lenses, and out of the five men present three wore spectacles. The two male students who did not belong to the seminar ('Mr D.H.L.' and 'Mr Faulkner', Sylvia privately nick-named them) sat together and hardly spoke.

When the group from the seminar class presented her with a bunch of yellow chrysanthemums, she exclaimed, 'Chrysan-themums in July! How splendidly unseasonal! A symbol of autumn in the height of summer. Does it mean you are already looking forward to September and work?' The students laughed uncertainly. 'Mr D.H.L.' and 'Mr Faulkner' gave her a box of chocolates. 'Just what I like. Just what I shouldn't have!' This also confused the donors.

Sylvia served them spaghetti and a salad (they cried out for ketchup, which she didn't have), followed by a trifle. The latter was new to them, and they approached it warily; however, it was all consumed. The evening was more like an extended lesson than a party, even though 'Mr D.H.L.' sang, to her surprise, 'Cherry Ripe' in a rich baritone. The students seemed in awe of her, and throughout the evening Sylvia had to hold forth as no one otherwise said anything. The girls drank soft drinks; the men beer, though offered whisky. By nine they had gone. More than ever did Sylvia wonder what they thought of her. Had they heard the rumour? They gave no indication of having any knowledge of it. Perhaps Matthew had invented it out of spite. But he wasn't like that, was he? The vacation began on an ambiguous note.

· 20 ·

Matthew and Jun had set off on their trip to Paris and London. Toshi had not telephoned. Sylvia began to hope he would. Afraid that she might run into him if she went to his bank, she used the branch in Ikebukuro when she required some cash. She wheedled one of the ushers into helping her manipulate the money dispensing machine. She was always amused when he looked away at the moment she dialled her secret number.

With Matthew gone and no work at the university, Sylvia was lonely. She thought of Mr Ogawa as she had done after leaving the temple dedicated to Benten on the day she had impetuously asked Toshi to leave the flat.

Dawn came excessively early owing to the refusal of the Japanese to adopt summer time. The glow of morning shone through the *shōji*, which Sylvia left partly open so that she could see the trees in the cemetery. At 4 a.m. it was light and Sylvia would stir and watch as the trees and a patch of sky became more

116

distinct. While she dozed or gazed she would think of Mr Ogawa and then of Toshi. Had she been unreasonable? But why should she share him with some frustrated housewife? Then Mr Ogawa would return to her mind's eye until he was superseded by the greengrocer. Mr Five-Four-Six's visits could never develop into a proper affair. He could never be a companion, but Mr Ogawa possibly could. He was nearer her age than Toshi; he spoke English and seemed to enjoy talking to her by the pool after their swim. He had, though, never hinted that he wanted to be more than an acquaintance. His goodbye outside the sports centre was businesslike; he turned and walked to his car parked nearby. He had not once offered her a lift. Was this due to his Japanese shyness, which seemed at times to be almost pathological?

In the summer the skating rink at the sports centre was converted into a large pool, the Mammothu Poolu. Part of the pool was reserved for those swimming lengths, while the other, much larger part was given over to those who only wanted to play in the water. There was an island planted with three plastic trees in this part and there were rubber boats for hire. Since Sylvia did not have to go to the university she went to the pool more often. This meant seeing more of Mr Ogawa. He became neither more nor less friendly. He had none of Toshi's charm or the greengrocer's forcefulness, and yet he was not unattractive. What could she do about him? There was no one she could ask. Matthew was away and to ask him would be humiliating, and in all probability his advice wouldn't amount to much more than saying, 'I've no idea.' She decided she'd try and get on more intimate terms with Mr Ogawa.

One afternoon when Mr Ogawa and she were sunbathing after their swim on the patio between the Mammoth Pool and the Winter Pool, she began with her usual gambit, 'How many lengths today, Mr Ogawa?'

'Twenty.'

'That means forty by English counting.' She had learnt that the Japanese reckoned once up and once down the pool to be one length. 'One kilometre. Very good. I did twenty, or ten by your counting. Mr Ogawa, are you staying in Tokyo all the summer?'

'I think so.'

'It's so humid.'

They were sitting in plastic chairs. Other sunbathers were stretched out on the concrete of the patio.

'Why don't you go somewhere?' asked Ogawa.

'I don't know where to go. I want to see Kyoto, but they say it is hotter than Tokyo and unpleasant at this time of the year. Tell me, Mr Ogawa, why are there so many hotels with funny names in this district? I mean those with names like "Duet", "Casablanca" and "La La". Who stays in them?'

'They "love hotels".'

'"Love hotels"? Do you mean they are brothels?'

'They for couples.'

'What are they like? The hotels, I mean.'

'Some are quite luxury.'

'I want to see one. I want to know what a "love hotel" is like, what is provided and so on, the charges.' Sylvia felt she was being too brash, so she added, 'I'm thinking of writing an article on Ikebukuro and I feel I can't do so without mentioning the hotels. They are such a feature of the district.'

'I see.' Mr Ogawa shut his eyes and leant back in his chair and with a slight smile on his lips began to bask in the sun like a contented cat.

Sylvia, irritated by his apparent nonchalance, spoke quietly so that she would not be overheard by nearby sunbathers, who, although their eyes were shut seemed engaged in an important occupation. 'Mr Ogawa, please will you take me to one of the hotels so I can get first-hand information?'

Ogawa opened his eyes. 'It difficult.'

'Why?'

'I live here, maybe they see me.'

'Does it matter?'

'It matter.'

'But I only want to see one of the rooms for five minutes.'

'It difficult.' He shut his eyes again.

'Oh, never mind,' muttered Sylvia, petulantly. She rose and went to the changing room, where, angry at being peeped at by prying eyes, she brazenly displayed her naked body to a couple of giggling girls. Her act of exhibitionism alarmed them. They looked away and became absorbed in their own dressing. Sylvia furious with herself and with Mr Ogawa's indifference, fumed all the way home.

Gordon Apartments,
London.
3rd August

Dear Sylvia,

Jun and I had a very pleasant time in Paris. We saw most
things. All very exhausting, but Jun had not been to Paris
before, so I had to show him round. Now we're in London
staying at Gordon Apartments off the Fulham Road. Not
bad. Jun has been to London before, so I don't have to trail
around with him seeing the Changing of the Guard, the Tower, the Abbey and so on. We did do a river trip yesterday,
which was very pleasant.

An extraordinary coincidence occurred last night. I met
your son Mark. Jun and I went to see *Candida* with Colin
Sibley as the Rev. James Morell, Patricia Howard as his wife,
Candida, and Mark as Marchbanks. I knew the actor, Peter
Cox, playing the part of Mr Burgess, and when we went
backstage to see him, he insisted on introducing us to Colin
Sibley, who told us he might be taking the company to
Tokyo in the autumn. Mark came into Colin's dressing-room
and when I said I was teaching in Japan, he asked me if I
knew you. We – Colin, Peter, Mark, Jun and I all dined
together.

Mark, who was very good as Marchbanks, is going to play
Ariel in *The Tempest*, which Colin will also take to Tokyo if
the tour can be arranged. It depends on their getting enough
sponsorship. 'I'm told', he said, 'one must take a
Shakespeare play.'

Mark complained that you never write and he was anxious
about you. He asked if you were lonely. I did not tell him
about Toshi. By the way, what has happened about him?
Have you made it up?

I wouldn't worry about the silly rumour that apparently

rumbled round the university before the end of term.

How are you enjoying the heat of the Tokyo summer?
Here the weather has been good, on the whole. Jun
complains about there being no proper air-conditioning
anywhere. Colin's theatre was supposed to be air-cooled, but
it was not as well cooled as a Tokyo subway station.

I wonder if you're going on any trips.

We'll be back at the beginning of September.

Yours,
Matthew

• 22 •

Sylvia wrote a short and unrevealing reply to Matthew's letter. It
was not much more than an acknowledgement. She did not mention Ogawa, or the greengrocer, or Toshi, whom she had been
missing. To Mark, she sent a brief motherly missive saying how
pleased she was that he was doing well, and that he might be
coming to Tokyo. She said nothing about Colin Sibley, whom she
had not met and did not want to. She did not like his influence
over her son.

Sylvia spent much of the sweltering summer in her air-
conditioned flat, reading and occasionally watching television.
Sometimes there were films whose original English soundtrack
could be heard by pressing a button on the remote control panel,
and some news bulletins were dubbed into English. It was such a
joy to hear people speaking in her own language (or almost her
own language, since most of the films were American) that she
found herself watching a lot of trash. Her visits to the pool
continued and so did her platonic relationship with Mr Ogawa,
who did not refer to her request to be taken to a 'love hotel'. She
would never know what he thought about her request, just as she
would never know what Mr Five-Four-Six thought about her. The
latter continued to visit her sporadically and she had to admit she
looked forward to his calling, but since he stayed only long

120

enough to throw off his clothes, push her on to the bed, and hurl himself on top of her, the performance was from her point of view incomplete. Too soon would he cry, '*Okā-san, iku. Okā-san, iku, iku, iku*', and then hurriedly dress and depart, leaving her in a state of frustration, her desire aroused, but not sated.

On some days Sylvia would in spite of the heat force herself out on excursions. She went to Kabuki which she greatly enjoyed, to various museums, to exhibitions in department stores, and to nearby places. She visited Kamakura to see the great statue of the Buddha, Oshino-Hakkai to see Mount Fuji (but the revered mountain was shrouded in cloud), and Nikkō to see the famous shrine and Lake Chūzenji. But going to these places on her own was not much fun. She needed a companion, not necessarily a lover, to accompany her. She could not ask Ogawa again as she was sure he would suspect her motive and decline.

More and more while Sylvia sat in her tiny apartment, travelled about Tokyo in the trains (her bottom was often pinched by lustful fingers; she didn't mind this because it made her feel desired), visited museums, swam in the *mammothu poolu* and sunbathed in the patio, and submitted to the greengrocer, did she think of Toshi. More and more she missed him. What could she do about him? Telephone? Call at the bank? Write to the bank? And what would she write, what would she say? Apology would be awkward, embarrassing.

And then one Friday evening, just after half-past nine, he telephoned.

'I very sorry,' he began.

'I too am very sorry,' she replied. Her heart began to thump.

'I lonely without you. I wan' see you, Siru-san.'

His using the nickname he had given her was touching. 'Come and see me now, at once, Toshi, darling. I long to see you.'

'I come tomorrow aroun' six o'clock. Okay?'

'Where are you now?'

'I in my *apāto*. Tomorrow awri?'

'Yes, of course, but make it six-thirty.'

'Okay, Siru-san.'

Matthew was worried as he suspected that Colin Sibley had taken a fancy to Jun. He had sat Jun next to him at the dinner after the performance of *Candida*, and had paid him much attention, asking him many questions about Japan.

Colin had the urbane manner of someone confident of his ability, his Thespian gifts. Not quite fifty and just under six foot, he was an impressive man with a firm profile, grey eyes, long dark hair speckled with grey and a fine physique. If he had been on the stage in the thirties he would have been a matinée idol. Women adored him, but the adoration was not reciprocated. It was reserved for his profession and for Mark. Mark had his mother's good looks: blond, nearly as tall as Colin, but unlike his mother, svelte. Colin tried not to show any favouritism towards Mark; in fact he would be stricter with him than with the other members of the company, although everyone of course knew that Mark was his lover; at the same time they respected his talent and thought he deserved the plum parts of Marchbanks and Ariel. Colin directed the company and played most of the leading roles. In a way he was in the tradition of the old actor-manager.

Matthew sat next to Mark at the dinner party. The young man plied the older one with questions about his mother, while Matthew tried at the same time to listen to what Colin was saying to Jun. Peter Cox, Matthew's old Cambridge friend and now a competent player of supporting parts, sat between Jun and Mark but did not contribute much to the conversation. Five is not a good number for a dinner party, Matthew reflected.

He overheard Colin mention Kabuki, about which Jun was pretty ignorant, so instead of letting Jun attempt to give answers he supplied them, to the annoyance of both the actor and Jun; Mark was also irritated at his questions about his mother being left in the air.

'Is my mother happy in Tokyo, do you think?'

'No Jun, the seventeenth century, not the sixteenth.'

'Is she lonely?'

'No Jun, the revolving stage was a Japanese invention.'

Matthew was cross with himself for showing his possessiveness and his jealousy. Colin was a glamorous person compared with him.

When Matthew and Jun got back to their flat in Gordon Apartments, Jun showed his displeasure.

'Mattu-san, why you not let me talk to Corin? You jealous?'

Weakly, Matthew replied, 'Yes, I suppose I am. Sorry, dear. I can't help it.'

'You very silly.' Jun said no more that evening.

· 24 ·

At ten minutes past six on the Saturday evening, Sylvia's bell rang. She was dressing after having a shower. 'Damn! I told him not to come before half past. Never mind. The little darling is so anxious to see me.' She put on a peignoir over her underwear and opened the door, not as she expected, to Toshi, but to Mr Five-Four-Six.

'Today not good, *kyō dame*,' she said through the half-open door. But the greengrocer was insistent. He pulled the door open and pushed his way past Sylvia into the sitting-room and proceeded to tear off his clothes. In no time Mr Five-Four-Six's cap was on the dining-table, his T-shirt was being pulled over his head and he was stepping out of his jeans.

She said, '*Kyō dame*. I am busy today. *Watakushi isogashī des.*' She had learnt a few words of Japanese, but she spoke them in a heavy English accent that made them incomprehensible. He took no notice and naked, approached her smiling. Should she scream? No. The best thing was to get it over as soon as possible. She gave in and soon the greengrocer's cries of '*Okā-san, iku, iku, iku*' resounded round the room, whose windows were closed because of the air-cooling machine.

Sylvia tidied the bed and then dashed into the back room and put on a dress. When she came back into the main room, Mr Five-Four-Six had lit a cigarette and was putting on his clothes slowly. Sylvia panicked, as she didn't smoke and Toshi would guess she had had a visitor and question her about him. She desperately wanted her reconciliation to begin on a harmonious note. The greengrocer usually hurled on his clothes but today he was taking his time. 'Please hurry,' she begged. '*Hayaku.*' At last he was dressed and with a puff of smoke was gone. She watched him walk down the passage and turn the corner to the stairs. She looked out of the passage window to see if Toshi was coming. The entrance road was empty. Soon she saw the greengrocer ascending on his motorcycle and just as he swung left into Hongo Avenue, Toshi in white shirt, loosened tie and jacket over his arm turned into the road. Mr Five-Four-Six and Toshi passed each other, but neither gave the other so much as a glance. Sylvia hastened into the flat, got the air freshener from the bathroom and began feverishly to spray the living-room in order to disguise the smell of the cigarette and of sex. The bell rang and with the spray still in her hand she opened the door.

Toshi leapt into Sylvia's arms before taking off his shoes. 'I sorry, prease forgive me,' he sobbed. She patted his back with the air-spray and said, 'There, there! It was my fault. I asked you to go. It was wrong of me.' With his forehead against her shoulder, he mumbled, 'I not go to "Crub New Love". I swear. I love you, Siru-san.'

'Come in. Let's have a drink.'

While he was taking off his shoes, Sylvia moved quickly into the living-room and sprayed the alcove ferociously, trying to obliterate any traces of the greengrocer and his cigarette.

'What are you doing?' asked Toshi.

'Spraying.'

'What for?'

'The air-cooler makes the room so stuffy.' She put her arms round her lover and held him close. How wanton she was! And Toshi had been on his way to her! She wished she had not succumbed.

They sat on the sofa and kissed for a while. How different Toshi was from Mr Five-Four-Six! So much gentler, and unlike the greengrocer, he loved kissing. Was it the brute in the greengrocer that made Sylvia submit to him? Was it the boyish charm in Toshi that made Sylvia fond of him? With Mr Five-Four-Six, there was no question of affection; it was just sex – exciting, irresistible sex. In a mysterious way, the greengrocer had a hold over her, a fascination.

'What you do with the spray?'

'Freshen the air.'

'Often you do this?'

'I find living with the windows shut and the air-cooler on all the time makes the air stale.' How awful it was to lie!

Later, in bed, Toshi cried out *'Iku!'* with as much feeling as Mr Five-Four-Six had done earlier in the day. When Toshi had lighted a cigarette and the two were lying on their backs resting from their exertions, Sylvia asked, 'What does *iku* mean?'

'It mean go.'

'Go?'

'Yes.'

Sylvia laughed. 'Oh, I see, you mean *come*. We say come, you say go. It would be so.' She laughed merrily.

· 25 ·

After lunch on the following day, Toshi, as had been his wont before the temporary rupture in their relationship, became absorbed in television. On this afternoon he was watching middle-aged housewives playing bowls. When Sylvia had washed up the lunch things, she joined him at the TV set. She wondered whether he found the hard-faced matrons attractive. Were they like the women he had entertained at the host club?

At last the bowling was over and Toshi switched off the set. 'I must go clean my room.'

'I'll come and help you.' How she hated vacuum cleaners, dusters, washing machines and irons! She did the minimum of housework in her own flat. Toshi had once remarked that the floor was dirty.

'They will see you.'

'Who?'

'The people near my *apāto*.'

'It doesn't matter, does it? They won't report you to the bank for having a foreign friend, will they? And if they were bank spies and did, would it matter? Couldn't you say, if you were asked, that you were my pupil? That you are having English lessons from me?'

'Maybe they not believe.'

'But it doesn't matter. It can't matter. You must live your own life without worrying about what the neighbours think.'

'We Japanese we always worry about what the neighbours they may think.'

Toshi's 'room', as he called it, was not very far from Sylvia's flat. With the walk to and from the stations at both ends, the changing of trains at Ikebukuro Station and the struggle there through the crowds, the journey took no more than forty-five minutes. At Nerima Station, Toshi went ahead up the steep flight of concrete stairs and stayed in front during their descent of the stairs that led to the exit. Sylvia caught him up at the traffic lights on the main road near the station.

'We are supposed to be together, aren't we?'

'I show the way.'

He crossed the road ahead of her and led her down narrow alley-ways brightly lit by shops and restaurant signs. It was getting dark. Sylvia liked the cosy, friendly atmosphere of this suburban warren. She caught him up again at some traffic lights controlling another main road, but off he went ahead of her to the other side. He turned down a dark, residential lane and waited for her to catch him up. 'Now it's safe, is it?' she said.

He did not reply. Perhaps he hadn't understood her sarcasm. They went down several more unlit lanes side by side, but not holding hands, until they came to a building faced with blue tiles. 'Library,' he said, going ahead into a small, parking space where there were three cars and a number of bicycles parked, and an iron staircase up to the first floor of an apartment building. Just before ascending the stairs, Toshi put a hand on the saddle of one of the bikes. 'My bicycle,' he said. 'So you ride to the station?' 'Sometimes.' He led the way up the stairs. At the top was a long balcony passage off which gave the apartments. Toshi's was the first one. He opened the door and went in. Sylvia stood in the tiny sunken entrance which was strewn with Toshi's shoes. 'Just a moment, please,' he said, and rummaged about for some slippers. He placed a well-worn pair on the step, and Sylvia knowing the drill took off her shoes and put on the slippers. Immediately to her right, in a row, was the usual equipment of a Japanese kitchen: a gas cooker with two burners and a grill, a sink, and a refrigerator with a microwave óven on top of it. The sink was full of dirty plates and cups with chopsticks poking out of the pile. 'Oh, Toshi, what a mess!' Sylvia exclaimed. Toshi slid open a door at the end of the 'kitchen' passage, stepped out of his slippers and went ahead into a tatami room and through it to another whose *fusuma* were open. Before he pulled the *fusuma* to, Sylvia glimpsed a mound of bedding whose covers had been thrown back carelessly, suggesting he had risen in a hurry on the Saturday morning. Had he really given up the 'Club New Love'? He had telephoned her after half-past nine. Probably it was the sort of place that started late in the evening. It was wrong of her to allow that devil suspicion to enter her mind.

In the little sitting-room with its windows of frosted glass were an armchair, a table strewn with books, papers and a jar stuffed with one yen coins, a television set on top of which was a cluster of dolls, a low table for floor sitting, and a glass-fronted cupboard holding some bottles and tumblers. On the floor over the tatami was an imitation Persian rug. Toshi bade her sit in the armchair. She did so, putting her handbag on the floor. She looked round the room. On the walls were two calendars: one featuring a scantily clothed Japanese girl peeping coyly through a motor tyre, the other of a Japanese couple standing on a beach and drinking a soft drink; both wore sunglasses and they were smiling at each other. A looking-glass hung near the sliding door, and a cuckoo clock, which was not working, its chains dangling, on the other wall. Except for the frosted glass windows, Sylvia did not find the apartment itself depressing, but she was disappointed in the furnishings and the decorations. Surely he could have better things on the walls than advertisement calendars and a cuckoo clock? Their tastes were wide apart.

'What you like?' Toshi asked.

'Nothing at the moment. I'm going to help you clean up the place. Let's do the kitchen first.' She rose and went into the passage kitchen rolling up the sleeves of her blouse. Toshi went into the bedroom and began to fold up the sheets. 'No, Toshi, come and help me here. I don't know where things go.' There was a ring of command in her voice, the ring of the victor. Toshi obeyed.

They washed up the dishes together, laughing; it was a happy time. 'And now your bedroom,' Sylvia said. She had put all the dirty clothes she could find into the washing machine in the tiny bathroom. Here there was also a Western-style lavatory, and above it a notice explaining how to use it illustrated with a diagram of two silhouettes, one standing, one sitting. The small, deep bath was covered with a plastic top. 'Do you often bath in that thing?' she asked.

'No. I go to *sentō*.'

'What's that?'

'Public bath.'

'Do you like it better than having a bath here?'

'Not so much trouble.' He smiled his winsome smile. 'I take a shower usually.'

'Have you a vacuum cleaner?'

'Yes.'

'Then get it.' She didn't realize that her managerial behaviour might damage their repaired relationship. Toshi produced the cleaner, plugged it in and started to work it. 'Give it me,' ordered Sylvia, and she took over the floor-sweeping task, while Toshi tidied his bedding; he folded the sheets and rolled up the *futon*. When the cleaning was done and the sweeper put away, the washing machine signalled that its job was completed. Sylvia and Toshi hung up the clothes in the bathroom. 'What about supper? Have you anything to eat?'

'I have some deep-freeze things.'

'Let's have a look.'

Toshi took out of the top part of the refrigerator two packets, one of which he called 'frozen rice', and the other 'sort of *ebi* in sauce.' Sylvia examined them. The 'sort of *ebi*' seemed by the picture on the packet to be a prawn dish with tomato and macaroni. 'I put them in microwave,' Toshi said.

'Fine. Where do you eat?'

'Here.'

'Standing up by the sink?'

'Yes.'

'Let's eat in the living-room.'

Sylvia sat in the armchair and Toshi gave her a bowl containing a mixture of the two packets. With an ease she envied, he, holding his bowl, went down on his knees by the low table and sat on his heels.

'What am I supposed to eat this with?'

'Oh, sorry.' He sprang up still holding his bowl. 'You like spoon or chopsticks?'

'Spoon, please.'

Toshi went to the kitchen and returned with the appropriate utensils and knelt again.

'Our sitting at different levels is unsatisfactory,' said Sylvia. 'Let me join you on the floor.' Clumsily she moved from the chair on to a floor cushion which Toshi placed for her. 'I must have something to lean against. Ah, this is all right.' She leant against the seat of the armchair and stretched out her legs under the table. Toshi sat in the polite fashion with his legs folded under him.

'Have you anything to drink?'

'I have coffee.'

'No, not coffee. Haven't you a proper drink?'

'I have whisky.'

'Let's have some of that.'

Toshi rose effortlessly in one movement and got out of the cupboard a bottle, half empty, of Johnny Walker Black Label, and fetched from the kitchen two glasses with lumps of ice in them and one filled with water. He covered the ice in Sylvia's glass with whisky, but only put a drop over his cubes and added a lot of water. 'That's not much of a drink,' remarked Sylvia.

'I don't want to drink.'

'I always need a drink in the evening. You are lucky not to want one. Well, cheers.' She gulped; he sipped.

'You like green tea?'

'No, thanks, but I'd like another whisky.'

Toshi poured out another generous measure into Sylvia's glass and after lighting a cigarette got up and made himself a pot of green tea. Before he sat down, he took out of the cupboard a photograph album. 'You like to see?'

'Yes, very much. I love photographs.' She turned the pages of the album asking every now and then who this was, who that was. There were school groups: 'Is that you? How adorable you were as a child!' She turned a page and found him at the top of a mountain with a solemn group of young men and women. 'Who is the girl you are standing next to?'

'One of my classmates at my university.'

'Did you love her?'

'Maybe, a little.'

Then came some photographs taken in what looked like a night club. 'This is the host place, is it?'

'Yes.'

'The women look very ordinary and badly dressed. Did you dance with her, that one, the one you're sitting next to?'

'Yes. She doctor's wife.' Toshi began to blush.

'Did you go to bed with her?'

'Of course not.' His deepening blush made Sylvia wonder.

'Who's that young man next to her on the other side?'

'That my friend.'

'He's very good looking. Is he married now?'

'He still work at crub. Not married. He gay.'

'Gay?'

'Many host they gay.'

'How extraordinary! You're not gay, though.'

'No, of course.'

'I suppose "Club New Love" is not a bad name for such a place,' said Sylvia, sarcastically, holding her glass up for a refill, which Toshi gave her. She turned the page of the album and came to more group photographs of men and women by the seaside; all of them looked so serious. Toshi was one of them. 'Where was this taken?'

'Our bank have holiday home near Ito.'

'You mean all the staff of your bank go to the holiday home together?'

'Not all, many.'

'How frightful!'

'Why?'

'To be with the people you work with all day, every day.'

'We have good time. We swim, or if it is in the mountain we go climbing or we ski. At night we drink and we play mah-jong.'

'You like these group trips?'

'Yes, of course.'

Sylvia shut the album. Except for those of the 'Club New Love', the photographs had only revealed the simplicity of her lover's life. The host club seemed to have been the most amusing experience he had had, but she didn't like the idea of his continuing his visits there.

'Toshi,' she said quietly, 'will you promise not to go to the "Club New Love" any more?'

'I not go. I promise. I told you. I swear.'

She leant round the table awkwardly and planted a kiss on Toshi's cheek.

'You like one more whisky?'

'Please. I wish you would have one too.'

Again he rose in one swift movement, and replenished her glass. 'Thanks. So you like the public bath better than your own tub?'

'Tub?'

'Bath.'

'Yes. It is friendly place. We Japanese we like to take bath with other people.'

'I don't. I hate undressing in front of others. In the pool I go to, the women try to look at my body.'

Toshi laughed. 'They wan' know what foreigner look like.'

Sylvia began to feel a little tipsy. 'Toshi,' she said.

'Yes?' He looked at her with his serious dark eyes; he obviously expected an awkward question. How quick he was to sense her mood!

'Would you come and live with me?'

'Very difficult.' She knew this meant 'No' and she was hurt. He must have noticed her disappointment for he added: 'I am sorry, Siru-san, it impossible. My correagues they find out. My company maybe they dismiss me if they know I live with a foreigner.'

'What the hell has your private life got to do with them?' His refusal and the whisky roused her.

'You no understand Japanese company; they control very much.'

'I think it's frightful. They don't own you. They may do so from nine till five, but after five they don't.' She was red in the face. 'It's monstrous.'

'That is Japanese way.'

Sylvia thought for a moment and then said, 'At least you could come and see me twice a week, couldn't you?'

'I try.'

'Darling!' Sylvia put her hand across the table, palm upwards, and Toshi at once put his hand on top of hers. 'I love you.'

'I love you, Siru-san.'

'Truly?'

'Yes, truly.'

But did he? Sylvia rose. 'You go and have your bath, and I – ' she swallowed 'shall go home.'

'I come with you to the station. It near the *sentō*.'

He led the way, keeping ahead of her in the narrow illuminated lanes. He bought her a ticket and waited until she had reached the top of the steps. She turned to see if he was still there. He was. They exchanged waves.

Part Three

· 1 ·

'I know *you* want to see them again,' said Matthew to Jun.
'Why?'

They were at breakfast in their flat in Gordon Apartments.
'Because you like Colin.'

'Not special man for me, Mattu-san.' Attempting to tease, he added, 'I think you like Mark.'

Matthew, serious and not taking up Jun's light mood, protested, 'No, I don't. You know I'm not turned on by Western people.'

'That why you not want to go to the dinner?'

'No, of course not.' In truth Matthew did not want to attend Colin's dinner party, which was to be held on the following Sunday evening, because he felt that Jun was or might become attracted to the personable actor with the charming manner. He was jealous. Colin had glamour; he had his name in lights outside a Shaftesbury Avenue theatre. He was famous, while poor bald, fat Matthew was just a teacher at a minor university in Tokyo.

Matthew knew that Jun had been fascinated by him because he was the first foreigner he had known, but he feared that when in the presence of the polished star, Jun might see him as he really was, ordinary and undistinguished. In Japan a foreigner, mediocre in his field, could pass himself off as a brilliant scholar. About foreigners the insular Japanese had little judgement; this was equally true of foreign literature. As far as the academic world was concerned, Japan was the kingdom of the blind.

135

• 2 •

Now reconciled to Toshi, Sylvia was happy even in the hot, empty summer days. She continued to go to the pool and to see Mr Ogawa. Neither of them mentioned the 'love hotels', and their acquaintance remained static. They did no more than exchange platitudes. There were certain people with whom one forever remained on the same level, neither falling out with them nor becoming more intimate; Ogawa belonged to this category.

In the middle of August came the O-Bon Festival, a sort of All Souls' Day when the spirits of dead ancestors were propitiated. Toshi had a few days off. His parents wanted him to go home to Hamamatsu for the holiday, which in spite of its name was a jolly time when there was folk-dancing in temple courtyards; at home flowers and offerings of food were placed in front of the Buddhist altars in which were kept little wooden stupas bearing the death names of departed ancestors. Toshi wasn't in the least religious and did not wish to celebrate the festival at home with his parents, who, he knew, would talk to him about marriage, a state he did not wish yet to achieve.

Therefore he did not need much persuading to agree to accompany Sylvia on a trip. After a long discussion (Sylvia had discovered that the Japanese enjoyed considering plans and going into minute details), they decided to go to Shimoda at the tip of the Izu Peninsula, the port where Townsend Harris, the first American consul to Japan, lived from 1856–7. Outside the town facing a little bay was the Grand Hotel and Sylvia, after lengthy negotiations in a travel bureau with the aid of instructions written down by Toshi in Japanese and her dictionary, succeeded in booking seats in a train and a room at the Grand for three nights. The cost of this little excursion was alarming, but paying for it by credit card mitigated the shock.

Matthew's jealousy was not allayed at Colin's dinner party, which consisted of six persons including the host and Mark, Matthew and Jun. The other two were Peter Cox, Matthew's old Cambridge friend, and Patricia Howard. Peter, who was Matthew's age, was slender and had a thick, grey thatch. He was right for Caliban, but a bit too thin for Mr Burgess; and though Patricia was too old for Miranda, she did well enough, and was perfect for Candida.

As before, Colin sat Jun on his right and Matthew on his left. The two visitors were unable to contribute much to the conversation as it concerned the stage and the London theatre. Matthew managed to squeeze in a remark about there having been competent Japanese productions of *Amadeus* and *The Dresser* in Tokyo, but this information didn't seem to interest the others, who were too taken up with what they had to say. The four members of the cast wanted to express their views and when they had done so, an argument would ensue in which they would become histrionic and hoot with laughter. Matthew felt very out of it, and so, he presumed, did Jun, who ate his roast beef which he liked quickly and with relish, and smiled and nodded, suggesting he understood what was being said. Matthew knew he didn't. How could he when Matthew himself was at sea most of the time? He thought it rude of the players to talk shop so much, but then stage people were invariably egoistic and always wanted to perform. It was Patricia who turned to Jun and sweetly said, 'Now Jun, please tell us about the Japanese theatre – Kabuki, Noh and all that.'

'Jun doesn't know much about the theatre in Japan, do you, Jun?' said Matthew, unkindly.

Colin said, 'He must know something about it.'

'He goes once a year to Kabuki and sleeps through it all,' replied Matthew.

'It can be very boring,' contributed Jun in a low voice.

'How?' asked Colin, to whom any information about any kind of theatre was interesting.

'It can be very static,' put in Matthew.

'Aren't the women's parts played by men?' asked Mark.

'Yes,' said Jun.

'Are they convincing?' asked Colin.

'Very,' said Matthew. 'They are so stylized, though, that they don't seem to belong to either sex.'

Colin frowned at Matthew and turned to Jun. 'Do you agree with that?'

'We know they are men, but we see them as women as they act women's parts.'

Everyone laughed, rather to the puzzlement of Jun.

'But some time,' went on Jun, 'when old actor he play the part of young girl, he look like old man.'

More laughter.

'And his voice?' asked Colin.

'He speaks in a special high-pitched tone,' explained Matthew, 'which is really neither female nor male.'

'Are there any beautiful young men who play women's parts?' asked Mark.

'We have Tamasaburo. The young girls they love him.'

'He fills any theatre he's playing at,' Matthew informed the table.

'You say the *girls* love him?' Colin asked, surprised. 'Why?'

'Because, because . . . how shall I say?' said Jun, unhelpfully.

'I've often asked my girl students this question,' stated Matthew, authoritatively, 'and the answer has always been "because he is so beautiful".'

'And is he?' inquired Mark.

'Yes,' answered Matthew, although the question was addressed to Jun. 'Especially in a dance; in a traditional Japanese dance he is superb, far better than any woman could be.'

'I have a feeling you're prejudiced,' remarked Patricia in her attractive contralto.

'Jun, tell them about Takarazuka,' commanded Matthew.

'Sounds like a dish,' put in Mark, facetiously.

'Takarazuka is the girls' opera,' explained Jun. 'All actors are girls and, er – '

'And,' interrupted Matthew, 'the audiences consist mainly of girls who have great crushes on the players, especially those who play male parts.'

'Heavens!' What a mix-up!' exclaimed Peter Cox. 'Japan sounds odder than I imagined. Men as women, girls as men. Both adored by girls. What do the young men like? The men dressed as women, or the girls dressed as boys?'

'They like the girls dressed as girls, I hope,' said Patricia. 'Am I right?' She turned to Jun.

'It depend,' said Jun, and everyone laughed.

Mark and Patricia rose to collect the empty plates.

'There's a female impersonator,' said Matthew, 'not a Kabuki actor, who plays Western parts. He-she was a very good Marguerite in *Richard III* and not at all bad as Judith Bliss, but rather an awful Edith Piaf.'

Mark and Patricia left the room with the plates.

'He good singer of chansons,' said Jun. 'His name Miwa. He sing once a month in a café called Paris.'

'Which is now closed,' capped Matthew. 'He is often on television being interviewed, on panels.'

Colin, ignoring Matthew, addressed Jun. 'What sort of audience does this chanson singer get?'

'Chanson lovers,' replied Jun.

'Are they men or women, or something in between?' asked Peter, but his question wasn't answered as Mark and Patricia returned with plates and an orange soufflé. Mark burst out with, 'Colin, we've an idea! So as not to confuse the Japanese, Patricia will play Prospero and you Miranda.'

'I've always wanted to play Miranda. Now's my chance!'

They all laughed.

When the meal was over they went up to the sitting-room on the first floor. Matthew chatted to his friend Peter Cox; Colin had much to say to Patricia; Mark spoke with Jun. After a while, Mark, interrupting the other conversations, announced excitedly, 'Mummy's got a Japanese lover. His name is Toshi. Isn't it marvellous!'

Matthew frowned at Jun. Colin and Patricia, who had never met Sylvia, expressed polite surprise and went on with what they were saying to each other. Matthew said to Peter, 'A cat has been let out of the bag.'

'Will it matter?'

'Well, I should have thought that the mother would have told her son if she had wanted him to know.'

On the doorstep, Colin said to Matthew courteously but not warmly, 'Awfully good of you to come,' and to Jun, whose hand he held for a few moments and whose shoulder he patted, 'Much look forward to seeing you in Tokyo.'

Jun dug into a pocket and produced a visiting card. 'My card,' he said.

Colin looked at it. 'But it's in Japanese.'

'Not other side.'

Colin turned over the card. 'I see. Jun Sakamoto.' He waggled the card. 'Good.'

While Matthew and Jun were walking away from the house, Matthew said, 'You shouldn't have told Mark about Toshi.'

'Why not?'

'I don't suppose Sylvia wanted Mark to know about him.'

'I'm sorry. It matter?'

'It's too late now. I'll have to warn Sylvia that Mark knows. She may not be happy about it. Oh dear!'

· 4 ·

On the Friday afternoon Sylvia, because of the powerful, humid heat and her heavy bag, took a taxi to Tokyo Station instead of going by subway as she had intended. At the station she found her way to the platform from which her train departed. It was a limited express called *Izuno Odoriko* ('The Izu Dancer'), after the title of one of the most popular stories by Kawabata Yasunari, who won the Nobel Prize. The story, which Sylvia had read, takes place on the Izu Peninsula, whither she and Toshi were bound, and concerns the theme of unrequited love, popular in Japan. This choice of name for the express revealed the uneasy relationship between Japanese sentimentality and realism. A kind woman passenger helped Sylvia find her seat. Sylvia chose the aisle one, leaving the window seat for Toshi.

It was five minutes before departure time and Toshi hadn't appeared. Had he been delayed by his possessive and pleasure-stingy bank, or by one of the patronesses of the 'Club New Love'?

140

No, that could not be. He had promised not to go to the club ever again. Anxiously, she looked at a platform clock visible from her seat. She wondered what she would do if he didn't turn up.

At two minutes before the train was due to leave, Toshi arrived in his light-weight blue suit, panting and carrying a small grip; there were little beads of sweat on his nose. '*Gomen nasai*,' he said to Sylvia as he took his seat. She might have been a stranger. Sylvia smiled. Toshi looked straight ahead and frowned. The train gently moved forward. It wasn't until they were well beyond Tokyo Station and travelling at speed that Toshi nudged Sylvia, returned her smile, and then, spreading out his newspaper so that it covered Sylvia's right knee, surreptitiously squeezed her hand. She reciprocated.

'I very afraid some bank people they see me,' explained Toshi.

'You'd think we lived in a village.'

Out of his bag Toshi brought a plastic container of sandwiches which he gave to Sylvia, and a box of rice balls wrapped in seaweed, and started to eat hungrily. A girl in a cap and apron pushed down the aisle a trolley bearing drinks and titbits. Toshi, without asking Sylvia, bought two cans of beer, a bag of peanuts and another of rice biscuits.

Sylvia drank the beer and ate the sandwiches to please Toshi. She disliked the bitter taste of beer and the '*hamu sandoitchi*' were made of bread so soft that it stuck to the roof of her mouth.

Darkness had fallen by the time they had started to descend the picturesque peninsula to Shimoda and they only got shadowy views of inlets and pines. The Grand Hotel, a modern barracks of a place, was comfortable enough. Their twin-bedded room looked on to a bay whose black-wooded arms enclosed a silver space.

'How wonderful to have a view!' exclaimed Sylvia. 'Toshi, come and look.'

Toshi was rummaging in the fridge. 'What you like?' he asked, bringing out a bottle of Coca Cola.

'Not that. Is there anything else?'

'Whisky.'

'I'll have some, please.'

'These drinks expensive.'

'Never mind.'

They sat opposite each other in small armchairs at a table in the window. Sylvia swigged her whisky and then put her glass down. 'Toshi, come here.'

'Jus' a minute.' He brought a camera out of his bag and took her photograph.

'Let me take one of you, Toshi.'

He handed her the camera and she took his picture.

'Now,' he said, taking the camera. He took another photograph of Sylvia, and then placing the camera on the dressing-table, focused it and then hurriedly sat on the arm of her chair. The camera clicked. They laughed.

Sylvia pulled Toshi to her and they began a long passionate embrace punctuated by affectionate mutterings – 'I love you,' 'Do you really, Toshi?' 'Yes, Siru-san.' 'Promise?' 'Promise.' Soon they were on her bed, and half-undressed with only their sexual parts exposed, they made love in a hurried, excited way. It was similar to one of Sylvia's flings with the greengrocer, and unfaithfully she thought of him.

Afterwards, they had a shower, not together because after sex Toshi became prim. He covered his genitals with a hand when he stepped out of the shower and cast a glance of disapproval at Sylvia sitting naked on the dressing-table stool and drying her feet.

The dining-room was shut so they walked up the dark hill hand in hand until they reached the town, where they found a noodle shop and greedily ate bowls of the worm-like pasta served in a soup.

'This *soba* good,' Toshi managed to say between slurps. He put his face near the bowl and sucked in the tubes of wheat. For Toshi, eating, especially something to his taste, was a serious business, a time for an exchange of grunts rather than light conversation.

'Isn't it,' agreed Sylvia, who tried to eat delicately with chopsticks but the pasta kept slipping back into the bowl. The weekend passed off well, except for one small incident which occurred when they were boating in the bay. Sylvia, in a black one-piece swimsuit sat in the stern, while Toshi in brief slips wielded the oars amateurishly.

Sylvia said, 'You know the pool I go to in Ikebukuro?'

'Yes,' replied Toshi, straining at the oars.

'Well, there's a Mr Ogawa I meet there. A sad man, he seems, but nice. As a sort of joke – I wanted to shock him – I asked him to take me to a "love hotel" and – '

'You what?' Toshi caught a crab, slipped off his seat and fell backwards, legs in the air.

Sylvia roared with laughter. Toshi did not look pleased when he recovered his perch and the oars.

'Oh darling! I am sorry. You haven't hurt yourself, have you?'

Toshi sulked. He returned the boat to the beach of grey volcanic sand, crowded with trippers and screaming children, and without a word waded into the water and swam away from the shore. Sylvia, a stronger swimmer, soon caught him up and when level with him she stretched out her arm and pushed his head under the water. When he emerged she let him do the same to her, and then she dived under him and ducked him again. He retaliated and they frolicked in the water, ducking and splashing each other, laughing. This gambolling dispersed Toshi's sullenness and after taking photographs of one another on the beach they returned to the hotel, a happy pair, but a sore one as they both had been burnt by the sun. In the bedroom they applied cold cream to each other's bodies. That night their skin was too painful for lovemaking. The following evening after dinner, dressed in *yukata* stamped with the name of the hotel all over them, and wearing *geta*, they went up the hill to the temple and in their cotton kimonos and wooden clogs they danced with the *O-bon* dancers.

· 5 ·

During the last two weeks of August and the first week of September, the affair went smoothly. No more mention was made of Mr Ogawa (Toshi accepted the fact that he was no more than a swimming pool acquaintance with whom Sylvia just passed the time of day), and Sylvia kept secret the greengrocer's occasional lust visit. Around 7 p.m. Toshi telephoned her. 'The seven o'clock love call,' he named it. Sylvia was content, happy for the first time since her husband dumped her. Toshi seemed to need her. But as well as possessiveness love breeds doubt, and in order to test him she would ring Toshi late on a Friday evening to see if he were home even if she had spoken to him earlier. She would invent some excuse like asking what he would fancy for the weekend meals. He had always been in. She felt he was completely hers.

'Are you mine?' she asked him one Sunday morning in bed.

'You belong to me,' he said.

She did not want the days to pass, for classes to begin, for Matthew and Jun to return. When September came, she did not tear off the August page of her calendar.

· 6 ·

The heat of the summer had not abated. At the end of the first week of September came the first day of term. People were still in summer clothes. Sylvia was too hot in her short-sleeved dress. She did not have a class but thought she would look in at the university on her way to the pool. She gave three taps on Matthew's door and was pleased to hear his pedagogical 'Yes?' in spite of its being a cry mingled with disinterest and irritation.

'I hope I'm not disturbing you, Matthew,' she said when he opened the door. 'I thought I'd look in to see how you were, to hear about your trip.'

'Good to see you, Sylvia,' said Matthew, coolly. 'Do sit down.' Sylvia sat in the chair nearest to Matthew, the one used by students for their tutorials.

'How did you find Mark?'

'He seemed fine. We saw him in *Candida* and in *The Tempest* and met him twice, at an after-show dinner and a Sunday lunch. The host, of course, was Colin Sibley.'

'What's he like?'

'Colin? An impressive actor, a charming man.'

'And how was Mark? I had a brief line from him. He's never written a proper letter in his life.'

'The young don't write letters. I thought he was charming too. He was good as Marchbanks and very good as Ariel. They're coming here.'

'I know. I wish they weren't. I don't want Mark to know about Toshi. By the way, it's on again between Toshi and me, and going better than before.'

'It takes a break to seal an affair.' Matthew laughed at his sententiousness. He wondered if he should forewarn her that Mark knew about Toshi.

'It was Toshi who made the first step towards our . . . our, er – '

'Reconciliation?'

The phone rang.

'Excuse me,' said Matthew, picking up the phone. 'Hellow? . . . Oh *hello*, Gordon. So you're back . . . oh you didn't go away . . . it's our first day . . . finding our feet, getting our fingers ready for the chalk – '. He laughed. 'Yes, we had a wonderful time . . . Paris, London . . . Yes, of course. . . . No, my dear, he wasn't a Charles Dickens character; he wrote a book called *Self Help*, which was very popular in Japan in the nineteenth century. The Japanese liked it as it suited their frugal nature. . . . You could look it up, you know, under Smiles in an encyclopaedia. . . . Not at all, pleased to be of help.' Matthew put down the phone and laughed. 'Oh dear,' he said.

'Who was that?' asked Sylvia.

'An ex-Hong Kong businessman who's taken up teaching here in his retirement. He's always being asked questions by his Japanese colleagues. His ignorance leads him into awful entanglements. He hasn't enough sense to say he doesn't know. He thought that *Antic Hay* meant "old grass", "Samson Agonistes" Samson in agony – one could almost forgive him for that – and that *Mansfield Park* was a writer of African adventures.'

'One might go on with this,' laughed Sylvia, 'and make it a sort of game: *Clayhanger*, a suspense thriller; *Daniel Deronda*, a Jewish dance, and – '

'And that Gertrude Stein wrote *A Sentimental Journey*. That was actually true.' Matthew dissolved into laughter again. 'It's unkind to laugh. But the muddles he's got himself into!' He mopped his eyes with a handkerchief. 'Oh dear!'

'Did you enjoy your visit to England?' Sylvia asked while Matthew was tearful from laughter.

'Yes. Yes, very much on the whole.'

'I do wish Mark wasn't coming here,' Sylvia repeated.

'He needn't meet Toshi, need he? There's no reason why he should.' Matthew again wondered whether he should tell her what Mark knew. 'Toshi is fine, you say?'

'Yes, we're like newlyweds. May it last!' She shut her eyes and put a hand on the edge of Matthew's desk. 'No more visits to the "Club New Love"; none as far as I know. I've rung him late on several Friday evenings and he's been in.'

'Why Friday?'

'It was his night there. He did what he called *arbeit* there.'

'I see.' Matthew picked up a biro and waggled it between his thumb and forefinger. He wasn't cynical enough to suggest that Toshi might have changed his night. He decided not to tell her that Mark knew about Toshi.

'Am I keeping you from something?' asked Sylvia.

'No, no.'

'How's Jun?'

'He's got to have an *o-miai*.'

'What's that? It sounds like an operation.'

'Well it is, sort of. It's an engagement meeting.'

'An engagement to be married?'

'Yes.'

'I thought he was er – '

'He is, but that makes no difference. He's had two before. This will be his third *o-miai*. It was arranged by his parents, who naturally want him to marry. All Japanese parents want their sons to get married, above all an only son.'

'I suppose English ones do too. I'd like Mark to marry. I can't imagine my arranging an engagement meeting for him, though. He'd just refuse. Can't Jun refuse?'

'No, but he can turn her down for some specious reason.'

'What will you do if he accepts her?'

'There's no danger of that. He has too much *on* to me.'

'Too much *on*?'

'It means obligation. But he has *giri* to his parents – a sense of duty. You should read *The Chrysanthemum and the Sword* by Ruth Benedict, a key book on Japan. I am afraid that his *giri* to his parents might outweigh his *on* to me.'

'There is a danger then.'

'Slight, slight, very slight.'

146

'What about Toshi? Do you think he is troubled by these things? Why did he ring me up and say he wanted to see me?'

'In his case, it's a matter of *amaeru*.'

'What's that, for heaven's sake.'

'*"Amaeru*,' Matthew began to expound in his lecturing voice,' 'means to be sweet; *amai* means sweet. A Japanese is *amai* on someone, usually someone older.'

'You mean like in English? He's sweet on her.'

'No. *Amai* doesn't mean sweet in that sense.'

'It wouldn't,' said Sylvia, a touch of irritation in her tone.

'It means dependence. Some Japanese need someone to be *amai* to, to be dependent on. There's a book about this by Professor Doi, a psychologist at Tokyo University.'

'In English?'

'Yes, it's been translated.'

'I must get it, and the other one too. One needs a guide-book to a Japanese relationship. So you think Toshi is dependent on me, and Jun has an obligation to you, and a duty to his parents. Doesn't Jun also have a dependence on you?'

'Oh yes. He's *amai* on me all right.'

'It's all very complicated. Or is it?' Sylvia rose. 'I must go to the pool, otherwise it'll fill up with housewives doing synchronized swimming; also, I may see Mr Ogawa there.'

'Mr Ogawa?'

'He's a swimming friend. Nothing more. I once thought . . .' She allowed her voice to trail away. 'By the way, no more rumours.'

'It's too early yet to know.'

'Suzuki didn't contact me throughout the summer, and he must have had lots of questions about Wilde's plays.'

'Not surprising he didn't contact you. He's lost face.'

'He hasn't much of a face to lose.' Sylvia picked up her bag of swimming things and went to the door. '"Bye, bye" as they *will* say here.'

· 7 ·

Although Matthew had told Sylvia that there was no danger of Jun's *o-miai* becoming positive, he wasn't certain that it wouldn't. Jun had sprung the news upon him as soon as he had come back from seeing his parents in Yokohama after they had returned from their holiday. Jun was now twenty-nine, the age at which most Japanese men marry. If a Japanese male hasn't found a wife before he is thirty, he will probably have to make do with a partner who is unattractive, divorced, or socially inferior in the eyes of his family. Of course this applies to arranged marriages, not to love matches, which were on the increase. Jun was not attracted to women at all. But then there was his *giri* to his parents, especially to his mother, and it was stronger than his attachment to Matthew. It had to be. Loyalty and obedience to his parents could not be overridden. It was too deeply ingrained in his culture. Matthew had not realized the true significance of Jun's statement when he once told him that he loved him more than his parents. For a Japanese to say such a thing, even in the heady moments of falling in love, meant much more than a Western person could comprehend. Jun still loved Matthew, but the pressure from his parents and his inherent feelings of duty were becoming implacable forces. Jun didn't tell Matthew this. He couldn't bring himself to. But this time, his third *o-miai*, he felt he must.

'Even if I marry,' Jun said to Matthew, 'I shall still go on seeing you. I shall spend one night a week with you.'

'It won't be the same. We've lived together for six years. We've become a partnership.' Matthew swallowed the lump in his throat.

'It's not until October, the *o-miai*.'

'That's next month, Jun.'

· 8 ·

Sylvia passed the hoardings by the railway lines, advertising 'Duet', 'Casablanca' and 'La La', and soon afterwards mounted the steep steps of the bridge. At the top, she paused to catch her breath. She took off her straw hat and dabbed her brow and watched a green train snake its way into Ikebukuro Station; on the horizon were the tower buildings of Shinjuku. She put on her hat and walked on across the bridge until she came to another steep staircase, which she descended. She continued along the alley-way of makeshift houses and turned the corner and came upon the entrance steps to the pool building. As she was going in, Mr Ogawa came out.

'You've had your swim, then?'

'Sorry?'

'You been swimming?'

'Yes, I finish.'

'I start. Many people?'

'Not so many.'

'Good.'

To her surprise, he said, 'Mrs Field, you like I take you "love hotel" in Yokohama?'

'Yokohama?'

'Here no good. Many people they know me.'

'No thanks. I wrote my article. I'm going to swim. Goodbye.' She went into the building. If, she told herself, he had made this offer before the reconciliation she might have accepted.

While swimming her steady crawl up and down the pool, she thought of her affair with Toshi and Matthew's affair with Jun. Both were anomalous. Were they evil? Some would say they were. She arrived at the end of the pool, pushed her goggles up on to her forehead, stood with her back to the side and looked up towards the other end. She and Matthew were both old enough to be their lover's parent. Was their influence bad? If Jun were able to get married, then Matthew had not done him much harm; and she had not been the first middle-aged woman Toshi had laid; and it was he who had stood over her bed on that Sunday morning in his undervest, his prick a tent-pole. Yet there was an innocence about him that made her feel guilty, a guilt caused by the difference in their ages. She wondered if Matthew ever felt guilty; after all, his liaison with Jun was less socially acceptable, but only a little less. Potiphar's wife was not a heroine, although her tempting Joseph had inspired painters. No, it was ridiculous of her to have qualms. Toshi obviously enjoyed her company, and during their estrangement he must have missed her, otherwise he would not have telephoned and asked to visit her again. What about the matrons at the 'Club New Love'? Sylvia decided that she must try and make herself regard the affair as an amusing pastime, and not get emotionally involved. That would be difficult; emotions ruled the head. A male swimmer appeared beside her. His response to her smile was puzzlement. He dived and swam off to the other end. She pulled her goggles over her eyes, waited a few moments and followed in his wake.

· 9 ·

The heat of the Tokyo summer had subsided by the end of September and October was pleasant. Sylvia and Matthew got back into the swing of their teaching schedules. Sylvia was enjoying her work. She found the students easier to get on with than her colleagues. They were polite, but they never expressed any interest in what she was doing. When she asked a professor what he thought of one of her graduate students, she received an evasive reply. 'Why can't they ever commit themselves to an opinion?' she complained to Matthew.

'Orientals don't like to express an opinion,' he replied, 'in case it contradicts yours. They hate to be contrary. They loathe a confrontation; they don't like to disagree to one's face. They believe in *wa*, harmony.'

'How can one get anywhere in a yes-man's land, Matthew?'

'Well, you can see for yourself how brilliantly the Japanese have got on. The system works.'

Sylvia sighed.

One morning at the university Suzuki tapped on her door.

'Mrs Field,' he said, drawing in his breath through his teeth and making a hiss, 'may I ask you a question?'

Sylvia was tempted to be sarcastic and remark that he had done very well without consulting her for months and to suggest he took his question elsewhere, but of course she didn't. She couldn't though, resist putting a tinge of sarcasm into her greeting: 'How good to see you, Professor Suzuki! I thought you had got a sabbatical or something. Do sit down.'

The professor gave no direct answer, nor did he obey her invitation. Standing a few yards from where she was sitting, he put his bulging black briefcase on the table and said, 'Mrs Field, I see in the newspaper that the famous British actor, Colin Sibley, is coming to Tokyo with his company, and that your son is in the – how shall I say – in the, er – '

Sylvia supplied the word. 'The cast? Yes he is. He's playing the parts of Ariel and Marchbanks. Did the paper mention my son?'

'No. Professor Bennet told me.'

'I've never seen Mark on the stage. Matthew, Professor Bennet, saw him in both parts in London and said he was good.'

'Mrs Field, I want to ask you a favour.'

'I'll be glad to help if I can. Is it a question about Wilde?'

'No, not exactly.' Suzuki looked down. 'I want to meet Mr Sibley. Please could you introduce me?'

'But I don't know him.'

'Your son he know him. You will see your son.'

'Indeed I hope so. But the company will only be in Tokyo for ten days and the actors will be very busy.'

'There will be a party?'

'Probably. I haven't heard about one.'

'If there is a party, can you get me an invitation?'

'I'll see. I can't promise.'

'Thank you very much, Mrs Field.' Suzuki gave a formal bow and left.

Sylvia immediately rose from her chair at the head of her table and called on Matthew in the next room. Her special three knocks indicated her anger. Matthew let her in. 'What's the matter, Sylvia? Why the imperious knocks?'

'I've a bone to pick with you, Matthew.'

'Oh?' He returned to his desk chair.

'Why did you tell Suzuki that Mark was in Colin Sibley's company?'

'I saw no harm in it. It was at one of the Thursday meetings. The company's visit was mentioned and I said I'd met Colin Sibley and that your son was in the cast.'

'Was that necessary?'

'Necessary? What do you mean? I was simply stating a fact.'

'Suzuki has just asked me to introduce him to Colin Sibley. I told him that I had never met him and that the actors would be very busy. He suggested that I get him an invitation to a party to meet the company, should there be one. I said I'd see but could not make any promises.'

'He would take that to mean you won't get him an invitation.'

'Well, that's fine.'

'It was too abrupt a refusal.'

'It wasn't a refusal exactly. I said I'd try but couldn't make any promises.'

'He'll take that as a refusal and feel rebuffed. What you should have said was "*Dekiru dake itashimasu*", which means literally "I shall do my best", but can mean "I shall do nothing". It's a vague expression, but it is not a direct refusal to help. If you'd said something like that, he would have thanked you gratefully, and all would be well. In Japan you never refuse to help. You agree to enthusiastically and take no steps at all.'

'I'll never understand this country.'

'A lot of foreigners say that. If you think about it, our conventions of politeness are not so very different.'

'But they are different. If one can't do something, one says one can't and that's that. We like to be straightforward. They prefer indirectness and prevarication. Why must we always adopt their methods of behaviour? They're learning or teaching English. They should try and understand our ways.'

'When in Rome, my dear . . .'

'Oh, rubbish!' Sylvia flung out of the room.

· 10 ·

Mark telephoned his mother as soon as he and the company had settled into their hotel, one of the Shinjuku towers, and one subway stop from the theatre. Although the entire cast knew about Colin's relationship with Mark, Colin did not like flaunting it, and when on tour he insisted on Mark's sharing a bedroom not with him but with one of the young actors. This arrangement had caused words between Mark and Colin. 'Everyone knows I live with you in London,' he told Colin.

'In London it's different,' the actor replied. "I don't want the Tokyo press to know. I understand that the Japanese newspapers and magazines love gossip and can be vicious.'

Mark, who was deeply fond of Colin, resented being treated as an ordinary member of the cast; his possessiveness made him jealous of anyone whom Colin seemed to like; he fretted when he was excluded from discussions about a play with Patricia or Peter Cox. At rehearsals Colin was at times so caustic that he brought Mark near to tears. 'You didn't have to go on at me like that,' Mark would complain to Colin afterwards. 'When I'm directing you, I direct you the actor, not you my lover,' was Colin's stern reply.

Those who did not know Mark well had no idea that his skin was not thick and he was not, as he appeared, hard and cynical, but on the contrary soft and sensitive. He suffered agonies of anguish when criticized; his histrionic ability helped him to disguise his true feelings. Sylvia was among those who did not know Mark well.

· 11 ·

Colin's company arrived in Tokyo on a Friday in early November. *The Tempest* was due to open at the Globe Theatre in Shin Okubo in Shinjuku-ku on the following Monday evening. Colin allowed his players to rest and get over their jet lag on the Saturday and Sunday. On the Sunday afternoon at four o'clock Sylvia met her son at the Red Gate. She had got rid of Toshi immediately after lunch.

Mark gave his mother a duty kiss on the cheek and they walked together to her apartment. The young man was shy of his mother. He hadn't seen her for nine months and had hardly communicated with her; even before Sylvia left for Tokyo she hadn't seen much of him because of his involvement with Colin and the stage.

153

During the short walk to Sunflower Mansions, Sylvia asked him the sort of mundane questions one would pose to an acquaintance. She inquired about his flight, his hotel, his impressions of Tokyo (which is what a Japanese would ask), and then she explained about her university work, her students. She painted an unflattering portrait of Professor Suzuki.

'He wants to meet Colin Sibley. Do you think he could come to the party tomorrow night after *The Tempest*?'

'Yes, I suppose so. There will be lots of people there, probably. One more won't matter.'

'But he wants to meet Colin.'

'I could fix that. But why do you want to be nice to him, if he is as ghastly as you've just described him?'

'He's an important professor in my department and it would be diplomatic to do something for him and thereby put him under an obligation. He's powerful. It's best to be on his side.'

They had reached the top of the gentle slope at the bottom of which rose the dingy block of apartments, its concrete front stained with damp.

'That's it,' said Sylvia. 'That's where I live, down there.'

'Oh Mummy, it doesn't look very upmarket.'

'It isn't.'

They entered the hall and climbed the cement stairs to the dark passage.

'A prison,' said Mark.

'Like many apartment buildings. Here we are!' She opened the metal door. 'Shoes off.'

'Why?'

'It's the custom.'

'You care about Jap customs?'

'When in Rome. . . . Put on these slippers.'

Mark pulled off his track shoes. He was wearing a blue pullover and jeans.

'Come and sit down, Mark. I'll make some tea.'

The young man went straight to the window and looked out. 'God! You look on to a cemetery. Mummy, how can you live in this crummy flat?'

'It's considered not at all bad by Japanese standards,' said Sylvia raising her voice as she was behind the curtain that screened the kitchen. When she crossed into the sitting part of the room, Mark was standing at her desk and looking at the photographs of her and Toshi which they had taken at Shimoda. She had forgotten that she'd left them on the desk. When writing she often paused and looked through the photographs. It had been a happy weekend.

'Is this your lover?' Mark asked, shuffling through the pack of photographs.

Sylvia put the tray of tea things on the occasional table by the sofa and poured out the tea.

'Is this your lover?' repeated Mark.

'Come and have some tea,' Sylvia was blushing.

Mark sat on the sofa by his mother; he still had the photographs in his hand.

'Give me those, Mark.'

'Who is he?'

'Never you mind.' She stretched out a hand.

'I want to look at him again,' said Mark teasingly. 'What's his name?' He leant away from his mother holding the photographs up to his face.

'Mark, give me those photographs.'

'Not until you tell me his name. I know you have a lover. Matthew's friend told me in London.'

'Oh he did, did he? His name is Toshi, if you must know.'

'Toshi? Do you call him Tosh?'

Sylvia sipped her tea, Her face was red with shame and fury.

'How old is he? He looks about eighteen.'

'He's twenty-six and works in a bank. Now, Mark, give me the photos, please, and let's not talk about him anymore. Please, please, Mark.'

Mark gave his mother the photographs. 'I'd like to meet him. He looks nice. You and he seem very happy together. Are you going to marry him?'

'Of course not.'

'It'd be fun to have a Japanese stepfather only three years older than me. Have you known him long?'

'Oh Mark, do stop asking questions about him.' Sylvia sniffed and put her handkerchief to her nose.

'I'm interested. I am your son, you know.'

'It's a private affair.' Sylvia swallowed and blinked. 'Toshi has helped me a lot. He provided solace after – ' she dabbed her eyes. 'I was so lonely when I arrived here and he asked if he could come and see me. He works in the bank I use and I met him there. And so it began. Our relationship hasn't been entirely smooth. At the moment it seems to be on an even keel.'

'Judging by the photographs it seems to be very much plain sailing. May I meet him, Mummy?'

'I'd rather you didn't.'

'You don't want him to know you have a son nearly his age?'

'He knows about you. I told him. It's just that I'd be embarrassed if you met him and so would he.'

'It seems so unlike you, Mummy, to take up with a boy.'

'Let's not talk about him, Mark. I want to hear about you, the plays, and your friend.'

'You mean Colin?'

'Yes.'

'You'll meet him at the stage party after the opening.'

'I don't want just to see him at a party. Couldn't you bring him here?'

'Might be possible next Sunday when the plays are over.' Mark tossed blond strands of hair away from his blue eyes. In looks he was very like his mother. The resemblance was immediately noticeable.

'Do you ever see your father?'

'Rarely. He doesn't approve of my relationship with Colin. Daddy never really liked me.'

'Oh, don't be silly, Mark! What a thing to say about your father!'

'It's true.'

'But you seemed to be on his side when he went off with that – '

'I didn't want you to divorce. I hoped his affair would blow over.' Mark paused, again tossed back his hair and said in a pleading voice, 'Mummy, you don't disapprove of my life, do you?'

Sylvia thought for a moment. 'I did. I disapprove less now.'

'Because of Tosh?'

'Toshi. Yes, I think that's the reason. I would be happier if you had a girl friend and were not – '

'Gay?'

'Yes. It'd be more natural. But then, Matthew is gay and I like him very much, and Jun, his friend, is a sweetie. Jun, though, may be getting married.'

'I feel sorry for his future wife. He's so obviously gay. The Japanese have to marry, don't they? Perhaps you'd be satisfied if I were like a Japanese son and married a girl of your choice I didn't like and lived unhappily ever after.'

'It's hard for me to accept fully your way of life.'

'But you accept Matthew's.'

'Matthew isn't a relation. Jun is not my son. I feel responsible for your being gay. It makes me think I brought you up wrong, that I didn't give you sufficient affection or too much or something.'

'Don't be idiotic, Mummy. It's in the genes.' Mark rose, 'I must go. Colin is calling a rehearsal tonight. Can you please phone for a cab?'

'Why not go by train? It's easy. I don't know how to call for a cab. No one seems to do so here. You can get a taxi in Hongo-dori, where I met you. I'll show you the way.'

They walked up the slope to the avenue, where they soon found a taxi. Mark kissed his mother. 'Goodbye, darling,' said Sylvia, 'and good luck with the play.'

When she got back to her *apāto*, she rang Matthew and remonstrated with him about Jun's indiscretion in telling Mark about Toshi. 'Did you know about it?'

'Yes. It was at the dinner party Colin gave for us in his house. I told Jun afterwards that he shouldn't have mentioned Toshi to Mark. But really it doesn't matter much, does it? Mark ought to be pleased you've found someone to make you happy.'

'If Toshi were Suzuki's age, then it wouldn't have mattered. The fact that he's just three years older than Mark does. Mark found the photos of Toshi and me taken on our trip to Shimoda. He said he looked like a boy. It's true, he does. Anyway, tell Jun I'm cross with him. No, don't. Leave it. The damage has been done. Next Sunday, I thought I'd give a lunch party for Colin and Mark. I'd like you and Jun to come.'

'Next Sunday's no good for lunch, I'm afraid. Jun's going to see his potential fiancée in Yokohama and I have an engagement.'

'Pity, but never mind. I'll see you at the stage party tomorrow night. You are going to it, aren't you?'

'Yes. I got Suzuki a ticket for the play. It's best to butter them up, even if they have behaved badly.'

'Funny, I've just said almost exactly the same thing to Mark, who said it wouldn't matter if Suzuki came to the stage party.'

· 12 ·

Toshi's seven o'clock phone calls had become very regular and Sylvia welcomed them, but she was surprised to receive one on the Sunday evening after Mark's visit as Toshi had been with her until the early afternoon. Sylvia told him it wouldn't be convenient to see him on the following weekend since she was going to the last night of *Candida* on the Saturday evening, and he informed her that he couldn't have managed to keep their habitual Saturday-Sunday 'meeting' anyway (he always referred to their trysts as meetings) as he had to go on a company journey. 'I forget to tell you when I with you today,' he said.

'Where are you going?'

'Atami.'

'Didn't we go through Atami on our way to Shimoda and you said it was a resort full of bar hostesses?'

'Yes, I don't want to go, Siru-San. I must obey to my boss.'

'You obedient Japanese and your bosses! I'm giving a lunch party for Colin Sibley, the actor, and my son next Sunday. Matthew and Jun can't come. It would have been lovely if you could have come. What a pity you can't make it!' It was devious of her to give the invitation when she knew he couldn't come. She didn't want him to at all, but she thought she might as well reap the merit of asking him, to pretend she wanted his presence. 'See you the Saturday after next, then. Goodbye, Toshi. I'll miss you next weekend.' It was a relief that Toshi had expressed no desire to see the plays. 'I not understand, Siru-san,' he had said when tentatively she had asked him.

158

Sylvia was disconcerted to discover Suzuki sitting in the aisle seat next to hers in the stalls of the Globe Theatre. He rose to let her by.

'Your son in this play,' he said, pointing to Mark's name in the programme.

'I know. He's Ariel. I've never seen him act before.'

'Sō?'

'Yes, sō.' She began to read her programme with rapt attention.

The auditorium was filling up. There were a few foreigners here and there sticking out like sore thumbs. Most of the audience consisted of teachers, or professors as they liked to be called, and students, who got tickets at a reduced price. In the first three rows were the British ambassador and his wife, some other diplomats and a number of representatives from the banks and the trading firms which had sponsored the tour. It had been hoped that the Crown Prince would attend, but for some reason he didn't appear.

The house lights went down and there began the noises of the storm, the shouts of the Shipmaster and the Boatswain. When in the second scene of the first act Prospero (Colin Sibley) summoned Ariel (Mark Field) and the airy spirit materialized, a chill went down Sylvia's spine. She could hardly bear to look at her son, who wore a scanty electric-blue loincloth spangled with sequins and whose hair glistened with sequins too. She supposed it was right for Ariel to be practically naked, but her son's nudity embarrassed her. He articulated the verse almost too carefully, perhaps because of the predominantly Japanese audience. But when he sang in a clear, sweet voice, 'Come unto these yellow sands, And then take hands' tears came into Sylvia's eyes. In spite of his costume (or lack of one) she was proud of her son. He gave the idea of being only partly of this world cleverly. She felt that there existed a special rapport between him and Colin, who was correctly avuncular and authoritative. At the end of Act Five when gently he addressed Mark, 'My Ariel, chick, That is thy charge: then to the elements be free, and fare thou well!' and then looked round, Ariel had already disappeared, evaporated into the air in the manner of the spirit he was meant to be. How had Mark done it? Prospero remained puzzled for a moment and then turned to Alonso and his train, 'Please you, draw near.' Sylvia almost blubbed. Mark had managed his exit so brilliantly.

At the party on the stage, Suzuki stuck to Sylvia like a shy husband. She moved towards Matthew and he followed. And when Mark came up to her, she had to introduce him, 'This is my son.' Suzuki bowed and said, 'Your mother and I are colleagues, and friends.' Mark muttered to his mother, 'Mummy, this isn't – '. Sylvia almost snapped, 'No, of course not.' She hoped that Suzuki hadn't understood. 'Mummy, you must meet Colin,' insisted Mark. 'Let's interrupt him. He looks as if he needs rescuing from that circle of bores.'

The 'bores' in fact consisted of the British ambassador and the ambassadress, the British Council Representative and his wife, and two middle-aged Japanese businessmen, delegates for the sponsors, and their wives. Mark, leading his mother by the hand, broke into the circle and took Sylvia up to Colin, who had exchanged his costume for a dark suit. He looked elegant and striking. Suzuki determinedly followed. 'I wasn't surprised at your superb performance,' Sylvia told Colin, 'but I was at Mark's. His being so good must be due to you.'

'He has talent, you know,' answered Colin. 'I believe I'll have the pleasure of lunching with you next Sunday, and – '

Suzuki pushed his way forward and presented Colin with his card, bowing and announcing his name.

Colin accepted the card graciously, giving a little bow; he then turned to Sylvia and said softly, 'I've so wanted to meet you. How like your son you are!' He then introduced Sylvia to the ambassador, 'This is Ariel's mother. I'm not sure that spirits are meant to have mothers.' The diplomat allowed his lips to form a watery smile. After uttering a few vacuous remarks, the ambassador left, and the party, which was only a drinks affair, thinned out.

Sylvia declined Mark's offer to dine with him and Colin at their hotel and slipped away on her own, leaving Suzuki standing as near Colin as he could and being ignored by the actor and those around him. She refused the invitation to dine with the actors as she feared that Suzuki would try and come too and she didn't want the embarrassing task of telling him he couldn't; it would not be difficult for Colin and Mark to fob him off.

· 14 ·

Sylvia only saw Mark once during the rest of the week and then just briefly for tea at his hotel. Matthew, she learned to her annoyance, saw more of him than she. After the performances and the official receptions which on several occasions succeeded them, Matthew, sometimes accompanied by Jun, guided Colin, Mark and Peter Cox to some of the gay bars in Shinjuku, which amused Mark more than the three older men.

Toshi telephoned every evening of the week except for the Friday evening when she called him and got no reply. She rang several times. Was he at the 'Club New Love'? She wished she knew where it was. Why hadn't he taken her there? She had asked him to.

Sylvia had thought of Toshi (not that he was ever far from her mind) when at the end of the play, Candida asked Marchbanks (Mark) to make a poem out of what she was going to tell him and said: 'When I am thirty, she will be forty-five. When I am sixty, she will be seventy-five.' Sylvia would have to tell Toshi to remind himself: 'When I am thirty-five, she will be fifty-nine. When I am fifty, she will be seventy-nine.' Of course her affair with Toshi could not possibly last. 'May it last a little longer,' Sylvia prayed to herself. 'Another year, please God!' It was when she had been unable to contact her lover that Sylvia felt melancholy and uncertain about him.

· 15 ·

What should she give them for lunch? Smoked salmon followed by roast lamb? She could get both at the supermarket in the department store at Ikebukuro. But wouldn't Colin expect something less English? She could buy raw tunny to serve as a first course instead of the salmon, and then do a Japanese stew which was named *shabu-shabu* because of the bubbling noise the boiling water made in the pot. One simply put slivers of beef and chicken into the water and fished them out again with chopsticks after a few moments. It was a good dish and the 'fishing' was fun. But Colin and Mark might not be able to use chopsticks. Foreigners often found them awkward. She wasn't very adept at using them herself, and she wasn't sure that she could buy the right kind of thin beef or the correct pieces of chicken. No, she'd settle for the conventional meal she'd first thought of, and make Mark's favourite pudding, chocolate mousse. What a pity it was that neither Matthew nor Jun could come. They'd be only three, which might make the occasion embarrassingly intimate. Although Colin had seemed charming at the stage party, to entertain him with her son without anyone else to help lighten the atmosphere and to prevent the conversation from becoming disconcerting was not an attractive proposition. What was she to say to Mark's amour, who was around her age? She could hardly mention their liaison, ask them their future plans as if they were an ordinary couple. All the week she had dreaded the visit and now it was upon her.

· 16 ·

Matthew had declined Sylvia's invitation to lunch because since Jun was going to Yokohama on the Sunday, he would be alone and free. This freedom gave him the chance to go to a certain cinema in Ueno, one of the cinemas which Sylvia and Toshi had passed and remarked upon on that Sunday during their first walk together nine months ago. His refusing Sylvia's invitation, which he could perfectly well have accepted and his telling Jun the lie that he would be going to lunch with her made him feel guilty. On occasions the temptation to stand at the back of the crowded cinema pressed as closely as in a rush-hour train to the other patrons was too great to resist. It was the initial moves that thrilled: the unzipping of a stranger's trousers, fumbling through the gap in his underpants and taking hold of his cock, and the stranger reciprocating. Such preliminaries might be interrupted by the soft-porn film ending and the lights going up or by a customer pushing past and separating the partners. Matthew never told Jun about his visits to the sordid little underground theatre in Ueno. He was ashamed of them; yet he often thought about them. The uncertainty of what might happen increased the excitement. Sunday afternoon was the most rewarding time of the week.

· 17 ·

Colin and Mark took a taxi to the Red Gate and from there they walked to Sunflower Mansions. As they were descending the short road that led to the block, they noticed a man in a blue suit ahead of them. He entered the building just before them and went up the stairs to the first floor as did they. When they reached the apartment the man was standing by the door having rung the bell.

'Ah, a fellow guest!' exclaimed Colin cheerfully.

The man turned and looked at the two Englishmen with alarm. At that moment Sylvia opened her door and seeing Mr Five-Four-Six hemmed in at the bottom of the step by Colin and Mark and unable to budge cried out, 'Oh, my God!', and then recovering from the shock, she shouted to the greengrocer, '*Kyō dame*. Not today, thank you.' Five-Four-Six understood and pushing the other two apart, fled down the passage.

'Come in,' said Sylvia, leading the way into the flat.

'We have to take our shoes off, Colin,' said Mark.

'Oh, do we?' Colin slipped out of his loafers and took off his short overcoat, underneath which he was wearing a red, polo-neck pullover and cavalry twill slacks. Mark had on his blue sweater and jeans.

'Such a good idea taking off shoes,' said Colin. 'I think I'll adopt the custom when I get back to London.'

'Mummy, who on earth was that?' asked Mark when he had

joined the others in the sitting-room section at the foot of the L.

'What, darling?' asked Sylvia, stalling. 'Do sit down.'

'Who was that man, Mummy?'

'Oh, no one.' She turned to Colin. 'What may I get you to drink?'

'Oh gin, I think, please. Gin and tonic, if that's all right. I can indulge as there's no performance tonight.'

'And you, Mark?'

'The same, please.'

Sylvia went to the kitchen area to pour the drinks.

'What did you think of that man, Colin?' asked Mark, quietly.

'The man at the door? Didn't see much of him.'

'He had silver teeth. I think he's Mummy's lover, but he looked older.'

'Older? What d'you mean older?'

Sylvia appeared with the drinks. 'I'm afraid Matthew and Jun can't come, so you've only got me.'

'Mummy, who was that man?'

"I've told you,' replied Sylvia, a little crossly. 'He's no one. He works for the drink shop and comes to collect empty bottles.'

'In a blue suit?'

The bell rang.

'Now who on earth?' Sylvia hurried to the door.

'Another bottle man, perhaps,' said Mark.

'How many lovers does your mother have, Mark? asked Colin.

They heard Sylvia say, 'Professor Suzuki! Good heavens!'

'I hope I am not late,' the professor said. 'I am sorry my wife could not come.' He was dressed in a blue suit and wore a red tie, the usual outfit for a professorial function.

'But,' Sylvia began, and then added in an unwelcoming tone, 'You'd better come in, I suppose.'

And in came Suzuki without any sign of embarrassment. Soon he was bowing and shaking hands with Colin and Mark. 'My deep congratulations to you both,' he said. 'I greatly enjoyed your performances. Seldom have I seen such good acting. You are both big stars. Well, one big, one little star.' He seemed pleased with his little speech.

'Thank you,' said Colin.

'Thank you,' said Mark.

'Please sit down, Professor Suzuki. And what will you have to drink?'

The professor looked at the other drinks and then said, 'A dry martini. Very dry.'

'I'm no good at making martinis. Come and help me, Mark.'

Mark followed Sylvia into the kitchen area behind the curtain. 'I didn't ask him,' she whispered, 'did you or Colin?'

'Of course not.'

'He's gatecrashed. The little swine!'

'Don't you like him, then?'

'No. He made a pass at me once, which I rebuffed. He ignored me after that until he heard that you and Colin were coming and because he wanted to meet Colin he made up to me again. Also, he spread – '

'Spread what?'

'Oh it doesn't matter.' Sylvia stooped to look at the joint in the oven.

'What were you going to say?' Mark was mixing the martini.

'Nothing. Please take him his drink. I wish I could put some poison into it.'

'I could pee into it.'

'Really, Mark! I must look at the vegetables and make some gravy. Go on, take him his drink.'

When Mark returned to the sitting-area, Colin was saying to Suzuki, 'It's quite his best play. Each act is perfect. I once played the part of Simon years ago.'

Mark handed Suzuki his dry martini. 'Your drink, Professor.'

'Thank you, Ariel, or should I say Marchbanks?' He laughed and jerked a bow at Mark and then turned to Colin again. 'We have production of *Hay Fever* some years ago. A famous actor, he plays woman parts always, he play Judith Bliss, you know.'

'How amusing. I should have loved to see it. And how did *Hay Fever* go down in Tokyo? Was it a success?'

'No.'

'Oh.'

Sylvia wearing padded gloves took the leg of lamb out of the oven, and just as she was placing it beside the gas cooker, there was a tap on her shoulder.

'Oh!' She looked round and there was Toshi smiling; he was

dressed in casual clothes and looked tired. 'Heavens! I didn't hear your key in the door.'

'I come in very quiet, to make surprise. You ask me come. I say no cannot. This morning at Atami I think I will say my correagues I must back to Tokyo. So I come. You not please?'

'Yes, of course. But Professor Suzuki is here and – '

From the other side of the curtain came Mark's voice, 'Mummy, may Colin and I have refills?' He started at the sight of Toshi. Sylvia quickly said, 'Mark this is Mr Toshihiko Yamada. Toshi, my son.'

Nervously, Toshi said, '*Hajimemashite*,' and then changed into English, 'It is first time we meet.' In the manner of a boy seeking approval from his mother, he threw a questioning glance at Sylvia.

'I've heard a lot about you,' said Mark, but Toshi didn't seem to grasp the purport of this utterance. 'What will you drink?'

'Give him a gin and tonic,' said Sylvia. While Mark was preparing the drinks, his mother took her lover to the other part of the room and introduced him to Colin and Professor Suzuki, who both needled him with curious looks. Toshi bowed to the professor, who whipped out his visiting card and presented it, and bowed and shook hands with Colin, who patted the empty place on the sofa saying, 'Come and sit by me.' Toshi obeyed. Suzuki fired off some questions in Japanese, which received more grunts from the young man. He clearly did not enjoy the interrogation. As soon as Mark had handed round the drinks, Sylvia took him back behind the kitchen curtain. 'Help me divide this smoked salmon, Mark. It's got to do for five instead of three.'

While helping his mother, Mark asked, 'Do you really love that boy, Mummy?'

'Yes,' she replied defiantly.

'He's so young.'

'He's twenty-six.'

'But – '

'If I asked you the same question, Mark, about Colin, what would you say?'

'I love him.'

'Well, there we are then.'

'Are you going to marry him?'

'You asked me that before and I said of course not. How could

166

I? I don't want to anyway. Please be nice to him, Mark. Don't ask him awkward questions. He's very sensitive. I don't want him upset. I was surprised he turned up. I didn't want him to.' She took out of a drawer a handful of cutlery and silver. 'Here, please lay two more places and tell them that lunch is ready.'

Suzuki had finished his examination of Toshi and was talking across him to Colin. 'I have great interest,' he was saying, 'in Oscar Wilde. Do you know his work, Mr Sibley?'

'Indeed.'

'Lunch is ready,' announced Mark.

'What do you think of – '

Colin got to his feet and so did Toshi. 'We are called to table.'

'Called to table?' echoed Suzuki. 'Is that a common English expression?'

'One could say "summoned to the board",' said Colin.

'Summoned to the *board*? What board?' Suzuki laughed.

· 18 ·

At about the same time that Sylvia and her guests were sitting down to lunch, Matthew set out for Ueno and the cinema. He enjoyed travelling about Tokyo, especially on the Yamanote Line, an elevated railway that circled the inner part of the city. He liked to look at the passengers, sum them up, and imagine where they were going, what they were going to do. He didn't mind standing, and he was less disconcerted than Sylvia had been when there was a free seat next to him and no one took it. But when someone stood by the empty seat deliberately not taking it, it seemed, he did feel a bit snubbed, even after his long sojourn in Tokyo. Sometimes he spread out and took up more room than necessary so as, he hoped, to return the snub. In a certain part of the train during the rush hour the same sort of feelies went on as in the cinema. But today was Sunday and the train was not crowded enough for misbehaviour.

Sylvia put Colin on her right, Toshi on her left, Mark opposite her at the other end of the table, and Suzuki next to Colin. She hoped that Toshi's proximity would enable her to protect him from any difficult questions that might come from the professor.

'Ah, this is pleasant,' said Colin, as he took his place next to Sylvia and Suzuki. 'It's good to be in a home.' He looked across the table at Toshi. 'Do you live here?'

Toshi looked confused.

Sylvia at once came to her lover's aid. 'He lives in Nerima-ku, a suburb, not far out.'

'My parents they live in Nerima-ku,' said Suzuki. He then switched into Japanese and asked several questions, to which the young man replied with grunts and monosyllables as he had done before.

'Did you understand any of that, Sylvia?' Colin asked his hostess.

'Of course she didn't,' said Mark. 'Mummy doesn't speak a word, do you, Mummy?'

Sylvia laughed apologetically. 'I can bring out a few phrases and grasp a few too. I say I speak "supermarket" Japanese. I can read the prices, of course, help myself from the shelves, and say "thank you" at the pay-out place. I can count a little, and I am beginning to understand when the price is told me, though in the supermarket I can cheat: it's on the machine.'

'"Supermarket Japanese",' said Suzuki. 'Very good.' He turned to Colin. 'Have you acted in a drama by Terence Rattigan?'

'Yes. I once played the part of the barrister in *The Winslow Boy*.'

'And you did *Separate Tables*, Colin,' Mark reminded the actor.

'So I did. I wasn't very good in the part.'

'Very interesting,' said Suzuki.

'This smoked salmon is excellent,' remarked Colin to Sylvia.

'It's Japanese. It comes from Hokkaido, I believe.'

'Ah, you have salmon in Japan?' Colin asked Toshi across the table.

Toshi said nothing, but Suzuki broke in with, 'Salmon is very common in Japan.'

Colin turned to his neighbour, said coolly, 'Really?' and then looked at Toshi. 'And what do you do in Tokyo?'

'He works in a bank,' Sylvia answered for him.

'Ah, a banker. Do you like banking?'

'I think he likes it, don't you, Toshi?' Speaking slowly, she added, 'You like the bank, don't you?'

'No, I like.'

Colin and Mark laughed, and Suzuki after a moment joined in.

'He means "yes",' explained Sylvia, and they all laughed again.

'I knew that "no" sometimes meant "perhaps",' said Colin, 'but I never knew it could mean "yes". It must complicate matters.'

'You take "no" for an affirmative answer, do you?' Mark asked Suzuki.

Suzuki replied didactically, 'It is due to your tag questions, "do you", "don't you". We say "No" in reply to "don't you" and "Yes" in reply to "do you", because we Japanese feel we must agree with the questioner. It is wrong, but we feel it is polite. I wrote a paper about this and gave a lecture.'

'Fascinating,' said Colin in a jocular tone. 'I do wish I had heard it.'

Sylvia rose. 'Mark, do help!' She didn't like to ask Toshi because doing so might reveal her intimacy with him. She and her son collected the plates and Mark handed round the helpings of lamb as she carved the joint behind the curtain.

'Mr Sibley,' began Suzuki, 'have you – '

'Have I what?' He frowned.

'Have you acted the part of Hamlet?'

'No. I say, Sylvia, this lamb is delicious.'

'It's from New Zealand. Frozen. You have to defrost it slowly.'

'We Japanese don't like lamb,' remarked Suzuki.

'Why not?'

'We say it smells.'

'Smells?' echoed Mark. 'It's a pleasant smell, I think.'

'If I had known you were coming,' said Sylvia pointedly, 'I would not have arranged for us to have lamb. Toshi likes lamb, don't you, Toshi?'

'What?'

'You like lamb meat, yes?'

'Yes, I like.'

'Some do,' said Sylvia, but Suzuki ignored her and turned to Colin. 'And what about King Lear?'

'What about the old bugger?' asked Colin.

'You play . . . I mean have you acted in the part of King Lear?'

'No.'

'What about Othello?'

'No.'

'But he was wonderful as Julius Caesar and Leontes,' stated Mark.

'And you, my dear, were a perfect Florizel.'

'We do not know about Leontes in Japan,' said Suzuki as if somehow such lack of knowledge was an advantage.

'Would anyone like some more lamb?' asked Sylvia.

'I'd adore some,' said Colin. 'It was so good.'

Mark rose. 'Would you like some more, Professor?'

'Me? No, thank you.' He had left his meat. He got up from the table and went into the little hall.

Sylvia looked at her other guests, turned her open palms upwards, splayed her fingers and shrugged. 'I didn't invite him,' she said softly.

Back hurried Suzuki with a camera and before anyone could object, he had taken five photographs. He spoke to Toshi in Japanese, gave him the camera, went round the table and stood behind Colin. Nervously, Toshi took their photograph.

'Please understand,' said Colin severely, 'that those photographs are to be private and not used in the press.'

Suzuki did not reply. He retrieved his camera from Toshi and returned it to his briefcase in the hall.

· 20 ·

Matthew changed his mind and instead of going by the Yamanote line he caught the Chiyoda line train, which would take him direct to his destination or very near it Jun had set off early to Yokohama for his engagement meeting, which he was dreading. For the first time in months, Jun had got into Matthew's bed and they had had sex. Matthew wondered if this was a compensating gesture on the part of his lover. He almost felt it was a kind of farewell. Sex had not been important for the prospering of their partnership. Desire had dwindled, but last night it had revived and it had been stronger on Jun's side than on Matthew's. To Matthew having sex was like eating chocolate: once he had had it he wanted more.

There were families on the train with rampaging children demanding attention. Instead of business suits and sober dresses, the passengers were in casual clothes: golf jackets, jeans, short sheepskin coats or cable-stitch pullovers of thick white wool. Matthew wore a raincoat over his tweed sports jacket and grey flannel trousers. The cinema was usually more productive in the winter and a raincoat could be an asset.

He alighted at Yushima Station near Ueno Park, crossed the road and took the path which skirted the lotus-growing side of Shinobazu Pond. The crowd of promenaders so resembled the passengers on the subway that the train might have emptied itself into the park. 'A homogeneous lot,' muttered Matthew to himself as he turned up an alley that brought him to the main street which led to the entrance to Ueno Park and after a twist to Ueno Station. He turned left, passed a cinema showing ordinary films and then after pausing and looking both ways, darted down a steep flight of concrete steps. He slipped a thousand yen note into the ticket-dispensing machine, took the change that spilled into the metal cup and diffidently handed his ticket to the man in the booth, who did not look at Matthew when he tore the ticket in half. Matthew was grateful for his discretion. But how could it matter? If he were seen it would be by someone with the same tastes. He pushed aside the curtain that screened the doorway and edged his way into the little auditorium, which was packed with men. There were some empty seats but most of the patrons preferred to stand in the gap between the last row and the back wall or down the side aisles. Matthew, causing a number of frowns and noises of complaint, gradually squeezed through the bodies and succeeded in securing a place against the back wall, the most desirable position.

171

'Please help, Mark,' said Sylvia, beginning to collect the plates. Suzuki returned to his seat by Colin. Toshi started to rise. 'You sit still, Toshi,' said Mark. 'I'll be parlourmaid.' Colin gave him a look. 'I mean butler.' He winked at Colin. Sylvia and he served the cheese, which neither Toshi nor Suzuki would touch.

'We Japanese do not like cheese,' said the professor.

'Because of the smell?' suggested Colin.

'We say it is like soap. We do not like to eat soap.' Suzuki let out his shrill laugh.

'But some Japanese like cheese,' said Sylvia. 'There're heaps of it on sale in the supermarkets. It can't all be for foreigners.'

'Maybe some Japanese they like cheese,' admitted Suzuki. 'but we do not have cheese in our . . . how shall I say? In our, er – '

'Diet?' contributed Mark.

'Yes, our traditional diet.'

'If we in England stuck to our traditional diet,' said Colin, 'our fare would be stodgy and dull. Travelling and the lack of servants have improved English food enormously.'

This platitude did not draw any reply. Sylvia, Colin and Mark ate their Brie in silence. Suzuki, though, addressed Toshi across the table in Japanese; as before the young man's replies were very brief and did not amount to much more than '*So des*' (that is so) and '*Ah sō, des ka?*' (is that so?).

'Professor Suzuki,' reprimanded Sylvia, 'it's not fair of you to speak in a language we don't understand.'

Suzuki did not reply. He looked down, muttered something and kept quiet. When he declined to take a helping of chocolate mousse, Colin said, 'The smell again?'

'We Japanese do not like sweet things after a meal.'

Colin glanced at Toshi, who was spooning his mousse into his mouth with speed. 'Some do, it seems.'

Sylvia blurted out, momentarily forgetting, it seemed, the presence of Suzuki, 'Jun loves mousse and cheese. The smellier the better.'

172

'I adore Jun,' said Mark. 'He's sweet.'

'He's having an o-something today, an engagement meeting, Matthew told me. And Matthew's got something on too. I don't know what. He didn't say.'

'*O-miai*,' said Toshi.

'What, darling?' And remembering Suzuki, Sylvia put a hand over her mouth and regarded her son at the other end of the table. 'Did you say something, darling?' she asked Mark.

'No.'

Sylvia jumped up from the table. 'Let's move into the other room, and then when I've done the washing-up, we'll go for a walk. I'd like to go on my favourite walk to Shinobazu Pond. Would you like that, Colin?'

'Very much. It would be good to see something of Tokyo on foot. I've only seen a bit of Shinjuku and the inside of the theatre.'

They all rose from the table.

'Mummy, I'll help.' Mark began to gather the plates.

Toshi, who rarely lent a hand with the kitchen chores, started to emulate Mark at the other end of the table. Colin collected glasses. Suzuki stood in the space between the dining-table and the armchairs. The others ignored him.

'I wish he'd go,' whispered Sylvia to Mark at the sink.

'Why not say you're busy?'

'How can I?'

The four continued to disregard the professor and carried on with the washing-up and the drying. While Colin and Mark dried the dishes, the silver, the cutlery and the glasses, Toshi put them away. Sylvia was surprised that he knew exactly where everything went. She wondered if Suzuki noticed and suspected this knowledge, which revealed that he was well acquainted with her apartment.

'We'll have coffee and then go on our walk,' Sylvia announced. Suzuki was now gazing out of the window at the cemetery. Sylvia said, 'We're going to have some coffee, Professor Suzuki. Have you time to have a cup before you go? Or are you in a hurry to leave?'

'Yes, please. Coffee I like.'

'Damn!' murmured Sylvia under her breath.

· 22 ·

The Japanese, Matthew had observed during his years in Tokyo, had the enviable ability to observe without obviously doing so. While he turned his head to look at the person next to him or a few feet away, that person would probably have surreptitiously scrutinized him. The men on either side of Matthew did not interest him, but further down the row against the back wall was a young man who appeared desirable. He could not see his features clearly in the obscurity but he seemed attractive and didn't he look at him? Matthew was too tightly packed in to move. He decided to do so when the film ended and there would be a reshuffle of the audience. He hated the soft porn film, an American hetero one with no subtlety consisting of swift approaches and hasty beddings down. The quick rise and fall of male buttocks could be exciting, but he found very full female bubs revolting. The film concluded with several couples having it off together. The lights went up.

The five-minute interval between films was embarrassing because the illuminated auditorium revealed one's presence and a foreigner stood out like a beacon, but it enabled Matthew to get a proper look at the young man, who returned his regard and allowed a slight smile to pass across his face. While the strident bell signalling the end of the interval was ringing, and just before the lights dimmed, Matthew surrendered his place against the wall and stood in front of the young Japanese. The fact that he prevented him from seeing the screen did not matter, since standing patrons mostly ignored the film, being otherwise engaged or hoping to be. Matthew put his hand behind his back. At once it was fondly grasped. He squeezed the hand and the squeeze was returned. Encouraged, Matthew let go of the hand and pushed his inside the open raincoat, found the tag at the top of the young man's zip, pulled it down, and then after some fumbling took out the small hard prick and held it in his fist. There was no objection. He fondled the vibrant member until his potential partner pushed his hand away and put it inside his trousers. Matthew felt rebuffed. However, he was wrong. The young man simply wanted to change places. Matthew now against the back wall and submitting to a sensual caressing by deft fingers, leant forward and whispered into the young man's ear, 'Hoteru', the Japanese for hotel, but he pronounced it to sound like Otaru, a port in Hokkaido. Since his apparently complaisant quarry made no reply, Matthew assumed he was one of those who preferred to do things on the spot, which Matthew did not enjoy. He adjusted his dress. Whereupon the Japanese looked round and gave him a hint of a nod. Matthew edged out from the wall, gave a tug to the young man's sleeve and muttering 'Sumimasen' (excuse me), gently pushed his way through the tight cluster of men, some of whom were distinctly displeased, to the exit. At the top of the steps, Matthew paused. Would he follow?

· 23 ·

'Well now, shall we go?' asked Sylvia, rising from her armchair. Again she tried to get the uninvited and unwanted guest to leave. 'Professor Suzuki, we're going for a walk. I don't suppose you want to come, so I'll say goodbye.' She held out a hand. 'It's been so nice having you.'

'No, I come with you to Ueno and catch my train from there.'

She turned to Toshi, 'Now you be the leader. We'll go first to Sanshiro Pond.'

They set out. It was a lovely November afternoon; the air was crisp, not cold. Toshi took his duty seriously and went on ahead like a tour guide. Mark walked with his mother and Colin with Suzuki. The professor began to ply Colin with statements and questions, to which the actor replied with the same sort of monosyllables that Toshi had emitted.

'I am a graduate of this university,' revealed Suzuki, after they had gone through the Red Gate on to the campus.

'Really.'

'It's the best university in Japan.' The professor waved a hand at an undistinguished block of lecture rooms.

'Really.'

175

When they reached Sanshiro Pond, Sylvia said, 'Now Toshi, tell us the story.'

Toshi began, 'Japan's number one story writer, Natsume Sōseki, he write – '

Suzuki drew in his breath through his teeth and then interrupted. 'No, not number one. You must say, "One of Japan's leading novelists" – '

'Please go on, Toshi,' said Sylvia.

Toshi nervously continued, 'He write famous story it call 'Sanshiro Pond'. This pond's name Sanshiro, the same as the boy in the story.'

Again Suzuki broke in, 'He was a student at this university, so more than a boy.'

'He have love affair, but it broken. He simple country boy and not understand city girl. She not love him – '

Suzuki again stopped Toshi. 'I think she did love him, but couldn't marry him. He was too young and she had to marry a rich man.'

'Sensible woman,' put in Colin.

'I wish you'd let Toshi tell the story, Professor Suzuki,' snapped Sylvia. She turned to Colin. 'He tells it so sweetly. Go on, Toshi, dear, I mean, please continue, Toshi.'

'No, I cannot. Professor Suzuki he can tell much better.' Toshi was clearly upset.

'I'll complete the story then,' said Suzuki. 'It was probably autobiographical and describes a calf-love. The student was broken-hearted when he lost his sweetheart and to console himself he walked round and round this pond, which is now called after him – Sanshiro.'

They continued their walk through the campus. Toshi, no longer in the lead, walked with Sylvia, and Mark joined Colin and Suzuki.

'I'm sorry, darling. You tell that story so well,' said Sylvia to Toshi.

'He know better. He professor.'

'I like the way you tell it.'

'What he think about me?'

'I don't know. It doesn't matter what he think, thinks.'

They entered the main street which descended to Shinobazu

Pond. The huge poster of the androgynous young man advertizing a shampoo caught Colin's eye. 'Who may that be?' he asked Suzuki.

'He is Kenji Kaneko. A pop singer.'

'Looks pretty gay to me,' said Mark.

Suzuki made no reply. Colin frowned.

The party continued their descent to the pond, and with Suzuki, Colin and Mark still in front and Sylvia and Toshi behind they began to cross the causeway that divided the boating part from the lotus-growing part of the lake, making their way to the temple dedicated to Benten, the goddess of luck.

· 24 ·

Self-consciously and hating every moment, Matthew waited in the street outside the entrance to the cinema. Loitering in this way was acutely embarrassing; although one rarely ran into an acquaintance in the immense city, one always feared one might. He felt conspicuous. He glanced down the steps to the entrance. Should he give up? The young man was probably groping someone else. He took a few steps in the direction of Ueno Park and the station, looked round and there he was, standing where Matthew had stood a few seconds before. They advanced towards each other.

'"Love hotel", okay?' suggested Matthew.

'Okay.'

Outside in the light the young man was better looking than Matthew had thought – it was usually the opposite. He had a full head of black locks, sexy dark-brown eyes and a sensitive mouth, the lips finely shaped. Dressed in slacks, a pullover and a light coloured raincoat, he was about the same height as Matthew.

'"Love hotel" you know?' asked the young man.

'Yes.'

'I have *karuma*. Car.'

'Where is your car?'

'There.' He waved a hand in the direction of Shinobazu Pond.

They walked down the alley-way that led to the path round the pond.

'Look! There's Matthew!' exclaimed Mark.

'Professor Bennet,' said Suzuki.

'Let's pretend we haven't seen him,' suggested Colin, who had immediately grasped the situation. But Sylvia had not. She called out, 'Hello, Matthew!'

Matthew quickly said to his companion, 'See you other side of park,' and came towards his friends.

'You old cheat!' teased Sylvia. 'You could have perfectly well come to lunch.'

'I had to see this exhibition of Edo period hairpins and combs in the museum.' Matthew had suddenly remembered reading about such an exhibition in the *Japan Times* the previous morning. 'I'm writing about it.'

'Who were you with?' asked Sylvia.

'I? I wasn't with anyone.'

'But you were with someone.'

'Oh that was no one. He asked me the way.'

Suzuki and Toshi stood aside from the foreigners, while they were engaged with one another.

Inwardly, Matthew cursed Sylvia. He was determined, though, not to give up his afternoon of dalliance. All of a sudden, like a puppet pulled into action, he bowed to Suzuki and Toshi, rapidly shook hands with Sylvia, Colin and Mark, saying, 'I must rush,' and made off.

Neither Colin nor Mark could contain their laughter. Sylvia remained puzzled. 'What has come over Matthew? He behaved as if he didn't want to see us.'

Suzuki made his excuses, bid his goodbyes, but offered no thanks, and went up the alley-way that led to the main street and the station. The others continued their circumambulation of the pond, Sylvia walking with her son, Colin with Toshi.

'Wasn't Matthew behaving oddly?' Sylvia said to Mark.

'Oh Mummy, didn't you see? He was with someone.'

'Only someone who wanted to know the way, he said.'

'Would a Japanese ask a foreigner the way? He was with a pick-up.'

'Oh, I see. Going to the exhibition was a blind. Poor Matthew! Jun's having an engagement meeting. I see.'

· 25 ·

Matthew's new friend rejected the 'love hotel' and guided Matthew to his car, a Toyota sports model parked in a back street where parking on Sunday was condoned. Soon they were stopping and starting along the clogged expressway to Yokohama.

'What is your name?' asked Matthew.

'My name Yamamoto.'

'Yamamoto what?'

'Yamamoto Kazuyoshi.'

'My name is Matthew. Where are we going?'

'Near Yokohama. I know good "love hotel".' Yamamoto gave a sly smile.

Now and then, when there was a gap in the traffic, the little bell that indicated that the car was exceeding the speed limit rang. Yamamoto paid no attention, and on they drove towards the port. Dusk was falling when they turned off the expressway and after a short distance, up a narrow lane to a black building with a neon sign on its roof in Japanese characters and 'Hotel Enjoy' in English. Yamamoto drove to the back of the hotel where there were garages attached to the building. As soon as the car entered one of these, the door came down behind them. Yamamoto got out of the car and spoke to someone through a microphone. He beckoned to Matthew and they descended a steep staircase to a door which opened into a bedroom. No member of the staff appeared. Yamamoto spoke to one of them through a little cubby hole.

The room was larger than many Tokyo apartments and furnished lavishly in the worst of tastes. The bed was huge, there were mirrors on the walls and on the ceiling; a box of tissues, a packet of condoms and a TV remote control instrument were on the bedside table. Yamamoto opened the refrigerator and brought out two bottles of beer. They sat for a while on a plush red sofa, sipping the beer. Soon they were in each other's arms.

'I love you,' said Yamamoto.

Matthew muttered, 'You're very sweet.' He could not bring himself to reciprocate the declaration of love, which he knew meant not much more than a conventional phrase.

They undressed, put on *yukata* (unnecessarily Matthew thought), went into the bathroom, which was equipped with every modern device except a bidet (like the English, Matthew thought, the Japanese don't know about bidets), took off their *yukata*, soaped one another, doused their bodies with hot water using the little plastic bucket provided for the purpose, sat in the tub together making it overflow on to the floor, dried each other with tiny towels, put on their *yukata* again, sat on the sofa again, sipped some more of the beer, embraced, and then at last (Matthew was getting tired of these preliminaries) they got into bed, slipped out of their *yukata* and made love – wildly. Matthew hated to admit that Yamamoto was better in bed than Jun had ever been – but then the first time is often the best.

Yamamoto insisted on paying for the room and driving Matthew all the way back to Tokyo although he lived in Yokohama, dropping him off at Yoyogikōen station, not at the apartment, and giving him his telephone number without asking for Matthew's. 'What wonderful discretion!' Matthew muttered to himself as he strolled home. 'Thank heavens for gerontophiles!'

· 26 ·

Oh Lord! What was he to do? There was no doubt about it. He had crabs. Matthew had had them before, but not since his meeting Jun. These body lice, these *papillons d'amour*, as the French in their typically facetious way called them, were (possibly because of the luxuriant pubic hair of the Japanese) common in the land of his adoption. And after all that washing too! But Matthew knew that crabs clung persistently and could not be eliminated by hot water however much one tried.

It was Tuesday. Jun had returned from his engagement meeting in Yokohama early on the Monday evening, Monday being his day off, and he and Matthew had dined together. It was on the

Tuesday morning that Matthew had begun to suffer the ominous itching in his crotch. What had he done last time? He had got some ointment, but he no longer had it and had forgotten its name. After Jun had gone off to school again on the Tuesday morning, Matthew examined himself under a reading lamp. Yes, there was one, and another. He picked the two nasty, transparent insects out of his pubic hair and squashed them between his finger and thumb. But of course there were others hiding or about to hatch out in the roots of his bush. Damn! And he had taken a superior attitude to Jun over dinner on the previous evening when the young man had confessed that he might have to go ahead with the engagement and eventually marry the young woman his parents had found and set their heart on as a spouse for their son.

'If you're truly gay, you must not marry,' Matthew had pontificated.

'I must obey to my parents,' Jun had protested.

'What about us?'

'I come and see you once a week. I promise.'

'Very different from living with me, sharing my life.'

'What can I do, Mattu-san?'

'You can tell your parents and your would-be fiancée that you can't go through with it.'

'I can't. I don't want to go to marriage. I must. I am nearly thirty.'

'Do you think you'll be able to fuck her?'

'I don't know. But I try.'

'Huh!', exclaimed Matthew, adopting one of Jun's favourite ejaculations. 'What am I going to do?'

'What you do before you met me?'

'I was promiscuous, but I wasn't happy. I have been happy with you, Jun. You know that. Living with you I have not wanted anyone else.'

Recalling this conversation, Matthew felt contrite. How could he have been so hypocritical? Jun had gone to bed tearful and apologetic and Matthew, to console him, had joined him.

On his way to the university, Matthew called at a pharmacy he often patronized. He hoped the man was there and not the woman, his wife, who sometimes served in the shop. He was. By a stroke of luck, Matthew remembered the Japanese for crabs.

181

Feeling abject, he blurted out, '*kejirami arimas*.' The chemist gave him a kindly, conspiratorial smile, went to the back of the shop, and after several minutes produced a jar of ointment. 'Try this. Rub on. I think they go in two days,' said the man.

Matthew paid for the ointment in a hasty, guilty way and hurried on to the station. His chief concern was whether Jun had caught the lice from him. As soon as he got to his office, he locked the door and pulled down his trousers. Then came Sylvia's knock.

'Just a minute,' he shouted, feverishly applying the ointment. Matthew quickly pulled up his trousers, shoved the jar of ointment into his jacket pocket and let Sylvia into the room.

'What on earth were you doing?' she asked, eyeing him suspiciously. Now that she knew him better her attitude towards him bore the mark of a sister rather than that of a colleague. Matthew slightly resented this new familiarity.

'I was writing something down in case I forgot it.'

Sylvia glanced at the empty desk on which there was nothing but a biro pen.

'In my diary,' Matthew added.

'I see.' Sylvia sat in the seat next to Matthew's revolving chair. Matthew took his place. 'They've gone, I suppose.'

'They left yesterday for Osaka by the bullet train. I saw them off. After two performances in Osaka, they fly on to Hong Kong.'

'Sorry not to have seen Colin and Mark again, not to mention my old friend Peter Cox.'

'You could have come back to tea when we met you by the pond.'

'I had an appointment to see Professor Saito – he's not at our university. I help him with his interminable essay on the Japanese socialist poets in the middle and late Meiji period. He's writing it in English for some inexplicable reason.'

'I see. What about your article on hairpins and combs?' She smiled mischievously.

He avoided her gaze and fiddled with the biro. 'It's coming along.'

'Wasn't Suzuki awful?'

'You mean at the party on the stage?'

'Yes, but also on Sunday. He came to lunch uninvited and behaved abominably. And to make matters worse, Toshi turned up too. He cut short his bank's trip to Atami and suddenly appeared for lunch. I had invited him but he said he couldn't come. Now, what am I to do?'

'About what?' The crabs were biting voraciously. He longed to scratch.

'About Suzuki's meeting Toshi. I'm sure he guessed he was my lover.'

'Oh, don't worry about that. The Japanese don't care about one's sex life provided you don't throw it in their face.'

'But I did throw him in Suzuki's face.'

'What did you do? Kiss him, or something?'

'No, not that, but I did call him darling and Suzuki noticed. I know he did.'

Matthew, craving a scratch, wriggled in his chair and involuntarily uttered, 'God!'

'Are you all right?'

'It's just a twinge.'

'A twinge?'

'Of my arthritis.'

'I didn't know you were a sufferer.'

'My knee,' said Matthew twisting in his chair.

'Don't you think it was monstrous of Suzuki to have gate-crashed my party?'

'Absolutely so. But he's like that. A tuft hunter. Pushy. Also, like some Japanese, he finds Westerners entertaining.'

Sylvia rose. 'I don't have a class today. I'm on my way to the pool. So you don't think I need worry about Suzuki meeting Toshi?'

'No.'

Matthew got up swiftly, turned his back on Sylvia as she was making for the door and gave his crotch a brief clawing. 'No, no need to worry. I know these people. They don't pry into one's private life.' He followed her to the door. 'See you,' he said and shut the door quickly. He took the jar of ointment out of his pocket, lowered his trousers and rubbed his crotch thoroughly with the paste, which stung.

The next day, Wednesday, while Sylvia was expounding on the use of the colon and the semi-colon to her composition class, she suddenly felt a sharp stab in her crotch as if she were being bitten. She longed to scratch but she couldn't in front of the class. To the puzzlement of her students, she sped up the pace of her lesson, moving about more than usual. She walked to the back of the class and was able to get in a scratch unseen. 'The use of the colon has come back today and is much more common. It is now over-used.' She returned to the blackboard and wrote out an example. 'One could have used a dash there,' she explained. Another pin prick made her announce, to the students' astonishment, and probably delight as she usually ended the lesson well after the bell had rung and there were still twenty minutes to go, 'That will do for today.' She hastened out of the room and dashed to her office, where under the harsh striplight she examined herself and found what Matthew had found the previous morning, a crab. She knew what it was as her husband had told her once about body lice years ago. She also knew that Toshi had given them to her as he had slept with her on the Sunday evening after Colin and Mark had had tea and gone back to their hotel. Toshi had not stayed all night as he had to go home to change for work the next day. Where had he caught the lice? What had he done in Atami? What was she to do? Ask Matthew. But he wasn't in his room. She went home. When passing the bank she dismissed the thought of trying to see Toshi; in any case it was five o'clock in the afternoon and the bank was closed to customers. As soon as she arrived in her flat, she had a shower, playing the jet of hot water directly on to her crotch. To no avail. She spent some time trying to catch the insects with the tweezers she used for plucking her eyebrows and hairs off her legs. She caught three. How horrible they were! At seven she rang Toshi. He was out. She then rang Matthew, who was in.

'Oh hello, Sylvia.' Matthew, who was in the middle of an awkward conversation with Jun put no enthusiasm into his voice.

'Do you know anything about Atami?' Sylvia sounded meek, very different from her brash manner on the previous morning.

'Atami?'

'Yes.'

'It's a seaside resort. Hilly, with lots of expensive hotels and inns. There's a new musuem there, rather cleverly let into the side of a hill. Why? Do you want to go there?'

'Would there be any prostitutes there?'

'Hundreds, I should think.'

'The little bastard.'

'I beg your pardon. What on earth's the matter, Sylvia?'

'Toshi spent Saturday night in Atami, no doubt with a whore. He slept with me on the Sunday evening and I have crabs.'

'How extraordinary! That really is quite funny.' Matthew began to laugh.

'I don't find it funny. The bites of the odious little beasts are like continuous bee stings. I feel dirty.'

'So do I.'

'So do you? What do you mean?'

'I mean I understand how you feel. I had them once; a long time ago, of course.'

'What should I do to get rid of the lice?'

'You can get some ointment at a chemist's.'

'What is it called?'

'I don't know. Go to a pharmacy and say *"kejirami arimas"*, which means "there are hair lice", and they'll understand. They are very common in Japan. Just a minute, Jun's signalling.'

'I don't want Jun brought into this,' Matthew could hear Sylvia's voice saying after he had put down the receiver. He went to the sofa on which Jun was stretched out. 'Did you gather what's wrong with Sylvia, Jun?'

'Yes, tell her to splay cockroach stuff on the er, on the down place. Wait ten minute. They fall down like rain. Then wash off.'

'Matthew went back to the phone. 'Have you got an anti-cockroach spray?'

'You know I have. You advised me to get one to drive away the disgusting beasts which infest this flat.'

'Jun says spray the stuff on and then wash it off after ten minutes.' Matthew laughed. 'He says they drop down like rain.'

'I don't know why you find it funny. I'll try it anyway. It won't give me a rash, will it?'

'Not if you wash it off. Good luck with your crab hunting!'

'Damn you, Matthew.' She rang off.

Matthew's smile had gone by the time he returned to his armchair. He and Jun had been having words about Matthew's infidelity and its consequences. Jun had caught some *kejirami* from Matthew, hence the discovery of the cinema escapade. Ointment had been applied to Jun's itching crotch. Jun broke a long silence by saying, 'Maybe it good if I marry. You do not care.'

'That's not true, Jun. You know it isn't.'

'Then why you go with a man you pick up in the cinema?'

'It's just sex, Jun. Not love. It didn't mean much more than masturbation.'

'Why you not masturbate?'

'It meant a little more than that. And you had gone off for your *o-miai*. I felt lonely. *Sabishī*. Suddenly I had the urge to go out and I went.'

'You cancel lunch with Sylvia-san?'

'Yes.'

'I see.'

After another silence, Matthew said in a jocular tone, 'Are the bugs still biting? Mine are, damn it. I believe their eggs hatch out in a matter of hours. I wonder what their life span is. Would you like me to rub on some more of that ointment?'

'Yes, please, Mattu-san.'

'You should have seen the face of the pharmacist when I said "*kejirami arimas*".'

Jun laughed and Matthew went into the bathroom to fetch the jar of anti-body-lice paste. When he returned and was examining Jun's pubic hair, he asked, 'How did you know that the cockroach stuff killed *kejirami*?'

'One of my friends he tell me.'

'I see.'

· 28 ·

The next morning Sylvia's torture by the *papillons d'amour* (in her case at least 'amour' did enter into it) seemed to have been quelled by the anti-cockroach spray. Her annoyance with Toshi had not. She rang him at six and after ten rings got a sleepy answer. 'Toshi,' she complained, 'you have given me *kejirami*, understand? *Kejirami*.'

'Yes. I have too. I no sleep.'

'Then come round here at once. I have some stuff.'

'Staff?'

'No. Stuff. Medicine. A cure.'

'Okay. I come.'

Toshi arrived in under an hour, letting himself in with his key. Dressed for the bank in a dark-blue suit, a white shirt and a blue and red striped tie, he came forward into the sitting area of Sylvia's room. He looked contrite. '*Sumimasen*,' he said. 'I am very sorry.' He bowed to Sylvia, who was at her desk correcting compositions. She looked at him over her pink rimmed spectacles. 'I should bloody well think so,' she replied. She rose and in the tones of a hospital matron commanded him to take off his jacket and trousers. Toshi hesitated. 'Take them off. You want to get rid of the *kejirami*, don't you?'

Toshi did as he was bidden and stood self-consciously by the sofa. Sylvia spread a sheet of the *Japan Times* on the floor by the desk. 'Stand on the paper. Take off your underpants.' Toshi showed reluctance. 'Take them off, for God's sake.' He obeyed. She aimed the desk lamp on his crotch, took her tweezers from the occasional table, lifted up his shirt. 'Now, let me see.' He recoiled. 'Don't be silly, Toshi. Stand still. Just a minute.' She fetched a magnifying glass from the desk and began to examine the thick black forest around Toshi's genitals. 'There! See?' She showed him a lice she had picked out of his pubic hair and dropped it on to a piece of Kleenex. 'Here's another. See?'

'*Gomen nasai*. I am very sorry.'

'What was she like, this woman you slept with?'

Toshi did not reply.

'Perhaps it's better that I don't hear about her. Now, the cure. She picked up the cockroach spray from the table and blasted a jet at Toshi's crotch.

He cried out, '*Itai*! Hurt. That for *gokiburi*.' He stepped back. 'No!'

'Yes!' contradicted Sylvia fiercely, and moving forward sprayed again.

'It danger,' complained Toshi.

'Rubbish.' Sylvia let off another squirt. 'Now you must wait ten minutes and then have a shower.'

'*Itai*. It danger.' Toshi looked alarmed and distressed; near to tears, he seemed no more than a boy.

Suddenly, Sylvia felt compassionate. After all, she reflected, if Matthew was right and crabs were common in Japan, she might easily have caught them from Five-Four-Six and given them to Toshi. When the young man came back from the shower, Sylvia insisted on repeating the treatment. He submitted. His shame made him complaisant. He agreed to return that evening from the bank for more treatment, which this time ended with their going to bed together for a lovemaking that exceeded in rapture and passion their normal performance.

Part Four

· 1 ·

Spot Out, a weekly magazine that had been recently launched in Tokyo as a rival to *Focus* and *Friday*, appeared on Thursday. It promised to be more scurrilous than the other two, which depended on their revelations about the peccadilloes and idiosyncracies of the famous for their healthy circulation. A week or two before one of the magazines had published a photograph of Edward Kennedy emerging from the sea naked. It was said that the purchase price of this prying picture was high.

On his way home from school late one Tuesday afternoon in November Jun took a discarded copy of *Spot Out* from the luggage rack in his train and while leafing through the magazine, he came across an article entitled 'Lunch Party for Lovers'. The subheading read: 'English Woman Teacher Plays Hostess to Gay English Actor and Their Lovers'. The article was illustrated with three photographs: one of Sylvia and Colin with the caption, 'Sugar Daddy and Sugar Mummy'; a second of Mark looking across the dining-table at Colin with the caption, 'Lover Boy looks at Father Figure'; and a third of Sylvia looking wistful, but Toshi was not in the picture. The caption for the last read, 'Is *okā-san* afraid of losing Sonny?' The article itself did not have much more to relate than the story told by the photographs and the captions. It said that Mark was the woman teacher's relation (it did not say son), that the woman's lover was a twenty-six year old 'salary man', and that Colin gave good parts to Mark because of their relationship rather than because of his talent. Mark's interpretation of Ariel was called that of a 'fairy'. The word was given in English and it was explained that a 'fairy' in this sense would be called in Japanese, an '*okama*', a pejorative for a homosexual. The article concluded: 'It is not known what happened after the meal. Did the lovers sleep it off in the king-size bed screened off by *shōji* but only three paces away from the table? Or did they have an orgy?'

Jun read the article several times. He was amazed and worried. He ran from the station to the flat and showed the magazine to Matthew as soon as he got in.

'*Spot Out*!' Matthew exclaimed in derision. 'Yes, I've heard of it. I understand it's more scandalous than those other rags. And what does it mean, *Spot Out*? Typical nonsensical Japanese English.'

'Look at this.' Jun opened the magazine at the article about Sylvia's lunch party.

'Good God! Sylvia! Colin! Mark! How frightful! What does it say?'

Jun translated the article and the captions.

'Suzuki, of course. He gatecrashed the lunch party. Took the photos. What a blessing Toshi's picture isn't included. He'd get into trouble with his bank. God, what a shit! We must tell Sylvia. Poor Sylvia. It's most unfair. Thank God I didn't attend the party. Worth getting crabs not to have done so.' He laughed. Jun didn't. 'It's monstrous. Scandalous. Who wrote the article?'

'It doesn't say.'

'Suzuki obviously wrote it, or inspired it. I'll have to tell Sylvia. I'll tell her on Wednesday. I see her then. Good thing he didn't find out about the *kejirami* saga.'

'Huh!' said Jun.

· 2 ·

'Can I sue for libel, Matthew?'

'Much better to leave it, Sylvia. Not everyone reads *Spot Out*.

It's a week old anyway.'

'That isn't long. Why should I take this lying down?'

They were in Matthew's room in the university. Matthew had just shown Sylvia the offending article.

'Your name isn't mentioned.'

'But my photograph is published. More people know my face than know my name. At least on the campus. Give me the beastly magazine. I'll go and beard Suzuki with it.'

'Better not,' warned Matthew.

'Damn you and your pusillanimous diplomacy!' She snatched the magazine and stormed out of the room and into the entrance hall. Seeing that the lift was on the fifth floor, she ran up the four flights of stairs to the staff room, which she entered, breathless. Five members of the department were seated in the room and one of them was Suzuki. Sylvia went straight up to the professor and brandishing *Spot Out* in his face, and said, 'What do you know about this, Professor Suzuki?' The other professors quietly retreated, leaving Sylvia with Suzuki and the woman secretary, whose desk was in the room.

'I know about it,' said Suzuki, smiling.

'Why did you write such damaging libel about me and my guests? You have abused my hospitality and my guests. And you promised Colin Sibley that the photos you took would not be used.'

Suzuki remained seated on a sofa. Sylvia, trembling with rage, stood over him. The secretary pretended to busy herself with some documents. Since Suzuki simply smiled without replying, Sylvia almost shrieked, 'I demand an apology and damages.'

Suzuki said, 'I did not write the article. I only showed the photos to a friend who work on the magazine. He ask to keep them. I did not think he use them for an article.'

'How am I to believe that? Don't you see the harm the article does to Colin, my son and to me?'

'I am sorry about it.' He kept up his smile. 'It is regretful.' He rose from the sofa. 'Excuse me, I have a class.' He left the room.

Sylvia turned to the secretary, whom she had always found kind and sympathetic. 'What do you think about it?'

'I don't know, Field-san.'

'What can I do?'

'I don't know, Field-san.'

Sylvia went to her room and waited for her favourite student to arrive. Mr Matsuda, after all, was married and the most mature of her graduate students; he might be able to give her good advice. He was due to submit the third chapter of his thesis on *Middlemarch* for correction. When he arrived and gave his usual bow and solemn, deep-voiced greeting, 'Good afternoon, Mrs Field,' Sylvia asked him if he had seen the previous week's issue of *Spot Out*.

He smiled. 'Mrs Field, I do not read such magazines.'

'You've not seen this then?' She handed him her copy open at the defamatory article, which Matsuda read with great concentration. After he had finished the short text and scrutinized the photos, he asked, 'Who wrote this?'

'I have an idea who inspired it.'

'And the photographs?'

'Professor Suzuki took them and gave them to someone on the magazine.'

'It true?'

'Yes. He forced his way into my apartment on the pretext that I had invited him to lunch and I hadn't. I was in fact giving a lunch party for my son and Colin Sibley. In the middle of the meal he took photographs. Those photographs – there!' She stood up and pointed to the pictures that illustrated the calumnious article. 'What can I do, Mr Matsuda? I challenged Suzuki just now with the article and his lame excuse was that he'd given the photos to a friend who works on *Spot Out* and didn't think he would use them or write a piece for the magazine. What should I do?'

'I don't know, Mrs Field.'

'What would you do?'

'It true?'

'Is the article true, you mean?'

'Yes.'

'It is true in a way. My son is gay and is Colin Sibley's lover, and I do have a Japanese boy-friend.' If Matsuda hadn't had a soft, sympathetic nature, Sylvia would not have confessed these facts to him. He looked at her and gave a smile of what could be interpreted as admiration. 'If it true, then you must do nothing. If they ask you, then you must say it not true.'

'So I must lie down under it?'

Matsuda gave her a quizzical regard. 'Lie down under?'

'I mean, I must not take any action against the magazine?'

'Do not take. It will not help you. Everyone they forget by next week.' Matsuda looked at his watch and firmly handed to Sylvia, who had resumed her seat at the desk, the typescript of the third chapter of his thesis. Sylvia took the pages and began to read.

· 3 ·

On Thursday afternoons all over Japan each university holds faculty meetings known as *kyojukai*, meeting of professors. The next day was Thursday and while Matthew had no classes he was expected to attend his faculty meeting, which began at 3 p.m. Sylvia was not invited because she was only a visiting professor and did not speak Japanese. Instead she had a class. Matthew felt it was such a waste of time his having to attend the meetings, whose deliberations often led nowhere. Round and round a subject would the professors meander. Some would fall asleep as a holder-forth droned on, and Matthew, who would fortify himself for the tedium by having two gin and tonics at a nearby Western-style hotel, followed by a hearty lunch and half a bottle of wine, would nod off too, thinking of the young waiter in the short mustard Eton jacket and tight black trousers who had served the meal. But just as he was about to leave his room in the Faculty of Literature to go up to the *kyojukai*, the phone rang. It was the department chairman, kindly Professor Maeda, whose English was rudimentary, in spite of his being an 'expert' on Iris Murdoch.

'Professor Bennet?'

'Yes?'

'This Maeda. Ju' to say not necessary for you to come to *kyojukai* this day.'

'Has the meeting been cancelled?'

'Not cancel. We discuss private matter.'

'I see. Thank you, Maeda-*sensei*.' Matthew rang off and then spent half an hour musing about his not being wanted at the meeting. Had they found out about his private life and decided to terminate his contract? But he had never flaunted his tastes at the university and also last year he had been granted tenure, although not with the universal approval of the Faculty members he learnt later from the secretary, who would often confide in him information about the professors and the students. Matthew liked Miss Ikeda, who spoke better English than many of the professors. When alone with her in the staff room, they would have a gossip. It suddenly occurred to him that she would be alone now as she did not attend the Faculty meetings. He went up to the staff room.

'Do you know why I was not asked to the meeting, Miss Ikeda?'

'They discuss Professor Field.'

'About the article in *Spot Out*?'

'Yes.'

'Oh dear! What will they decide?'

'I don't know. Many professors they are not pleased abou' the article.'

'Nor is Mrs Field. It's not her fault.' Matthew lowered his voice to a whisper, 'It was Professor Suzuki who – '

'I know,' Miss Ikeda whispered back.

'They will sack her, will they?'

'Some professors think they must sack her.'

'It would be most unfair if they did.'

'They think the article in *Spot Out* very bad for the university.'

'But everyone knows that *Spot Out* is just a malicious scandal sheet,' said Matthew, adding to allow for Miss Ikeda's limited vocabulary, 'a bad magazine that tells lies.'

'I know.'

'I must warn Mrs Field.'

'Please do not say anything to her until the professors decide. Maybe they not sack her.'

Matthew took Miss Ikeda's advice and did not tell Sylvia about the meeting.

On the following evening, Friday, Sylvia rang Toshi several times, but he was out. Of course, she conjectured, he might well be with his colleagues or still at work in the bank tussling with figures, or whatever he did, but she had a suspicion, and she did not know why, that he might be at the 'Club New Love'. This suspicion was reinforced when she telephoned him at midnight, but when he came to see her the next evening it evaporated as he was so sweet and loving.

They had discussed the *Spot Out* piece over the previous weekend. Toshi had sympathized with Sylvia, though he had not hidden his relief that none of the photographs taken of him had been included. A week had gone by since Sylvia had seen the offending and offensive magazine and while it had not faded into her unconscious, the worry about it was no longer gnawing all the time. She and Toshi spent a happy weekend together and on Sunday afternoon she had accompanied him to his apartment to help him with his domestic chores. After their little meal of instant noodles which they had sitting on the floor, he came with her to the station and up the steep concrete steps to the ticket machines. He waited until she had gone through the barrier and when she turned to wave, he was still there to wave back. It was like the first time she had gone to his *apāto*, or to his 'room' as he called it. 'Thank God for Toshi,' she said to herself, often, especially when he telephoned her in the evening.

On the following Wednesday the complacency that had set in over the *Spot Out* affair was shattered. Just before leaving her room for her reading class there was a knock on her door, and in answer to her, 'hello?', Professor Maeda entered. He was wearing his habitual Harris tweed sports jacket, flannel trousers and brown brogues. From his neck down and from the rear he looked English. He had once told Sylvia that he loved England, which he had visited many times but didn't really know or understand.

'Oh, Professor Maeda, how good to see you!' exclaimed Sylvia. 'Do sit down.' She gestured towards a chair. 'I was just going to my class.' The professor remained standing. 'I have something to say,' he said.

'About Iris Murdoch?' Sylvia put on her generous party smile.

'No.' He seemed confused. He made an obvious effort, drew a breath and said, 'Mrs Field, at the faculty meeting last week we discuss the organization of the Faculty, and we decided that we have to er, to er, reduce, cut down our members. And I am sorry to tell you that we have to terminate your contract at the end of this academic year, that is, next March. We are very sorry for this, and we appreciate very much what you done for the students, especially the graduate students. You been a big success, but – '

'But,' interrupted Sylvia, her smile gone, 'I have signed a contract for two years. You can't push me out after one year.'

'In your contract it say you on probation for first year.'

'But probation has to do with behaviour and you have just said that you were satisfied with my work.'

'We very satisfy, Mrs Field,' said the professor, clearly hating the task he had to perform for he was a mild and pleasant man. 'But it is this cut-down of staff. University cannot afford another foreign teacher.'

'It's nothing to do with economy, is it, Professor Maeda? You're sacking me because of that article in *Spot Out*, aren't you?'

'*Spot Out*?' Maeda uttered the name as if he had never heard it.

'Yes,' Sylvia insisted fiercely. Her anger was aroused. 'The magazine, *Spot Out*. The one that had that article and the photographs about my lunch party for Colin Sibley and my son which Professor Suzuki attended uninvited.'

Professor Maeda looked down. 'I do not know about *Spot Out*. I know abou' our reducing staff.'

'Professor Maeda, I do not believe you are sacking me because you have to reduce the staff. I believe you are sacking me because of the article in *Spot Out*. And it is grossly unfair.'

Still looking at the floor, the rather pitiful professor, who manifestly did not enjoy what he had been delegated to do, repeated unconvincingly, 'It is because we must cut down, Mrs Field. Truly we regret, but you are the only professor we can ask to leave. I wish it not so. We all like you very much, Mrs Field. We are sorry.'

Sylvia sighed. 'I must go to my class. They are waiting. I am late.'

She went out of her room leaving the professor behind. Her

students seemed unusually responsive that afternoon. Was this because they had heard about the article and sympathized with her, because they admired her for having a lover, or simply because they were in a good mood? Their moods varied. On some days they were like a brick wall, on others, this afternoon, they were lively, co-operative and interested. At the end of the class, Sylvia had that feeling of exhilaration that teachers get after giving a good lesson which has been well received, and what Professor Maeda had told her seemed of small importance. It was just stupidity on the part of the Faculty members. She would see the President. He would rescind their decision for sure. How could they dismiss her when she was so obviously a success and she felt that the students liked her? And she enjoyed her work. She hastened to the Faculty building and rapped three times on Matthew's door.

'Yes?' came the Englishman's bored, irritated cry. Sylvia opened the unlocked door and still in her exuberant mood, she blurted out, 'I've decided I'm going to see the President. You've heard they've sacked me?'

'No!' Matthew exclaimed, hoping to appear shocked and surprised. Miss Ikeda had imparted the news to him that morning before Sylvia had been informed of it by Professor Maeda.

'I'm going to see the President of the university,' repeated Sylvia. 'I'm sure he'll reverse the decision of the Faculty of Literature. Professor Maeda said that my dismissal was due to a need to cut down staff, which I don't believe. Will you take me to see the President?'

Floored by the question, Matthew stammered, 'Well I, I, I don't know whether I, I could possi – '

'But you speak Japanese. You could interpret. Let's go, Matthew.'

'Now? The President speaks English anyway.'

'Your being with me would help,' Sylvia said. 'I want to get this thing settled now.'

Matthew wanted to tell her that a *démarche* to the President would be useless. Instead he said quietly, 'It would be much more effective if you went with Professor Maeda.'

'But it was Professor Maeda who sacked me. I'll go along now, barge in, if necessary.' Sylvia snatched up her teaching books, which she had plonked down on the desk. 'I thought you might have helped.' She tore out of the room.

'It won't do any good,' Matthew cried, just before she slammed the door.

To Sylvia's disappointment Matthew was right. She managed to see the President. Her distraught state caused his secretary to take pity on her and conduct her into the presence of a small, bald, bespectacled man in a dark-blue suit sitting behind a huge, polished desk in a room twice the size of her apartment. There were armchairs and a sofa arranged round a square occasional table at the side of the desk. In a corner on a pedestal was a brown pottery vase filled with three yellow chrysanthemums at different levels and some bare branches sticking up above them at odd angles. On one wall hung an oil painting of a mountain and river scene with saplings tinged with autumnal colours in the foreground. Under the painting stood a bookcase full of Japanese tomes. A window behind the President's desk was curtained, and another at the opposite end of the room looked on to a lawn. When Sylvia was ushered obsequiously into the room, the President rose, came forward and shook her hand, grunting something as he did so. He stretched out a hand in the direction of the sofa and chairs; in the other hand was a cordless telephone.

Sylvia perched on the edge of one of the chairs, while the President engulfed himself in the sofa, the toes of his shining black, child's-size shoes just touching the Persian carpet. He placed the telephone by his side. 'Tea? Coffee?' the President asked.

Sylvia hesitated. 'I just wanted to – oh tea, please.'

The President muttered to his hovering secretary, who hurriedly left the room.

Sylvia felt somewhat awed by the President; small in stature though he was, he exuded, with the assistance of his luxurious office, an air of inexorable authority. How was she to address him?

'Sir,' she began, 'you may have heard about my dismissal.'

The President winced. Sylvia thought that her broaching the subject so bluntly might be tactless and not win her any sympathy. Just as she was about to make another attempt, the telephone rang. The President picked it up and talked into it at some length.

A woman attendant in a short skirt and sleek black hair which tumbled to her waist appeared with a tray on which were two cups of tea, milk, slices of lemon, sugar and a plate of biscuits. She fussily placed one cup in front of Sylvia and the other by the President, who ignored the bow the attendant made after serving the tea and before she left the room, and continued his conversation. When it had ended, he said, 'You take sugar?'

'No, thank you.'

'Milk? Lemon?'

'Lemon, please.' She leant forward and plopped a slice of lemon into her cup. 'Sir,' she began again, 'you may have heard – '

'Have a cookie,' said the President, indicating the plate of biscuits wrapped in plastic bags.

'No, thank you,' replied Sylvia, irritably. She braced herself for the third time. 'Sir, Professor Maeda told me this morning that my contract which was for two years is to be terminated at the end of this year.'

'I have heard. I am sorry about it. I had good report of you.' The telephone went again and the President again became engaged in another long conversation. Sylvia drank her tea. When the President had finished talking, he said, 'You like one more cup?'

'No, thank you. Don't you think it is unfair to cancel my contract because of the article in *Spot Out*? It wasn't my fault. Surely no notice should be taken of a magazine that thrives on making scandalous statements about people?'

'*Spot Out*?' The President uttered the word as if it were unknown to him.

'There was an article about me in this muck-raking rag *Spot Out*, and because of it you are sacking me. It is monstrously unjust.'

In reply the President picked up his telephone, dialled a number and proceeded to have yet another conversation. Sylvia felt so exasperated she wanted to scream. The only words spoken by the President which she recognized were 'Field-*sensei*'. At least he was talking about her and, she hoped, telling Professor Maeda to alter the decision made at the Faculty meeting. When he had switched off the phone, he turned to Sylvia and said, 'I am very sorry, Mrs Field, the Faculty have decided that they must cut down expenses and as you are the latest to join they must ask you to leave. They are very sorry. You have done good job.'

Sylvia was roused. 'But why did they advertise for a teacher and then when she arrived discover they can't afford her? That's an invented excuse. It's *Spot Out* that is the real reason.'

'I am President of this university, elected by the professors. I cannot change decisions made by the professors of a Faculty. Faculty control by the professors of Faculty. Only I can approve the decisions they make. They engage the professors and they can change arrangements as they wish.' He turned and regarded Sylvia with a helpless look. 'I am sorry there is nothing I can do.' He moved his body forward and rolled on to his feet, not forgetting to pick up the telephone, which rang the moment after he had done so. '*Moshi, moshi,*' he said into the speaker. '*Chotto matte.*' He held out his free hand to Sylvia. 'Thank you for coming, Mrs Field.' He gave a slight bow with the telephone to his ear and then began to talk into the instrument. Sylvia made a meek exit.

· 5 ·

'Poor Sylvia,' remarked Matthew to Jun over supper. They were having spaghetti with garlic and prawns, which Jun had knocked up. He had forgotten it was his turn; he got home earlier than Matthew on Wednesdays. 'It's egregiously unfair. She saw the President this afternoon, but got no joy from him.'

'He refuse to help?'

'Said he couldn't override a Faculty decision. Lot of balls. Of course he could if he wanted to, couldn't he?'

'It difficult,' explained Jun. 'If Faculty members they vote against keeping Siria-san, it hard for President not to agree.'

'Is there any cheese left?'

Jun shook the container of grated Parmesan. 'It finish.'

'There's that Emmental. We could grate some of that.' Matthew left the table and went into the kitchen and grated a slice of the Swiss cheese. On re-entering the living room, he said,

'When Sylvia came back from seeing the President, she wasn't seething with rage. She was quite calm. She told me about her interview and that she was going to the pool as she usually does on Wednesdays after her classes. I admired her composure.' Matthew did not add that she had said in the tone of voice a grown-up uses to a child not equipped with the ability to help, 'I had hoped more from you, Matthew. I can see now that you don't want to compromise your position.'

· 6 ·

Just as Sylvia's body lost its weight while she ploughed up and down the pool, so did her mind lose its concern about her predicament. She found swimming calmed her, and she was pleased when each time she passed Mr Ogawa doing his perpetual backstroke, he smiled. It was a generous smile. She wondered whether if she had accepted his invitation to go to Yokohama, her life would have been different. She decided that it was better that he remained at arm's length. A closer relationship might have led to disillusionment. She smiled at her 'sour grapes' conclusion. They chatted after their swim and then bade each other *sayōnara* on the sports centre steps.

She had not been back in her flat more than a few minutes when the doorbell sounded twice, and there on the threshold stood the greengrocer, beaming. He was in his work clothes and wearing his peaked cap with 0–546 on it. The pleading look of desire in his dark eyes made him irresistible. She let him in. By the time she had taken off her overcoat and lit the gas fire, he was in his underclothes, and quite naked before she had rid herself of her dress.

There was something desperate about his brief and ardent lovemaking, as if guilt ordained that he should get it over with as soon as possible. The inevitable cry of '*Iku, iku*' came too soon, but nevertheless the swift, rough tumble was more elating than a successful lesson, a thirty-minute swim, or an interview with the President. He put on his clothes as speedily as he had taken them off. When he was about to leave, Sylvia offered him a glass of whisky. His reply was to wave a hand in front of his face and make for the door. '*Gia*,' he said, and giving an apology of a bow he put on his cap and left. It was only six fifteen and his shop didn't close till eight, so Sylvia supposed that the ten minutes or so he had spent with her had been stolen from his working hours. She emitted a happy gurgle of a laugh and poured herself a large tot of whisky from the bottle she had proffered him. Still in nothing but her peignoir she sat in an armchair. The room was pleasantly warm and her flesh glowed.

At seven precisely Toshi made what he sometimes referred to as his 'love call' and Sylvia was especially affectionate. But on the Friday there was no call and when she rang his *apāto* late at night there was no answer. On the next evening over dinner (large prawns with mayonnaise, followed by thin, lean slices of pork dredged in flour and sage and cooked in white wine), she asked Toshi, who pleased her by praising the meal, where he had been the night before. She knew she shouldn't make such inquiries, that they invited prevarication, and besides what would she have told him had he asked her about her activities between five past six and six fifteen on the previous evening? He gave his habitual answer 'with my correagues'. And when she pressed him to be more explicit, he said, 'We go to *karaoke* bar and we sing.'

'And what did you sing?'

'I sing Japanese song. We all sing song.'

'I see.' Somehow she didn't believe him. The weekend passed off well enough, but at times he seemed *distrait*, yet he evinced disappointment when she said she was too tired to accompany him to his room. Was the disappointment due to the fact that she was not going to help him with his housework? How convoluted her speculations about Toshi's motives had become! Were her suspicions justified? Hadn't his performance in bed lacked enthusiasm? Was this due to a late night at a *karaoke* bar or to satisfying the demands of a sex-starved housewife from the 'Club New Love'? She must go there. She rang Matthew and asked him if Jun could take her there the following Friday evening.

'Well, I don't know,' said Matthew. 'I'll ask him, of course. He normally gets back late on Friday. He has a long day at school. Just a minute.'

Sylvia could hear mutterings in the background and then Jun's voice. 'Okay, I'll do it. I don't want to but I'll do it.'

A minute or two later, after scrabbling noises caused by his picking up the receiver, Jun came on to the phone.

'I very sorry about your trouble at your university, Siria-san.'

'Thank you, Jun. They have been beastly.'

'Mattu-san say you want me to take you to "Club New Love" next Friday. Okay I take you there. I'll meet you at the corner by Isetan Department Store in Shinjuku, you know?'

'Yes, I know. At what time?'

'Ten o'clock. Okay?'

'That's fine. It is good of you, Jun.'

'Not at all.'

· 7 ·

Sylvia spent much of the Friday wondering what she should wear for her visit to the 'Club New Love'. She decided on a dress she had worn at the last cocktail party in London she had attended, a navy-blue, three-quarters length, long-sleeved frock. It was well cut and still fitted her comfortably. With it she wore a gold necklace with an emerald pendant and large gold ear-rings in the shape of hoops – her 'gypsy' rings her husband had called them. On her left hand she put her wedding ring, which she didn't always wear, and next to it a ruby and diamond one that had been given her by her mother; the third finger of her right hand she adorned with a plain jade ring, rich green in hue; her left wrist displayed her gold watch and her right one a jade bracelet which matched the ring. Over her dress she donned a dark-blue serge coat. She was pleased with her appearance when she regarded her reflection in the pier-glass in the back tatami room, where she dressed. Her elegance clashed with the shabbiness, the drabness and the untidiness of the room like a Ming bowl on a dust heap.

Feeling too chic for the subway and its ladder-like concrete stairs, she took a taxi to her rendezvous with Jun. She was much relieved when the taxi drew up outside the Isetan store to find him waiting. During the journey she had worried about his being late and her having to stand conspicuously on the pavement. She had read in the press of a Western woman being picked up by the police for patrolling for immoral purposes when all she was doing was waiting for her husband.

'How good of you, Jun,' she said on alighting from the taxi.

'You look very smart, Siria-san.'

'Thank you.'

'You do not look like a teacher.'

'I'm glad of that. Teachers hate to look like teachers.'

'I don't mind.'

They were waiting for the traffic lights to change. They crossed the street, went down a narrow lane of bars, crossed another wide street and entered a warren of bars glittering with fluorescent signs in red, blue, green and yellow. They arrived at the 'Queen of Heart' building, each of its eight floors blazing with coloured signs.

'This is it,' said Jun, leading the way into the entrance, where there was a lift. They ascended to the fifth floor. On either side of the landing was a bar. One had 'Club New Love' on its door in brass letters, and the other 'Mr Lady' in green striplighting.

'What on earth does that mean – "Mr Lady"?'

'That special gay bar.'

Jun pushed open the door of 'Club New Love'. 'I know manager, I introduce you. I cannot stay.'

'Oh, please, Jun.'

'Sorry.'

Sylvia and Jun stood just inside the door scanning the scene. The room was discreetly lighted. The atmosphere was warm and plush and contrasted sharply with the utilitarian plainness of the entrance, the lift and the landing, which gave the impression that the architect had his budget cut and had had to make economies. The decoration of the bars was left to the tenants, who took over bare rooms. 'Club New Love' boasted a wine-red carpet and banquette seats of the same hue, a small dance floor, a bar hedged by five hosts in dark suits with sleek short hair, and a white grand piano, on which stood a large white lamp in the shape of a male torso with a red shade, and a red vase containing white gladioli. The taped music was of the big band kind and the numbers were 'oldies'.

The five hosts turned to stare at the newcomers. One of them slipped off his bar stool and approached. He was handsome but not young. He bowed and while Jun was addressing him in Japanese, his black eyes ran up and down Sylvia in an appraising way, not missing her jewellery; she felt uncomfortable. Jun turned to her. 'This Mr Naito,' he said. 'He look after you. I explain to him you not member but want to see the place and then you may join. He says okay.'

'Thank you.' Sylvia hesitantly glanced round. Now her eyes had become accustomed to the dim lighting, she noticed that several tables were occupied by middle-aged Japanese women and young Japanese men. Mr Naito took her overcoat and showed her to a banquette table by the door. 'Can't you stay awhile, Jun?'

'Sorry. Not allow. I am going to "Mr Lady" bar. If you want me, I be there.' Jun hurried away. Sylvia took her place at the table, her back to the wall. Mr Naito bore her coat away. From her place near the door, Sylvia had a good view of the club and its members. The hosts were attending to the patronesses with studied diligence: pouring drinks, lighting cigarettes and listening to them patiently. Such chivalry, Sylvia imagined, was what the neglected wives, the widows, the disappointed divorcées or whatever they were, paid for.

An unattached host from the pool at the bar came up to her table. 'Wha' you li' drink?' he asked.

'What have you got?'

'We got whisky, wine. You li' champagne?'

'Yes, please. I'll have a glass of champagne.'

'No have *garasu*. We have bottle.'

'I suppose I'd better have a bottle, then.' The young man, who looked about twenty, returned to the bar.

Two hosts and their partners were dancing cheek to cheek to a tape of 'People Will Say We're in Love'. The eyes of the four were closed. The women's faces bore smiles of rapture; the men's no decipherable expression, except perhaps that of boredom.

The champagne arrived in an ice bucket brought by the same young man on a tray with two glasses and three plates of tidbits. With a bow he sat down beside her and poured out the wine. He raised his glass. '*Kampai*. You know *kampai*?'

'Yes,' she said. '*Kampai*!'

'You name Hideki. What my name?'

Sylvia laughed. 'Your name Hideki. My name Sylvia.'

'Siruvia. Very difficult.'

The dance ended and on to the floor with her partner, a tall young man in a navy blue suit and an expensive looking blue and red striped tie, came a stout little woman of uncertain age in a short dress. Her legs were sturdy and her hair had that dead blackness which dye produces. The host took from the top of the piano a microphone and made an excited announcement in the manner of a professional compère.

'What'd he say?'

'He introduce her.'

'Is she a famous singer?'

'She customer.'

The big band music increased in volume for a few bars, then quietened, and having accepted with a slight bow the microphone from her host, the little dumpy housewife launched herself into 'One Enchanted Evening', half in Japanese and half in English. She sang off-key in a hooting contralto, gesticulating wildly with her free arm and furrowing her brow. While she sang, her host stood at the side of the floor, slightly behind her. He did not trouble to hide his contempt, turning at one point to the boys at the bar to exchange a mocking grimace. Sylvia felt sorry for the woman, more because of her partner's disdain than for her own pitiable performance. If only she had the ability to laugh at herself, thought Sylvia. Her seriousness made her more pathetic. The fervent claps given by her host when the painful song ended emphasized his insincerity. There was no other applause apart from a few scattered duty claps from Naito-san and the boys at the bar. The woman gave a solemn bow to the room, handed back the microphone to the host and regained her seat.

The cruel indifference of the tall, young host set Sylvia thinking about her relationship with Toshi. Did he despise her in his heart of hearts? Was she a convenience, a digression?

Hideki refilled the champagne glasses. 'Thank you,' said Sylvia. She held up her glass and looked into his eyes for a moment. He had a roundish face with a snub nose; his eyebrows were neat and wide apart; his lips were finely chiselled; and his teeth were white, better than Toshi's; he had a sexy look too. She wondered as she regarded him if he wouldn't have done as well for a lover as Toshi, in spite of his limited English. Perhaps all the hosts were interchangeable, that is if one didn't go above the level of carnality. With the greengrocer she certainly did not rise above that level. It seemed that Matthew had succeeded in arriving at a relationship with Jun that wasn't based purely on sex, but at the same time it was one that could not be permanent as was shown by Jun's being engaged to be married, or at least about to be. Her affair with Toshi could not be anything but fragile. It definitely could not end in marriage.

The big band music was playing 'I Get a Kick Out of You'.

'You li' dance?' asked Hideki.

'No, I don't think so, thank you.'

'You wan' change host?'

'Change?' Had he read her thoughts?

'Have other host?' Hideki looked at his watch. 'You have me thirty minute. You have other host thirty minute, same price. Maybe you li' other host better than me.'

Sylvia was taken aback, both by the outspokenness and the realization that she was paying for Hideki's company. 'No, I don't want another host. I like you.'

'Thank you.' Hideki bowed his head. 'You li' have me one thirty minute more?'

'Yes.'

'Okay.' Hideki moved along the banquette closer to Sylvia, who became a little alarmed that her engaging him for a further half hour might make him think that she wanted some light flirtation. What would happen if Toshi appeared and caught her canoodling? It would defeat the object of her expedition, which was to catch him. Would he appear?

'Do you know Toshihiko Yamada?'

'Toshi-san? Yes, I know.'

'Does he come here?'

'Yes he come here. He do *arbeito tokidoki*, sometime on Friday.'

'Has he been here tonight?'

Hideki did not reply at once. He seemed to be ruminating over his response. '"Scu" me, what you say?'

'Toshi-san, he come tonight?' asked Sylvia, hoping that incorrect English would be more easily understood.

'He no come. His rady wait for him. She over there, near piano. How you know Toshi-san?'

Sylvia looked towards the piano. In the corner by its narrow end sat a Japanese woman alone. She was smoking, and there were a bottle and an ice bucket on her table, but the dimness of the lighting prevented Sylvia from seeing what she was like. Without answering Hideki's question, she said, 'Let's dance.'

The band was playing 'It's a Sin to Tell a Lie'. Hideki rose and Sylvia and he joined three other couples who were slowly circulating the small dance floor and clasping on to one another like young lovers. Hideki automatically held Sylvia close. She enjoyed his lithe body pressing against hers. Toshi's 'rady' looked a pleasant woman, motherly, kindly, but thin; her face was pale, her hair neat, her dress simple; she certainly didn't resemble a dragon lady or a *femme fatale*. Sylvia was surprised to see that she was drinking brandy. After a few more turns round the dance floor and the same number of peeps at the woman, Sylvia said she had had enough and Hideki at once switched off his amorous attitude, released his hold and conducted her politely to her table. In 'Club New Love' the hosts were courteous to their sugar-mummies in a Western way, letting them go first on to the dance floor, first back to the table, acting over-respectfully. But once out of the club, they apparently left their duty manners behind. Toshi had never been obsequious, except for that time when he had caught crabs; then he had shown he could cringe.

What was she to do? Wait for Toshi? Go and so avoid a confrontation? She would go. 'May I have my bill, please?'

'Sorry?'

'My bill, my check, *kanjō*. I want to leave.'

'You go now?'

'Yes. I go.'

'Okay.' Hideki looked at his watch and went to the bar. He soon returned with the bill on a plate. Sylvia was shocked at the price. At first glance it seemed to be forty-three-thousand yen, about one hundred and seventy pounds. She put on her reading glasses. Yes, it was undoubtedly that amount. How frightful!

'Credito cardo okay,' said Hideki, as if he had sensed Sylvia's embarrassment.

Sylvia fished her credit card out of her handbag and it was whisked away. Soon Hideki came back with her coat, her card and the forms, which she signed. The young man kept up his practised politeness till the end. He helped her on with her coat, saying, 'Thank you very much. I enjoy.' He opened the door, saying *Mata dōzo*. Prease come again.' He followed her on to the landing and pressed the lift button. The lift was ascending. Sylvia had a prescience that Toshi was in it. She dashed up a few steps of the unlighted stairs to the next floor and stood in the darkness surveying the illuminated landing.

Her premonition proved correct. Toshi came out of the lift, exchanged a grunt with Hideki and went into 'Club New Love'. Sylvia descended to the landing, where Hideki was still standing. He seemed to have grasped the situation. She pulled a ten-thousand-yen banknote out of her handbag and gave it to the young man. 'Please do not tell Toshi that I was here, 'understand?'

'I no tell,' he said conjuring the note away into a pocket.

The lift had been summoned from the ground floor. On the spur of the moment, Sylvia crossed the landing and went into 'Mr Lady'.

'That bar not for you,' cried Hideki.

· 8 ·

'I disagree. It was wrong of you to go into "Mr Lady",' said Matthew for the second time. He was lunching with Sylvia on the following day, Saturday.

'You haven't explained why,' cried Sylvia from behind the kitchen curtain. She was making a hollandaise sauce to go with the scallops she had fried. She had called Matthew to the table so there would be no delay between the readying of the sauce and the serving of it. They had each imbibed three gin and tonics, over which Sylvia had recounted her escapade in 'Club New Love' and her visit to 'Mr Lady'. She appeared from behind the curtain holding two plates of scallops with a dollop of sauce beside them.

'I thought hollandaise would go well with these,' she said, giving him his plate. 'I haven't tried it before. Do help yourself to wine, Matthew, and give me some too.' She sat opposite him. 'Why was it wrong of me to go into "Mr Lady"? I found it amusing. Everyone was very sweet to me. There was a much nicer atmosphere in the place than there was in "Club New Love", which reeked of the clip joint. How grotesque they looked! The men all made up, and one of them in a dress, an awful dress that didn't fit properly. One man thought I was a man *en travestie*. It was too funny.' She laughed. 'And Jun introduced me as "Mr Woman". It took some minutes for the man to realize we were joking. Then the man in the dress did a strip-tease. It was hilarious. Dear Jun, he was so sweet to me. He is a darling. I adore him.'

'Did Jun have on make-up?'

'No.'

'He usually does, I believe. These scollops or scallops, I've never known which to call them, are really scrumptious, to use an epithet from my youth.'

'Do you go to that bar?'

'I have been to it.'

'Did you put on make-up?'

'I did once as a joke, together with Jun.'

'I would have loved to see you, Matthew. Why was it wrong of me to go into that bar? No one seemed to object to me. They were very friendly.'

'It was wrong because men – especially Japanese men – do not like women to see them wearing slap.'

'Slap?'

'Make-up.'

'Why do they want to wear it?'

'It gives them a feeling of liberation. It makes them feel they are in a different world from their office and their home. It gives them a little holiday from work and from their domestic environment, which many of them find boring. Most of them are married. Not all, but most.'

'Are they gay, then?'

'Yes, but they had to get married.'

'Like Jun?'

'Jun may get out of his latest entanglement. He doesn't really want to go through with it, and I certainly don't want him to.'

'I couldn't possibly marry Toshi, not that I've ever seriously thought of doing so, and certainly not now I've learnt he has another mistress about my age too.'

'Disraeli was thirty years younger than his wife, and they had a happy marriage. Mrs Porter was nineteen years older than Johnson.'

'I don't', laughed Sylvia, refilling Matthew's glass and then her own, 'think you can compare Toshi with either the wily Jew or the revoltingly ugly doctor. And I could neither be a Mrs Disraeli nor a Mrs Johnson. They both helped their spouses inestimably. If I married Toshi, an absurd hypothesis anyway, but say if I did, it would wreck his career in the bank, and probably cause an irreparable break with his family. It would ruin his life. I couldn't take him to England. I can't stay here now that I've got the sack. I'm not sure that I want to anyway. Besides, he's been deceiving me all the time. Deception kills love, didn't you know?'

'It need not,' replied Matthew, taking a gulp of wine. 'About his mistress, the Japanese woman you saw, he probably has to see her out of obligation. He met her before he met you presumably.'

'And has to go on meeting her?'

'Yes. After all she's a permanent fixture here. You're not. Toshi doesn't want to burn his boats.'

'What about you,?' asked Sylvia, crossly. 'Are you staying forever?'

'Till I retire. That's in ten years' time. Ten years! All sorts of things may happen before then.'

'I've decided to mete out to Toshi his deserts.'

'How are you going to do that?'

'I'll tell you my plan when I've fetched the cheese.' Sylvia rose from the table. 'I bought some *chèvre* today.'

'Extravagant woman! I'm all agog,' said Matthew.

'For the cheese?'

'Yes, and for your revelation.'

'Sylvia's stark raving mad,' said Matthew to Jun as soon as the young man had come into the flat that evening. 'Do you know what she proposes to do? Or has done by this time?'
'What?'
'I'll tell you when you've taken off your things.'

Sylvia went out to the local shopping street when she had washed up the lunch things. '*Sutēki futatsu*,' she said to the smiling butcher, who, his smile not fading, cut off two slices from a lump of beef. She took the parcel after paying for the meat and inclined her head in response to the butcher's, '*Arigatō gozaimashita*'. What a mouthful 'thank you' was! Sylvia continued down the street, her heart thumping. Would he be there? He was. She could see him when she was sixty yards away. The large peak of his numbered cap was pulled over his eyes. Sylvia ostensibly scrutinized the vegetables and the fruit until Mr Five-Four-Six was free and ordered from him potatoes, French beans, bananas and persimmon. While he was putting the brown paper bags into a plastic carrier bag which he said was 'sarvice' (meaning gratis) he gave Sylvia a wide argentine grin. Sylvia said to him quietly, '*Roku-ji-han, dōzo*. Okay?' In reply the greengrocer dropped his hooded eyelids over his dark eyes and gave a shadow of a nod, but a second later when he reopened them they said nothing. He took Sylvia's banknotes to his wife, (his sister? his mother?) behind the cash-register machine. '*Arigatō gozaimashita*,' he cried while handing Sylvia her change and the other assistants took up the cry; it was an automatic cry emitted over and over again throughout the day. Sylvia bought a 'France *pan*' from the young woman in the baker's shop – would he like bread? – and returned to her apartment. She knew she had said 'half past six, please' correctly, but would Mr Five-Four-Six come?

It was just after five when Sylvia got back to her flat. She prepared the steaks and the vegetables, laid the table for two and then reclined on the sofa trying to read *The Princess Casamassima*, which a graduate student had chosen to write about in spite of her advising against it. Her agitation, though, did not allow her to concentrate on the turgid novel. In these days the Princess would have gone to bed with Hyacinth, if anyone could have slept with a man with such a silly name, and with Paul Muniment. Then there would have been a stronger case for Hyacinth's jealousy. People didn't realize what a big part jealousy plays in life. Would Mr Five-Four-Six come? Would Toshi turn up at the same time? It was Saturday and he was due at six-thirty. Twice Sylvia went to the door with the intention of cancelling the invitation. But to do that would be impossibly awkward. She had put her plan into motion; it was too late to stop it. Who would arrive first? Would they arrive together? At twenty-five minutes past six the doorbell sounded its two notes, timidly, as if the button had been pushed lightly by an uncertain finger.

Sylvia went to the door and admitted Mr Five-Four-Six. He was in his working clothes: blue jeans, a pullover and shirt of the same colour and his cap. '*Gomen nasai*,' he said, apologetically.

'*Dōzō*,' replied Sylvia, ushering him into the sitting-room. 'Food? *Shokuji*?' She went behind the kitchen curtain, picked up the frying pan and showed the greengrocer the steaks. 'You like, *ski des ka*?' she asked.

'*Kekkō des*,' he replied, waving an open hand in front of his face. Sylvia knew that the word for enough was used to denote a refusal. 'Later, perhaps, *ato-de tabun*,' she suggested and returned the frying pan to the stove and switched off the gas under the kettle. When she emerged from behind the curtain, Mr Five-Four-Six had already taken off his cap, his pullover and his trousers and was sitting on a dining-room chair and removing his socks. His hair was quite long now and this improved his looks, making him appear less fierce. Sylvia put a hand on his head and let it run gently down to his nape and tugged lightly the end of the long strands. Mr Five-Four-Six pushed her hand away and frowning, rose. He tore off his shirt and faced Sylvia in his spotless

215

underwear. He then approached her and gave her one of his closed-lipped kisses on the mouth and signalled to her to undress. She obeyed, matching the greengrocer's speed.

In an instant both of them were naked and lying on the bed clasped in a tight embrace. Would Toshi arrive now? In a way it was thrilling, this double suspense. Soon, too soon as usual, came the cries of '*Okā-san, okā-san!*', followed by '*Iku iku!*', and after a pause and a grunt Mr Five-Four-Six uttered a contented groan and released himself from Sylvia's clutches. From the bed Sylvia watched the greengrocer pick his underclothes off the floor and slip into them in three quick movements. Mr Five-Four-Six stood first on one leg and then on the other putting on his socks. Just as he was stepping into his trousers there came the sound of a key in the door and then Toshi's voice, 'Siru-san?' Mr Five-Four-Six started as if galvanized by an electric shock. The door into the living-room opened and before Toshi had time to say anything the nimble greengrocer dashed out of the room, his cap in one hand, his pullover, his shirt in the other. The front door opened and slammed to. Toshi regarded Sylvia with consternation as she stood naked by the bed.

'I no understand,' he said. 'Who that man?'

'He works in the vegetable shop,' said Sylvia donning her peignoir. 'I don't know his name.'

'He your lover?'

'Not exactly. He just comes for sex sometimes.'

'You let him, Siru-san?'

'Yes,' she replied. 'You have your friend in "Club New Love", I have the greengrocer.'

'What you mean?'

'I went to "Club New Love" last night and saw your lady friend.' She nervously swallowed a laugh caused by her using such a genteel term, but 'woman friend', 'girl-friend' or 'mistress' would have sounded wrong.

'You go to "Club New Love"?'

So Hideki hadn't told him. 'Yes, and you went there too to meet that woman. I saw you go in.'

'How you know?'

'I tell you, I saw you go in, enter the "Club New Love". You go there almost every Friday, don't you? You have your lady friend,

I have the greengrocer. It's tit for tat.'

'Tit?' Toshi, repeated, puzzled.

Sylvia nearly laughed again. Exchanging accusatory remarks in broken English was highly comic somehow. 'No, not tit. Retaliation. I mean you have your lady friend, I have the greengrocer, so we're equal.'

'Gleenglocer?'

'That man, the vegetable man, the man you saw just now.'

'You love him?'

'God no! I don't even know his name.'

'Then why?'

'Do you love that woman?'

'She very kind to me when I student. I mus' see her some time. She telephone me many time. I say I cannot see you. She very sad, so I see her.'

'You go to bed with her?'

'I been, yes.'

'You go to bed with her last night?'

'Yes, li' you go to bed with that man.'

Sylvia slid to the *shōji* of the bedroom alcove, and sat in an armchair. 'So we both go to bed to please our secret partners,' Sylvia remarked. Toshi said nothing. He stood by the dining-table, on which he had placed his briefcase, looking down.

'I go now,' he said.

'All right, Toshi.'

'You don' mind?'

'Of course I mind. But perhaps it is better.'

'What is better?'

'That we call it a day. I mean that we finish. I am sorry but I think it better that it end.'

With a sob in his voice, Toshi, his face tear-stained, looked at Sylvia. 'I not see you again?'

'Better not, Toshi.'

'I swear I not see my rady more.'

'I can't promise I won't see the vegetable man again. It's better we say goodbye now.'

Toshi did not reply. He took up from the table the briefcase that Sylvia had given him, and sped out of the room. Sylvia did not move for a few minutes, then she rose and went to the door to see if it had been locked. She found Toshi's key on the hall step. She picked it up and sighed. 'Have I done the right thing?' she asked herself aloud. 'I shall miss him. He was so sweet in many ways, and he's so young, young for his age. Ah well!' She went back to the armchair and opened the Henry James novel, put it down after two pages and went to the telephone.

'I've done the deed,' she told Matthew.

'And what happened?'

'Tears and flight.'

'Whose tears, and who fled?'

'Toshi's tears and they both fled. The greengrocer made a dash for it as soon as Toshi arrived on the scene. He nearly caught us *in flagrante*.'

'That was the idea, wasn't it? You wanted to give Toshi shock treatment, didn't you?'

'Not really. I wanted him to see me entertaining the greengrocer. I had bought two steaks. When I showed them to the greengrocer, he waved his hand across his face and said, "*Kekkō des*". I know *kekkō* means enough. Did it mean he had already eaten?'

'Not necessarily. It's a sort of negative. Rather abrupt. Not all that polite.'

The doorbell sounded.

'There's someone at the door. I must go, Matthew. I'll ring you back.'

'The greengrocer who has changed his mind about the steaks or a contrite Toshi?'

'We'll see.' Sylvia put down the receiver and went to the door. It was Toshi. She let him in. He stepped out of his shoes, took off the short topcoat he was wearing, hung it on a hook in the hall, and said tearfully, 'I mus' speak with you, Siru-san. I been thinking.'

'All right, Toshi.'

Once inside the main part of the flat, Toshi threw himself at Sylvia, put his head on her shoulder, and sobbed, 'I been very bad. I love you, Siru-san. I can't reave you. Prease we discuss our situation.'

Sylvia stroked the back of Toshi's head and gave his hair a few gentle pulls. 'There, there, Toshi. You go and get yourself a whisky and pour me out a gin and tonic. I must put some clothes on. I bought two steaks. We'll have them for dinner, shall we?'

Toshi nodded in eager agreement.

· 11 ·

December had arrived and with it Christmas songs and carols, the pale-blue skies and crisp air of the Tokyo winter, the red or white blooms of the ubiquitous camellia bushes, the blaze of cyclamen and poinsettias in flower shops. The golden leaves of the ginkgo trees littered the pavements and were constantly being swept up by shop assistants and housewives. There was the expectant thrill of coming festivity in the air. Christmas was no holiday in Japan but the New Year brought the biggest festival of the year, *o-shogatsu*, which lasted officially from 1–3 January, but in fact for many began on 30 December and continued until 5 January or even a few days later. The university had just over two weeks' holiday. The department stores and other shops exploited the Feast of the Nativity, although the number of Christians in Japan compared with the population was negligible, and there were plastic Christmas trees with winking lights, tinsel baubles and cotton wool in many a shop, restaurant and store. Fortunately for the retailers there was a custom of giving presents at the end of the year and these had got combined with Christmas gifts, though as one of her students said to Sylvia, 'Christmas means nothing to us Japanese.'

Sylvia resented the carol 'O Come, All Ye Faithful', which she had loved as a child, being boomed out in stores, supermarkets and even in her swimming pool along with 'I'm Dreaming of a White Christmas', 'Ave Maria' and 'Jingle Bells.' Nevertheless the atmosphere of the vast city became friendly and on the campus there were smiles. One morning Professor Maeda knocked on her door at the university.

'May I speak with you, Mrs Field?' he asked diffidently and respectfully. Since her dismissal, she had avoided meeting her colleagues as much as possible.

'Of course, Professor Maeda. Can I be of any help, or have you some more bad news?'

The professor seemed taken aback for a moment. 'No, as a matter of fact, I have some good news.'

'They've rescinded their decision?' she asked, eagerly. 'I always thought – '

'Not that, but – 'he paused. 'Do you want to stay in Japan?'

'How can I?'

'I have job for you at a publishing company. The salary it is good and they will pay your rent. You can stay on in Mrs Ota's apartment, if you like. It is company that has a strong foreign section and they need an editor.'

'Are you sure they would employ me after the *Spot Out* article?'

'Yes. The president of the company is a friend of mine. He understand it all. I explain to him.'

'What about the other people in the company?'

'No problem. Are you interested, Mrs Field? If you are, I will arrange a meeting with the president. He is very keen to meet you.'

'May I think it over until after the New Year holiday?'

Professor Maeda agreed and left the room with a bow.

Sylvia liked him and was grateful for his trying to help her, but did she want to stay in Japan? On the other hand did she want to return to live in England? The flat which she had got as part of the settlement with her ex-husband, was let. She could stay in Hove with her mother, but she had never got on with her, and her widowed parent had her own life, her own friends, bridge, parties, outings to a matinée in London, to the Theatre Royal in Brighton on Thursday afternoons when prices were reduced for senior citizens, and to the Festival Theatre at Chichester in the summer. Not a bad social round for a woman of seventy-five. She drove her Mini with aplomb. But Sylvia was only fifty, and the thought of staying, even temporarily, with her mother was unappealing. So Professor Maeda's offer had its attractions. Should she accept it? Did she want to continue her relationship with Toshi? She would decide after the New Year holidays. For the time being, she and Toshi had become reconciled, and they had both promised not to see their rival lovers, though Mr Five-Four-Six could hardly be called a rival. They had never exchanged more than monosyllables, and Toshi and his 'rady' could communicate much better than she and Toshi were able to.

And there was her life in Tokyo. It was a pleasant city to live in, well run and safe to walk about in; one could go practically anywhere with impunity; if one wandered drunk through a dark park it was unlikely that one would be molested. There was something very engaging about life in Tokyo. The city bewitched her, yet remained alien. She didn't feel she really belonged, yet she was perpetually fascinated. There were two main disadvantages, though: the occasional earth tremors and the expense. The first time her building had been shaken in a tremor she had been in bed with Toshi at dawn. They had awakened and she had watched his eyes, open, alert and anxious. The crockery had rattled, a book had tumbled from a shelf. 'Is this it?' she had asked, gripping his hand. 'It all right,' Toshi had replied. The tremor had only lasted a few seconds, but they had seemed long ones. Now she took no notice of the tremors and carried on with what she was doing, but she did wonder. The second disadvantage, the expense, was tempered by her large salary. She had been able to save an impressive amount. Tokyo was a city which throbbed with success – the lavishness of the decoration of the opera house at Ikebukuro was ample evidence – while London was dangerous and seemed to be running down. The subway system was excellent. One could go anywhere easily. There were first rate concerts to go to, and Kabuki, which she greatly enjoyed. It was a pity that Toshi liked neither classical music nor the traditional theatre, but she could go to these on her own. Toshi provided home entertainment. In England there wouldn't be a Toshi. There might be a greengrocer, but he would never be as obliging or as self-effacing as Mr Five-Four-Six; he wouldn't tactfully flee when surprised by her lover, he would probably stay and fight. So should she stay in Japan? She decided she would stay until the end of this academic year. By then, Toshi would be twenty-seven and marriage would be looming large, marriage to a woman of his parents' or his bank manager's choice. It was unlikely that Toshi would fall in love with an eligible girl as he preferred older women. If she accepted Professor Maeda's offer, then she would stay on until Toshi got married, and then she would bow out. But how easy would it be for her to do so when the time came? Wouldn't it be better for her to cut and run now when the reconciliation was only just freshly cemented and not yet set?

· 12 ·

'And Sylvia. We'd better invite her. She doesn't seem to know anyone apart from us, Toshi and the greengrocer,' said Matthew to Jun. The evening meal was over and they were going through the list of guests they had invited to their annual Christmas Day party, an evening and an all-male affair.

'She'd be the only woman,' objected Jun.

'We could ask Michio to wear one of his dresses, and I might put on mine to keep her company. You said she liked "Mr Lady". We can't leave her on her own.'

'What about Toshi?'

'He'd be sure to have a "forget-the-year" party, a *bonen-kai*. I'll ring Sylvia now.'

'I don't agree, Mattu-san. She spoil the party.'

'No, she wouldn't. She can be fun. We must be charitable.' Matthew rose and picked up his telephone on the desk. 'Is that you, Sylvia?'

'Yes, it is, Matthew.'

'Are you alone?'

'Yes, I am.'

'Jun and I were wondering if you'd like to come to our Christmas party – dinner on Christmas Day. Just a few old friends. But you'd be the only woman. Would you mind that?'

'Not a bit. But I won't be here. I've managed to get a flight to London for the holidays.'

'Oh, really? How long will you be away?'

'About ten days. My flight is on Christmas Eve.'

'I see. Well, have a good trip. Have you stopped teaching? I have. I usually give my students the last week off. They don't mind.' Matthew gave a feeble laugh. 'So, if I don't see you, Happy Christmas and all that!'

'Same to you, and to Jun.'

Matthew put down the phone. 'She's going to England for Christmas.'

'Good,' said Jun. 'Maybe she not come back.'

'Oh, I'm sure she will,' said Matthew, and then after a reflective pause, he added, 'but I wonder!'